THE ULTRA VIOLETS

WRITTEN BY
SOPHIE BELL

ILLUSTRATED BY
CHRIS BATTLE

razor
bill

An Imprint of Penguin Group (USA) Inc.

The Ultra Violets

RAZORBILL

Published by the Penguin Group
Penguin Young Readers Group
345 Hudson Street, New York, New York 10014, U.S.A.
Penguin Group (USA) Inc., 375 Hudson Street, New York, New York 10014, U.S.A.
Penguin Group (Canada), 90 Eglinton Avenue East, Suite 700, Toronto, Ontario,
Canada M4P 2Y3 (a division of Pearson Penguin Canada Inc.)
Penguin Books Ltd, 80 Strand, London WC2R 0RL, England
Penguin Ireland, 25 St Stephen's Green, Dublin 2, Ireland (a division of Penguin Books Ltd)
Penguin Group (Australia), 250 Camberwell Road,
Camberwell, Victoria 3124, Australia (a division of Pearson Australia Group Pty Ltd)
Penguin Books India Pvt Ltd, 11 Community Centre,
Panchsheel Park, New Delhi – 110 017, India
Penguin Group (NZ), 67 Apollo Drive, Rosedale, Auckland 0632,
New Zealand (a division of Pearson New Zealand Ltd)
Penguin Books (South Africa) (Pty) Ltd, 24 Sturdee Avenue, Rosebank,
Johannesburg 2196, South Africa

Penguin Books Ltd, Registered Offices: 80 Strand, London WC2R 0RL, England

10 9 8 7 6 5 4 3 2 1

Copyright © 2013 Penguin Group (USA) Inc.

ISBN 978-1-59514-603-8

Library of Congress Cataloging-in-Publication Data is available

Printed in the United States of America

For Fiona Butterfly

Prologue
{That Means It Happened Before Now. Four Years Before, If You're Counting.}

IT WAS A DARK AND STORMY MORNING. OR A BRIGHT and sunshiny night. Overcast with a chance of gumballs and not a cloud in the sky. But what really matters is that it was a Wednesday in September. Or maybe a Monday in May.

It was four years ago for sure, okay?

The Setting: the Highly Questionable Tower, or HQT, a rock-crystal skyscraper carved out of the side of a snoozing volcano. At its top: the secret, see-through Fascination Laboratory, or FLab, on the forty-second floor. At its base: a twenty-four-hour fro-yo shop. Its location: smack in the center of the stainless steel, totally tubular, sci-industrial complex of SynchroniCity. Sync City, for short.

The Actors: none. This isn't a play! Whatever gave you that idea? It ain't no party, ain't no disco, ain't no fooling around, neither. The girls *wish* it were that frivolous. What girls, you ask?

The four best friends at the sleepover.

Normally, a lab would be a very strange location for a sleepover. But all four girls' moms were big-deal scientists who worked at the FLab, and were all out at the same big-deal party hosted by the mayor. Also, this is Sync City. Nothing about it is normal.

"Candace. Hey, Candace? CandaceCandaceCandace-CandaceCandace? Look at me, Candace. Look!"

Iris Grace Tyler, grape lollipop sticking out of her mouth, was practicing cartwheels, her blond ringlets tumbling with her like curly ribbons on a tossed birthday present. "RiRi," as her friends sometimes called her, had hair so long and golden, you almost wouldn't blame a jealous Rapunzel for running with scissors behind her.

But Candace was more interested in the wriggly amoeba she'd squashed between two microscope slides. "That's nice, Iris," she tossed over her shoulder. Even though, for all she knew, it could have been the rare nasty cartwheel. Candace had just made an educated guess. Being a genius at fourteen, she was good at those. Being the

2

babysitter of four seven-year-olds running wild in a lab, she probably should have been paying better attention.

Iris finished flipping out and stood on two feet, stumbling a little to keep her balance. "Ta-da—*whoa!*" she said, with a shaky bow. "Sit still, you guys, you're making me dizzy." And she flopped down onto the lab floor next to her three best second-grade friends.

Cheri giggled, the red-and-white stripes of a peppermint candy flashing between her teeth. "How can you be dizzy when you're already Iris, Iris?" She paused to ponder this as she dabbed a sparkly coat of polish on her nails.

Iris closed her pale blue eyes and crunched on her lollipop. When she opened them, the room was right side up again. "Why do we have to wait at the FLab?" She pouted. "It's so metallic and *brrr* in here!"

"AND there's no TV!" Scarlet made a fist, even though she knew that

3

punching out the creepy lab skeleton hanging in the corner would be kind of pointless, considering he probably wasn't responsible for the lack of a plasma screen. She couldn't pants him, either, because he didn't have any clothes on (as the old saying goes, dead men don't wear pants). Scarlet Louise Jones, also known as Scar Lo, sometimes Scar Lo Jo, and occasionally as SLJ, was master of the stealth pantsing. Just short enough that nobody saw her sneaking up behind them. Just freckled enough that everybody mistook her for innocent. Frowning beneath her licorice-black bangs, Scarlet took her frustration out on her bubble gum instead, snapping it in anger.

"It is a bit *brrr* and boring." Cheri lifted her head from her mani-in-progress. When a stray strand of her berry-red hair fell across her nose, she crossed her emerald eyes and tried to blow it away. "They have a strict no-puppy policy at the door!" she complained between puffs. "This place is the *anti* warm-and-fuzzy!" Imagining litters of soft labradoodles and silky-eared spaniels scampering beneath the Bunsen burners, Cheri heaved a deep peppermint sigh. The stray auburn strand hovered in the air in front of her face for an instant before falling right back down onto her nose. "But," she said, sending an air-kiss to the baby boy skunk in a cage on the shelf, "they do have a skunk! As soon as my nails are dry, I'm taking Darth Odor out of his cage." Cheri Henderson never met a puppy, a pony, or a glitter nail polish she didn't immediately-and-madly love. But as of this sleepover, her heart belonged to the FLab's accidental mascot, Darth. She waved her shiny fingertips at him, and the skunk squeaked in excitement, blinking back at her adoringly.

Scarlet eyed the little skunk with suspicion. He might have been cute, but he was still a skunk. To be on the safe side, she pinched her nose. "Why is there a skunk here again?" she asked in a nasally voice.

"Mmm, your moms said they'd been doing some tests on scents as defense mechanisms in nature," Candace mumbled as she twisted a knob on the microscope. "But skunks only spray when they're threatened. So we're perfectly safe."

"He's so tiny and cute, I bet he smells like cookies!" Cheri said.

Even though Scarlet seriously doubted that, she let go of her nose. And made a mental note not to bully the skunk by accident.

From behind the microscope, Candace talked on about the scentsational world of skunks. Cheri was fascinated because Darth was adorable. Scarlet listened hard so that she'd be prepared in case of a stink attack. And Iris, who always packed colored pencils, was absorbed in her portrait of the baby skunk. Opaline saw her chance to sneak away. She got up from the group and padded over to the giant crystal windows. The truth was, Opaline Trudeau found Scarlet Jones just as scary as the skeleton. Maybe even scarier. She was loud. And she was a stealth pantser. Who was to say she wouldn't pants Opaline? Plus, the thought of sleeping over in this spooky lab made Opaline nervous. What if she had a nightmare and screamed out loud and woke everyone up? What if she wet her sleeping bag? She was going to have to use the bathroom at some point, even though the sound of flushing toilets made her blush all the way up to her amber-brown eyes. But Opal didn't want the other girls to know how uncomfortable she felt. "At least the view is pretty," she whispered, so softly she didn't think anyone would hear. Her breath formed a small foggy spot on the crystal windowpanes as she stared down at the twinkling city, then up at the gritty charcoal clouds circling the massive antenna on the FLab's domed roof.

"Super pretty!" Cheri chimed in from behind her, holding up her newly sequined nails to admire them.

Candace twirled around on her stool at the long lab table to face her babysittees. First she pushed her plastic goggles up on top of her head. Then she pulled the one-eye magnification loupe down on its elastic strap: It jutted out from her pointed chin like a giant robot-wart. Then she propped her thick black-framed glasses on top of the goggles. She rubbed her eyes and squinted. Candace may have been a teenage genius, but she hadn't figured out how to cure her severe astigmatism. (She'd do that later, in senior year.) Suffice it to say, without her glasses, the girl was blind as a bat.

"Hey, girls," she began, propped on her seat, hands on her knees, speaking not to the girls but in the general direction of a supply cabinet. "I know it's a *drag* to be stuck in the FLab when your moms are out partying at the mayor's gala—*drag* being the oppositional force exerted upon an object in motion, FYI."

The girls just blinked at her.

"But you can all hang together. With a baby skunk! That's fun, isn't it? How many second-graders can say they had a sleepover on the forty-second floor in the FLab?" To demonstrate the width of funness, Candace flung her arms wide open, missing a row of test tubes by exactly three millimeters.

"It's *flab*ulous!" Iris sang, throwing her arms open, too. Cheri and Scarlet burst out laughing, and even Opal had to smile. Scarlet could be scary sometimes, but something about Iris always made her feel safe.

The Highly Questionable Tower was indeed a highly questionable spot for a sleepover. Exhibit A: the skeleton, Skeletony, looking out at the lab with his one citrine-green gemstone eye. Beside him was a cluster of strange chambers. Some stood tall enough for a grown-up to fit

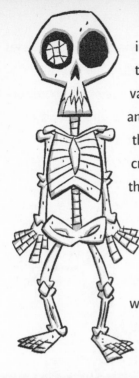

inside. All had coiled wires connected to their lids. Gnarly instruments, vacuum-sealed jars, gleaming vials, and stiff cardboard boxes crowded the shelves. Iris noticed skulls-and-crossbones stamped on some of them. That meant whatever was inside was poisonous. Their moms had positively forbidden the girls from touching a single item in the FLab, warning they'd ground all four of them for a month if even one of them dared. But they couldn't help looking. And that night, whenever the dark clouds parted, random shafts of moonlight would shine through the rough crystal walls to the glass jars on the shelves, revealing their contents. Opal had yelped when she saw what she thought was a piglet with a crocodile tail coiled up in the murky water of one jar. But Iris gave her hand a reassuring squeeze and told her she bet it was really just a jumbo jar of pickles her mom had forgotten to bring home.

Secretly, Iris wasn't so sure.

9

Against this soothing backdrop of giant pickles and boxes of do-not-touch stuff, Candace wrapped up her pep talk: "And since I'm here, I can finish my advanced chemistry homework using all this cool, high-tech equipment!" She gave a tip of her head to the cabinet, thanking it for its undivided attention. Then she spun back around and groped blindly across the tabletop until her hands came upon a big beaker bubbling with a gelatinous liquid. As she held it aloft, it flashed red, then blue, then red again. "I am so getting an A," she declared, squinting at the strange-'n'-smokin' substance like she was mesmerized by it.

Opaline's eyes widened in wonder. But Scarlet was not impressed. "Wow," she said, stifling a yawn. "Warm blueberry Jell-O. How exciting. For you."

"Wait, I've got an idea!" Iris piped up, springing to her feet and waving her arms in bhangra Bollywood flips. "It's fun," she said, looking at Scar. "Not scary!" She smiled at Opal. "And super-sparkly," she promised Cheri.

"Sparkly's my *favorite*!" Cheri squealed. Her sequined nails reflected the light as she clapped. "What is it?"

"We could put on a talent show!" Iris announced. "Right here in the FLab! And perform it for our moms when they come to pick us up."

"*Brilliant* idea, Iris," Candace said. Being a teenius, she knew brilliance when she heard it. (In this particular case she just couldn't *see* it, because she still hadn't put her three layers of glasses back on.) She placed the flashing beaker back down on the countertop, unbrilliantly close to the edge, between a bunch of steaming containers. For dinner they'd ordered Japanese takeout, and all the other vats of chemicals nearly camouflaged Candace's quart of spicy udon noodles. A pair of chopsticks poking out of the soup was the only way to tell it apart.

As the girls watched, Candace peered at the cluttered lab table, picked up a can of solvent strong enough to melt rubber, and raised it to her lips.

"Nooooooo!" they screamed together just before she took a sip.

"Common mistake," Candace said nonchalantly, putting the solvent back down and finding her chopsticks. "Mistakes are a vital part of any scientific process!" She fished a piece of broccoli out of her soup. A drop of broth dribbled down her chin and pooled in the robot-wart magnification loupe. "I'm not exactly sure what it is your moms *do* up here during the day, but this lab has got EVERYTHING! I guess when you're Sync City's top research scientists, you get to have the most advanced equipment and, like, a virtual supermarket of formulas and chemicals! And as your babysitter, *I* can borrow those chemicals to test out my theory of . . ."

At this point, the four girls zoned out. Admit it, you would have been bored, too, if Candace started lecturing *you* about biomolecular compounds and cold fusion and a theory of everything that was based on vibrating guitar string*zzzzzzzz*—humph, whazzat? Dozed off for a moment there. Where were we?

Talent show!

The girls knew their moms worked on some sorts of uber-secret projects. But with cartwheels to turn and bullies to pants and skunks to snuggle and toilets to avoid, their moms' experiments didn't exactly make their lists of Top Ten Interesting Things.

Instead, Cheri took Darth Odor out of his cage, and the four girls huddled together to plan their performance.

"*I'm* going to be the ninja princess guarding the temple," Iris growled, dropping into a tiger's crouch and scanning the lab for hidden dragons.

"How delicious!" Cheri beamed, squeezing the little baby skunk. "Because *I'm* going to be the ninja princess *inside* the temple, having tea and strumpets with my special guest, Darth!"

12

Stretching a neon green salamander Silly Band from her wrist, Scar Lo gathered her black hair into a sumo topknot and folded her arms across her chest. "*I'm* going to be a samurai warrior! Hi-ya!" she shouted, chopping down an entire line of invisible invaders. "Opal, what about you?"

"Um, I don't know," Opaline mumbled, toying with the zipper on her hoodie. "What do you guys think I should be? Schoolgirl in a sailor suit?" Iris might not think a talent show was scary, but to Opal, performing in front of her friends was as upsetting as a public toilet. In their kindergarten musical about the first Thanksgiving, she'd played the part of the baked potato. Mean Duncan Murdoch told her she looked like a dog turd in her costume, and she cried and forgot her one line about melted butter.

Ever since then, Opal much preferred being in the audience.

"Candace. Hey, Candace? Candace-CandaceCandaceCandaceCandace?" Iris began again. "Look at me, Candace! Watch

13

this!" And after three warm-up jumps, she leaped into the air with an especially spectacular ninja Rockette roundhouse kick. A kick higher than Iris herself. Higher than the stool Candace sat upon, higher than the laboratory countertop. Just not higher than the big honking beaker of blue-red goo sitting on its edge.

Her toe clipped the lip of the glass container, and it teetered on the edge of the counter, threatening to take a dive.

"Nooooooo!" It was Candace's turn to scream as she reached out to catch it—but clutched onto her chemistry textbook instead. Babysitter, put on your glasses!

The four girls held their breaths. Outside, the thunder grumbled. Inside, the beaker teetered. And then that troublesome strand of hair slipped out from behind Cheri's ear and tickled her nose again. And she couldn't push it away because her hands were full of skunk.

"Ah-ah-ahchoooopsie!"

It was the daintiest of sneezes, really. Exactly the kind of sneeze you'd expect from Cheri. If sneezes could qualify as cute (yuck, no, but if), this would win the gold medal: a high-pitched little squeak that wouldn't scare a skunk.

But that was all it took. The teeny-tiny squeak-sneeze caused just enough of a change in the air currents to blast that beaker not just over the edge of the table, but clear across the room.

Compelled by the laws of gravity, it rotated in slow motion—that's when, Candace would tell them later, things look like they take a lot longer than they actually do. Then the glass hit the wall. At the precise moment of impact, the entire FLab shook with an enormous thunderclap, the lights went out, the beaker shattered to pieces . . .

. . . and blue-red goo splattered all over the ninja-princess-samurai-schoolgirls. Plus one baby skunk.

"Gesundheit," Scarlet muttered.

"Thank you," Cheri answered. Just because she was covered in chemicals was no reason not to be polite.

It felt like they stood there, shocked and slimed in the dark, for fifteen minutes. It was really only five seconds, though. Then the lights flickered back on.

Opaline winced. She wondered if this was worse than a whole symphony of toilet flushes and decided it was.

Iris's ringlets hung flat and limp all the way to her waist under the weight of the gunk.

Cheri looked down at her recently sequined nails, now coated with sticky stuff and skunk fur. "Purple," she said to a dripping Darth Odor. "Why is it purple?"

"That's what you get when you mix red with blue." Iris's voice was muffled underneath all her hair. "Purple. Or maybe it's more of a violet?"

"Whatever color it is, it's all over my sneakers," Scarlet said "And my T-shirt. And everything."

"And. It's. Ewww!" Cheri concluded.

Candace snapped out of her shock and into panic mode. "That wasn't *the* beaker, was it? Please tell me it was just the free miso that came with the takeout. And not," she added under her breath, "Heliotropium, *the liquefied post-atomic hybrid particle capable of genetically altering any bio-organism on earth.*"

If the girls had been befuddled before by Candace's definition of *drag*, they now stood completely gape-mouthed and gob-smacked at this confusing stream of syllables.

"Helio-huh?" Scarlet said with a shake of her dripping hands.

Glasses and goggles back in place (*finally!*), Candace slid down from her stool, careful not to step in any puddles of her assignment. She surveyed her goo-covered charges. "Your mothers *can't* know about this. If they find out, they'll . . ." Candace seemed to be searching for the right words. "They'll . . . never let you have another sleepover again." Even through the double layer of lenses, the girls could see her left eye twitching a little.

"Sorry about drop-kicking your homework to infinity and beyond, Candace," Iris said, twirling a gummy, plummy strand of hair apologetically around her finger.

"What homework?" Candace said to all four girls, with a wink so exaggerated they knew it wasn't just a third-degree twitch. "Forget there ever WAS homework. If only my Neuralyzer were past the beta testing stage, I'd wipe all your memories right now!"

The girls, grabbing each other's hands, took a step backward as one.

"We've still got a couple of hours till the party ends and your moms come to pick you up. When you will be fresh and clean and fast asleep in your jammies!" Candace ranted, too distracted to sense their fear. From the back pockets of her jeans, she whipped out two flourescent orange flags and directed the girls with the expertise of a flight attendant. "Decontamination showers! Now! Down the corridor, second door on the right. Go power-wash those chemicals down the drain while I clean up this mess. And remember"—she leaned in close—*"This never happened."* Tossing the neon flags over her shoulders and into her udon, she grabbed a pair of latex gloves out of a box. She snapped them on like a doctor. "Cheri," she said, "hand over that skunk."

"No!" Cheri said, holding him close. "I love him!"

Darth chittered back his love for Cheri.

"I just need to rinse him off," Candace said calmly, bending over to look Cheri in her bright green eyes. "He's too tiny for those showers. I'll wash him here in the sink, okay?"

After planting one last kiss on his nose, Cheri reluctantly passed the skunk baby back to the babysitter. Then she trudged after Scarlet and Iris toward the showers. Only Opal remained in the FLab.

"So . . ." she asked, "no talent show?" If only she didn't have to face the showers, she would have been relieved.

"Sorry, sweetie." Candace shook her head. She was already mopping goo from Darth's white stripes. "Maybe next time." As Opal obediently shuffled off, too, the babysitter said to the empty room, "I don't think your moms are ready for radioactive ninja princesses tonight."

Iris, Cheri, and Scarlet were already in the hallway, but Opaline trailed behind. She'd stopped cold in her Crocs, a chill running through her soaked hoodie, when she realized that the citrine-eyed skeleton was missing from his corner.

Eventually the girls forgot all about the shattered beaker and the shower of goo. Or almost. They forgot to stay besties, too. They didn't mean to, but it happens. It happens to the besties of us, unfortunately. The Tylers moved away when Iris's mom got a job at NASA (an abbrev for the National Aeronautics and Space Administration, not the Nocturnal Affiliation of Strange Accents, the Noisy Association of Silent Artists, or the just plain Nice Alliance of Sassy Assassins, though those are all perfectly respectable organizations, if your mom works at any of them). Dr. Trudeau transferred Opaline to an all-girls' academy where the bathrooms were private. Cheri and Scarlet still saw each other in school, but between karate lessons (Scar) and kraft kircle (Cher), lil' mechanics club (Scar) and volunteering at the vet's (Cher), they lost touch. Before long, Cher was hanging out with the most fashionable girls in primary school. And Scar became the sidekick of some of the toughest boys.

For little did the foursome know then, on that snowy Friday in July four foreboding years ago, that their lives had been changed—*cue frenzied xylophone solo*—four-ever!

The Not Quite New Girl
{Four Years Later}

SHE WONDERED IF ANYONE WOULD NOTICE. *Of course they will*, she thought, shaking out her damp curls after she tugged on her T-shirt. *How could they not?* She stared at herself in the bathroom mirror, as she had so many times since "the change." *She* was still surprised by her own reflection, so the kids at school definitely would be. Would anyone recognize her? Would anyone even remember her? It *had* been four years.

She took a deep breath, closed her eyes, and imagined for a moment the best possible day. A day when everyone welcomed her back and she found all her classes and nobody made fun of her. That was her vision.

She was an artist, after all. And an artist had to have vision.

When she'd left her three best friends behind and moved to a new city, she forced herself to look at it as an adventure.

When she was left alone while her mom was lost in space, she tried to see it as an opportunity to be independent.

And when her mom came down to earth and told her they were moving back, she decided to approach it as a chance to start over.

It was a vision thing.

All that stuff had been hard. This, she told herself as she opened her eyes again, was just her first day at Chronic Prep, the middle school named after the middle word in SynchroniCity.

If beauty is truth, she mused as she laced up her boots, *the truth is: This is who I am now. I've got to own it.*

She grabbed an apple from the kitchen, slung her messenger bag over her shoulder, and checked her reflection one last time before she headed out the door. Her hair was almost dry now, and the thick strands spiraled down her back. Ultra vibrant. Ultra vivid. And ultra weird.

"Oh, well," she said to herself with a small smile. "Here goes."

The gawking began in the elevator. On the monorail to school, the other passengers whispered. In morning assembly, the students murmured. They muttered in class. And on the playground, they straight up ogled.

She just smiled, sucked on her lollipop, said hello to the occasional familiar face. In the cafeteria, she took a seat at a table all by herself.

She was taller now, but she still trembled with energy: Her periwinkle eyes were just as true blue. Only the cascading ringlets, once blond, were now . . . different.

"Iris?"

Balancing a tray of mac-and-cheese and a carton of chocolate milk with one manicured hand, hiding a dachshund in a tote bag with the other, Cheri slowly approached the table. "O-M-Jeepers. It really *is* you." She paused, trying not to stare and uncertain of what to say next. "Can I—"

"Sit down, yes, please!" Iris finished the question for her. After a lonely morning, her positive vision was kicking in. Yay!

Cheri slid into the opposite chair, placing her tray on the table and tucking her hot dog under her seat. She gave a little wave to her usual group of friends, the trendster girls over on the other side of the cafeteria, who all looked at her questioningly, wondering who on earth Cheri was hanging with. Though she wasn't sure why, she felt a bit embarrassed. It wasn't Iris's wild new style: Cheri considered fashion the ultimate in self-expression and always applauded daring choices. But maybe too much time had gone by, and her memories of their childish ice-cream birthday parties and spectacular Saturday afternoon talent shows belonged in the past. Maybe, Cheri wondered, Iris was thinking the same thing.

She poked at her macaroni with a fork while Iris set aside her iCan, the digital canvas she'd been doodling in. Cheri stole a glance at the drawing. It was a rainbow all in blues.

Then Iris said, "I really like your lip gloss."

"Ooh, merci boocoop!" Cheri said, and flashed a bright smile. "My mom says I'm not allowed to wear it. But it's just a sheer rose. With a hint of shimmer. Very natural-looking. Me, only shinier!" Cheri could host a daylong symposium on the sticky goodness that was lip gloss. But she realized she was beginning to babble, so she just blurted, "I wipe it off before I get home. Don't tell your mom."

"Of course not!" Iris said, placing her hand on her heart. "Friend's honor!"

So they *were* still friends! *smiley face!* Encouraged, Cheri decided to address the pink elephant in the cafeteria. (There wasn't actually an elephant in the cafeteria— thankfully, because that would have terrified the dachshund. And it wasn't pink, either. But since this metaphor may be confusing, let's let Cheri get to the point.) She looked Iris straight in the eye and began, "I heard some boys in assembly this morning saying that there was a new girl whose hair was—"

"Get. OUT!" The command came from over Cheri's shoulder, cutting her off mid-sentence.

Cheri stiffened in her seat, refusing to dignify the rudeness by turning around. "I absolutely will *not* get out," she stated, miffed to be interrupted. "I just sat down. And I was here first. Or second, after Iris. But definitely before you!" With a defiant toss of her auburn waves, she turned to face the boy who'd been so obnoxious—and instead found herself nose-to-freckled-nose with Scarlet. The tiny girl with the big voice dropped into the chair beside her, banging a Batman lunch box onto the tabletop.

"No, I didn't mean 'get out' get out," Scar Lo explained, popping open the lunch box and picking up her tuna fish on rye. "I meant, 'get out,' oh *swell* no! As in, believe the hype. As in, Iris, you're back, and your hair really is—"

Then Scarlet lost her nerve, turning from Iris to Cheri to her sandwich. It dawned on her that she was sitting at a lunch table with not one but two past-tense besties. One who'd moved away years ago, and another she barely said hey to in the hallways anymore.

"Hey, Cher," she started over, swallowing hard.

"Scarlet," Cheri acknowledged.

"Long time no see," Scarlet tried.

"We're in all the same classes," Cheri replied.

"Are you aware there's a small dog under your chair?" Scarlet asked.

"His name is Salami," Cheri said without missing a beat. "Are you aware you've got a Batman lunch box?"

"Batman's cool!" Scarlet said.

"If you like your heroes gloomy," Cheri countered, sipping her chocolate milk through a straw. "He should freshen up his look. A tangerine-orange cape would really pop against all that goth."

Scarlet gawked at her, briefly speechless, before saying, "Whatever, it's my brother's, all right? Not everyone is obsessed with My Little Pony."

"But Friendship *Is* Magic!" Iris tried to break the tension with a joke and get her happy vision back on track. Her mom

always said she had a sensitive personality. And right now she sensed that this snippy chitchat was just a way for Scarlet and Cheri not to deal with the awkwardness that was her return.

"Excuse me, um, hi?"

The three girls looked up in surprise. Opaline stood at the end of the table. Clutching her brown paper bag like a security blanket, she cleared her throat and tried again. "Remember me?"

"Remember you?" Iris echoed, leaping to her feet just like she used to do in their talent-show days. "I've totally missed you!" She gave Opal's shoulders an affectionate squeeze, then grinned at Cheri and Scar. "I've totally missed *all* of you!"

Opal hesitated for another second, until Scarlet slid down in her seat to nudge out the last empty chair with her foot. Then Opal shook off her shyness and took her place at the table.

"Welcome back, Opal!" Cheri said breathlessly. "To stay, I hope? You're not just here on the foreign lunch exchange program, are you? Because if you are, heads-up: It's Wonderful World of Cabbage week."

Opaline blushed at the attention. After four years at the all-girls' academy, she was still adjusting to life on the outside. But here they all were again, reunited, and it felt so good. It was weird, kind of. Coincidental, some might call it. The way things worked out.

"I guess my mom took your mom's old job at the FLab?"

Iris said, stirring her spoon in her cup-of-soup. "I think that's what she said."

"Oh, did she?" Opal said, unwrapping her cucumber sandwich. "Because—"

"But what about NASA?" Scarlet cut her off, swallowing down a mouthful of tuna. "What about outer space?"

"Ends up my mom was claustrophobic," Iris said, shaking her head. "That's when small spaces stress you out."

"But isn't outer space as big as you can get?" Cheri asked, confused.

"It is," Iris agreed, "but her spaceship was not. My mother spent so much time away, training for her mission to Venus, and after the blastoff . . ." Iris paused, a faraway look in her eyes. Then she seemed to remember where she was again. "Those were my astronaut offspring boarding school years!" she declared. "Kind of like an all-girls' academy." She gave Opal a wink. "Twenty-four hours a day."

"Wow, really?" Scarlet said. She lived in a rambunctious bluestone townhouse with three older brothers and a basement and a big backyard. To her, boarding school sounded like prison. "What was that like? Was it hardcore?"

"It was . . ." Iris paused again, as if she was trying to find the right words. "It was, um, 'character-building.' It was okay."

Somehow, the way she said it didn't sound very okay.

"Did they allow pets at astronaut offspring boarding school?" Cheri asked, reaching under her chair to pat Salami on his head. "Did you have a mascot like Darth Odor?" It had been four years since Cheri had met the baby skunk, when their first night together was cut short by goo. But not a day went by that she didn't think of his darling little black-and-white face.

"Nope, definitely no pets," Iris said between sips of her soup. "It was more like military school. You know, push-ups at six in the morning. Kitchen Patrol. Lights out by seven. That kind of school."

"Yikes," Scarlet muttered. She couldn't even do one push-up at two in the afternoon.

"Anyway," Iris went on, "after nine-and-a-half weeks up in her rocket ship, the Deep Space Nine-and-a-Half, my mom started to go stir-crazy. When her mission splashed down, she was ready to come back to Sync City."

"That's funny," Opal said hesitantly. She waited in case anyone spoke over her again, but they all just looked at her, waiting for her to continue. Opal could feel herself blushing all the way up to her barrettes. "Because my mom was so ready to leave. She got a job across the river, at this bio-cosmetic company called BeauTek."

"So she took you out of the all-girls' academy?" Cheri asked.

"Yes." Opal nodded, her chestnut brown bob swinging just above her shoulders. "Chronic Prep is closer to her new job."

"And bonus," Cheri said with a twinkle in her green eyes, "there are lots and lots of boys here!"

Scarlet wrinkled her nose as Opal blushed all the way down to her shirt buttons.

"Well, I'm psyched that you're here," Iris said warmly, grinning at Opal. "We can be old newbies, or new oldbies, or whatever we are, together. Right?"

Opal nodded again. Scarlet burped, Cheri rolled her eyes at the etiquette fail, and Opal had run out of places to blush, so she clasped her hands over her mouth instead. (Although she'd mostly outgrown her toilet phobia, bodily functions still equaled gross.) Iris just smiled at her old friends.

So much has changed, she thought. In the four years she'd spent out of Sync, she'd learned a lot. With her mom in the space program, she'd learned about astronomy: planets and galaxies, black holes and comets, satellites and supernovas. More important, between moving away and then having to fly solo herself while her mom was in orbit, she'd learned to be independent. When it came to climbing a rope, pitching a tent, building a fire, spotting poison ivy, or making the bed, the girl had mad skillz.

Iris knew things were different now, but she was ready. She didn't know for what. For anything, for really.

Because, she thought, *so much also stays the same.* After all, here she was, chilling at the lunch table with her three best friends from second grade.

Of all the things she'd learned about space, her favorite subject was the stars. So far away, but close enough you could almost touch them if you stood on your tippy-toes and reached high. Whenever she made a painting of the sun, Iris was reminded that it was a star, too. It made her happy to know that, day or night, starlight was always shining on her. And on her friends!

Friends, she pondered, *are like sparkly stars.* Sometimes, when skies are cloudy, you can't see them, but that doesn't mean they aren't still there. Sometimes, they could be millions of miles apart, but somehow they'd still be connected in a constellation.

As Iris considered this, she reached one hand across the table, linking pinkie fingers with Cheri. Then, with her other hand, she did the same with Opal, at her side. Scarlet hastily brushed her hands on her jeans and hooked pinkie fingers with Cheri and Opal. Together, they formed a diamond shape.

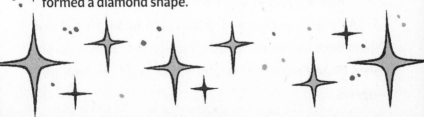

Her mom would say it was just her sensitive personality acting up again, but Iris was sure she could feel a kind of energy coursing through them, electrifying the diamond. She wondered if the other three felt it, too.

The *brrrraaang!* of the bell snapped her back to reality.

They all got up to go to their next class, but before splitting—not for four years, just for the rest of the afternoon—Scarlet wanted to seal the deal. She gave Cheri a playful punch on the arm, then stuck out her palm to shake.

"Friends again?" she asked, her voice cracking, much to her annoyance.

Cheri eyed Scarlet's open hand but didn't take it. "Scar," she said, pursing her lightly glossed lips and planting her hands on her hips. "I think we can answer that question with three little letters. Gimme a *B* . . ."

"Gimme an *F* . . ." Opal chimed in softly, grinning as she petted the dachshund in Cheri's bag.

"Okay, fine," Scarlet said, "gimme *another F.*"

"For F-r-i-e-n-d-s Forever!" Iris shouted, doing a cartwheel in the cafeteria for old times' sake.

They came together in a BFF hug.

As they hugged it out, it occurred to Iris that they'd spent the entire lunch period gossiping and catching up, but after those first few awkward moments no one had even mentioned—

"Hold on!" Scar exclaimed. "Rewind." They'd unhugged themselves at last and had started walking toward the stairwell, but now the other three girls pressed PAUSE.

"Ooh, yeah," Cheri agreed, catching Scarlet's eye and remembering the pink elephant she'd started to ask about before.

"Iris," Scarlet said. "Awesome that you're back. But *what* is up with the ***purple hair***?"

The Mall of No Returns

WE'LL GET BACK TO IRIS'S PURPLE HAIR, PROMISE. For now, just picture it in all its lavender loveliness, glossified and gleaming and as sparkly as grape soda. Picture the pretty. Pretty please? Because things are about to get ugly.

In the fours years that had passed since her extra-gooey babysitting gig at the FLab, Candace had zoomed through high school. Her parents wanted her to have all the classic experiences—homecoming, student council, varsity football, prom—so Candace had stayed in her grade. Officially, though, she'd earned her diploma as a sophomore. Now she sat in on a couple of college science classes for credit, but she had a pretty free schedule. Which is why she decided to apply for an internship at this new bio-cosmetic company, BeauTek, located in the vacant mall just across the Joan River. An internship would really score points on her college applications.

Candace had an interview that morning with the company's president, Develon Louder.

As the ferryboat sailed the short distance, Candace stood out on the deck. It was a clear if chilly day, and she wanted to enjoy the ride. But as she gazed into the waves, something under the water caught her eye. Peering closer (she'd cured her astigmatism, though she still wore glasses), she realized she was witnessing some unusual sea-life: strange creatures, in colors she'd never seen before— stingrays crisscrossed plaid; otters with coats that flowed lush and long and slightly highlighted on the ends, in that fashionable pattern known as "ombré"; fish flashing electric red and blue, blinking through the currents while they swam.

"That's fishy," Candace said, as the ferryboat bobbed into the dock.

Candace teetered down the plank. To look more mature and professional, she was wearing a pencil skirt and black patent pumps, but they were hard to walk in. As she made her way to the bank, she wiggled and wobbled this way and that, nearly falling into the water. A cold wind was blowing off the river, but Candace kept the straight bangs of her dirty blond bob so short that they hardly budged on her forehead.

When she reached dry land, she tucked her chin into her black turtleneck sweater and peered through her square-framed glasses. After the strange sightings on the ferry boat, her scientific mind wanted to document any new peculiar plants and animals. She clicked the button on her MP5 player to record her initial scientific observations.

"Cattails at riverside appear to have a, um, *mutation* that has resulted in feathery wings," she noted, looking closely at the vegetation that bordered the dock. Other ferry passengers jostled past her as she talked. "More atypically," she added, "the heads of these reeds seem to have lips. With red lipstick on them."

Swaying in the wind as if they could hear her, the cattails turned toward Candace and bobbed above her head with their shiny, smiling mouths. Unnerved, she wiggle-wobbled backward, her heels sinking in the mud.

"Eek equals m-e scared," Candace muttered, hurrying away from the cattails and stepping up to the top of the dock, where a large willow tree stood. As its fronds blew in the breeze, Candace was astonished to see that the tree was sobbing.

"A literally weeping willow? Now *that's* scientifically improbable," she said. Her first instinct was to offer the tree a tissue. Her second instinct was to catch one of its strands. Candace switched her eyeglass setting to MAGNIFY and stared so close that her nose touched the leaf. Passersby gave her funny looks. Candace was too absorbed to notice. "No, they're not tears after all," she said, "but some sort of resinous byproduct. Another mutation?" Underneath the willow's canopy, the drops set into stiff amber stalagmites as they fell to the ground.

"Curiouser and curiouser," Candace mumbled, snapping off the leaf and dropping it into a clear zip-top pouch for later analysis. She left the riverbank and approached the entrance of BeauTek.

"The Mall of No Returns," Candace read. The sign arched above the main entrance in three-foot-tall neon letters. The second L in MALL flickered on and off like a mosquito-zapper, and the final S had come loose, hanging upside down from

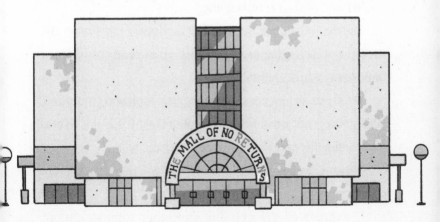

just one hook. It swayed back and forth precariously in the breeze, and the whole sign shone dully in the bright morning sun. But Candace knew the words glowed to life every evening. She had seen them often enough from Sync City, a sulfurous yellow beacon on the other side of the river.

Shaky in her shoes, Candace buzzed at the entrance and spoke her name into the intercom. "I have an eleven o'clock appointment with Develon Louder?" she said, phrasing it like a question even though it was a fact. Between the flashing fish and laughing cattails and crying trees, Candace was feeling a tad out of her element. But once the doors slid open, she was met in the lobby by a familiar face.

"Dr. Trudeau?" Candace said with surprise, recognizing the mother of her former babysittee Opaline. "But I thought you worked at—"

"I quit the FLab, Candace," Opal's mom said with a tight smile, leading the teenius down the mall corridors. "You could say I hit the crystal ceiling."

"I see," Candace responded seriously, the way she thought a scientist would. "Had you been conducting antigravity experiments?"

Dr. Trudeau just gave her a quizzical look and continued. "I've got a great position here at BeauTek. It's like a hybrid job: media director slash lead researcher."

Now it was Candace's turn to look at Opal's mom questioningly.

"I oversee all the publicity and other communications

for BeauTek," Dr. Trudeau explained. "And I also run a big research lab here. We call it the Vi-Shush." She gave a short, sharp laugh.

Victoria's Shush

"That's a little BeauTek joke," she said, like she was letting Candace in on a secret. "Because it's in the old Victoria's Shush store."

"Cool, can't wait to see it!" Candace enthused, her voice filling the hallway. Too late, she realized that sounding excited was not the mature thing to do.

"Oh no," Dr. Trudeau said sternly, shaking her head. "No no no no no. Absosmurfly not. Access to the Vi-Shush is for authorized personnel only." She seemed nervous. "I should know," she yammered. "I drafted the confidentiality clause!"

Candace wasn't sure what to say next, so she just concentrated on not tripping in her heels as she took in her surroundings. Each of the mall's former storefronts now housed its own specialized lab.

FOREVER 20-FUN

"The team in Forever Twenty-Fun tests antiaging serums and wrinkle-reversing creams," Dr. Trudeau stated, resuming the tour. "In the Build-a-Girl Workshop, we're developing synthetic growth hormones targeted to individual body parts." Candace's eyes passed over its window, filled with naked doll parts. They gave her the creeps. "And in what used to be the Cinnaubonpain," Dr. Trudeau continued in an overly cheerful voice, "lab technicians are whipping up aromatherapy to cure everything from

BUILD·A·GIRL WORKSHOP

CINN-AU-BON-PAIN

backne to ingrown toenails with little more than a sniff! You don't have backne, do you, Candace?" Dr. Trudeau asked.

"Uh, *no*," Candace said, taken so abackne that she veered to one side in her runaway heels. She grabbed onto a water fountain to regain her balance.

Dr. Trudeau waited, standing beside a windowless silver door. "*I wouldn't drink the water*," she hissed from across the hall to Candace, shaking her head insistently. Candace straightened her skirt, slightly embarrassed, and took tiny steps until she was beside Dr. Trudeau again.

"Well, your new job sounds brilliant," Candace said, though it actually sounded confusing.

"What? Oh, hmm," Dr. Trudeau answered, distracted. "Though the hours are *murder*..." Something about the way she lingered on the word gave Candace the creeps all over again.

Dr. Trudeau rapped on the door, then dropped her voice to a whisper. "If she curses you out," she said, "don't take it personally."

"Excuse me?" Candace said, confused again, but Dr. Trudeau had already begun to back away.

"Oh, and I meant to ask," Candace called after her. "How's Opaline? I always thought she was the sweetest, most polite little girl."

But then the silver door opened, just as Opal's mom disappeared around a bend.

"SWEET?" a voice bellowed. "POLITE? THAT WON'T GET YOU FAR IN BUSINESS!"

40

This time Candace's baby bangs did blow back, the woman shouted so forcefully. Closing the door, she directed Candace to a patent-leather couch as shiny as Candace's shoes. And just as uncomfortable. Even though the cushions were stiff as boards, Candace was just glad not to have to walk anymore.

Using her fingers, she combed her bangs back into place.

As Candace sat in silence, the woman paced back and forth in front of her. With her wasp-waist pantsuit, impeccable silver chignon, and dramatically lined eyelids, she looked elegant if severe, like one of those hairless cats. In a boa-tight grip, she grasped a snakeskin purse in front of her chest. Solid black, except for a thin transparent panel around the top, it was a custom-made designer Burkant bag, the ultimate accessory.

A rattling sound caught Candace's attention. Turning toward the corner of the office, she thought she saw a scaly tail, as acid yellow as the mall's sign, slip into the drawer of a file cabinet. The woman bumped it shut with a crisp swish of her hips, not even bothering to look, and continued pacing.

Candace swallowed. She wondered if she was supposed to say something first. But just as she was about to open her

41

mouth, the woman spun on her six-inch stilettos, raised the black Burkant to cover her face, and peered down at Candace through the transparent strip.

"DEVELON LOUDER!" she shouted, by means of introduction.

Candace's short bangs stood on end again. She might have been a teenius, but no amount of IQ points could have prepared her for this odd behavior. She looked up at the woman's beady eyes through the bag's clear panel, then extended her hand to shake. But Develon shook her head no. Candace could see her silver chignon twisting above the bag like a Christmas tree ball.

"Candace Coddington?" Candace said, as if she wasn't even sure of her own name anymore.

Develon circled around to her desk and sat down, propping her elbows on the tabletop. She never once lowered the bag.

Candace was at a loss. First Opal's mom, so stressed out, and now this strange shouty woman, using her luxury handbag like a helmet. Not to mention the possibility of a neon rattlesnake in the file cabinet. Candace finger-combed her bangs down once more. Then she tried to make conversation.

"I already have my high school diploma," Candace began, "and I'm taking Intro to Physics at Sync U. An internship here at BeauTek would—"

"*Shush!*" Develon Louder said from behind her black bag.

Candace fell silent. She felt like she was back in grade school!

Then it occurred to her: Maybe this was a test. And maybe that was a hint. "Oh!" she began again, relaxing a little. "The Vi-*Shush*! Yes, that sounds like an interesting laboratory, I—"

"Shush!" Develon Louder said, more loudly this time, still peering out from behind her black bag. "Never speak of that lab!"

"But—"

"Shush!"

"I just thought—"

"SHUSH!"

"Don't you want to know why—"

"SH*$%#SH!"

Candace was completely taken aback again. Had this woman just cursed her out from behind a designer handbag?

Develon Louder lowered her Burkant at last. She shuffled some papers on her desk. Then, as if the whole crazy shout-down had never happened, she started chatting to Candace about BeauTek and its bio-cosmetic research and all the coffee runs she'd be expected to make as an intern at the company.

Candace nodded along politely. But Develon had lost her somewhere around the second "Shush!"

As soon as I get out of this strange place, she thought, *I'm calling the FLab.*

With any luck, the FLab would have an opening for an intern, too. Because Candace knew—the way you know before you even get to school that there will be a pop quiz that day— there was something seriously creepsville going on at BeauTek.

The BFF Ritual

PICTURE, IF YOU WILL, CUTE PAJAMA PANTS PRINTED with jelly beans and ice-cream cones. Four sleeping bags arranged in a circle. Three movies ready to be downloaded at the press of a button. Two playlists of tunes—SLEEPLESS and SNOOZIN'—chosen especially for this most auspicious occasion. And one ginorm bowl of popcorn.

Let us party.

The sleepover was Scarlet's idea. Every other week, it seemed, she was called to Principal Dingelmon's office for "going into hyperdrive" during dodgeball and bonking some other kid smack on the nose by accident. Or "throwing down" with an eighth-grader, instigating an arm wrestling match that ended in a sprained wrist. For her opponent. Then there was that kid she forced to "eat her sand" for copying off her vocabulary quiz. Not to mention a near-constant string of pantsings. Her victims were almost always boys—mean boys! Boys

Scarlet swore were bullies. Dingelmon wasn't so sure. To see Scarlet Jones sitting in a corner of the principal's office, still too short for her feet to reach the ground, her ponytail bobbing in agreement as she accepted her latest punishment, she could have been the picture of innocence. But then the principal would turn his back and Scarlet would stick out her tongue and wrinkle her nose and the freckles would dance across her face in a ballet of bad intentions.

Blame it on growing up with three older brothers. All that roughhousing! Laser paintball in the backyard! The Saturday morning fight club! But secretly Scarlet was excited Iris was back. Already she could feel the calming influence Iris had on her—on the three of them, really. If Scarlet was a tough cookie, then Iris was a cool glass of milk.

Of course, that didn't stop Scarlet from detonating a spectacular glitter bomb-a-thon when Iris bounced down into the basement that Friday night.

"Surprise!"

Cher and Opal shook their glitter out of old plastic trick-or-treat pumpkins. But Scarlet, for that extra somethin'-somethin', had loaded her Super Soaker for a hydraulic glitter blast. With zero windshield factor, she had a fifteen-foot range.

Shiny foil squares floated down to nestle in Iris's ringlets and on her shoulders. She pulled out her lollipop, and silver squares stuck to that, too. Throwing her head back like a diva, waving her lolly like a wand, she sashayed into the center of the room. Glinting pieces trailed behind her. Then she tossed aside her bag and spun around in place, looking like her own private purple mirror ball. The light caught the flecks in her hair, and the flashing reflections on the basement walls inspired the other girls to do a little disco dance, too. Glitter flew all over the place! Scarlet let off another blast from her Super Soaker to declare the end of the beginning of the party. The air-blown burst of glitter hit the ceiling and rained down over them.

"You guys!" Iris exclaimed, flopping down on a sleeping bag dotted with tiny yellow Pikachus that must have belonged to one of Scarlet's older brothers. (Pokémon: a classic now and forever.) "It's not a surprise party if we all already know about it!"

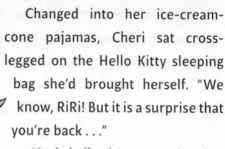

Changed into her ice-cream-cone pajamas, Cheri sat cross-legged on the Hello Kitty sleeping bag she'd brought herself. "We know, RiRi! But it is a surprise that you're back . . ."

"And, hello, it's a surprise that your hair is purple . . ." Scarlet said, stalking the corners of the basement for invisible beasts to glitter-bomb into submission.

"And," Opal added, wishing she had a sleeping bag as cute as Cheri's as she knelt down on a weathered Ninja Turtle one that had seen its share of campouts with Scarlet's other older brother, "the last sleepover we had, before you left, was interrupted by goo, remember?"

"So it's a sleep-*do*-over," Cheri concluded, proud of her joke.

Opal smiled. Scarlet snorted. Iris's pale blue eyes met Cheri's vivid green ones and they burst into a glittery giggle fit.

Scarlet joined the group, placing her glitter-soaker in the center of the circle and settling back on her *other* other brother's Blueberry Muffin sleeping bag. He was the most open-minded of her brothers. Also the best cupcake baker in the family. To practice his *ice-ice-icing*, he had baked a batch for the party. Scarlet didn't even have to ask. She helped by sticking Sour Patch worms, Gummi bears, and red-hot jawbreakers on top of the frosting. Now the cupcakes waited on a table against the basement's back wall. Opal got up again from her turtle's nest and wandered over to the table to admire them.

"Hey, Opes, while you're there, can you grab the popcorn?" Scarlet called.

Opal picked up the bowl and was about to bring it back to the group when Cheri piped up. "Oh, and Opes? Would you be a lambie and bring me a pomegranate juice, too?"

"Sure, Cher," Opal said, shifting the bowl of popcorn to

the nook of her arm and taking a juice from the table.

"And a bendy straw, pretty please?" Cheri called after her.

"Bendy straw," Opal repeated softly, turning back to the table for a third time and tucking a couple of straws into her shirt pocket.

"Oh, and apple-cranberry for me," Scarlet added.

Balancing the bowl of popcorn between her elbow and her hip, gripping Cheri's and Scarlet's juice bottles at their bases, with two bendy straws poking out of her pocket and a can of peach soda for herself in her other hand, Opal shuffled back to the sleeping-bag circle. Just as she was crouching down, she slipped a little. A few kernels of glitter-dusted popcorn fell to the floor, but Opal managed not to wipe out completely.

"Eeks," she gasped. Her heart was pounding, and she could feel her cheeks start to burn. What if she had spilled popcorn all over their heads? But no one else seemed to have noticed the near miss. Scarlet just picked the stray pieces off the carpet and popped them into her mouth.

"Five second rule!" she said with a smile, plucking her apple-cranberry juice out of Opal's hand.

Settled in the circle, sitting atop their sleeping bags

with their juices and sodas and bendy straws and a movie on MUTE in the background, the girls began to talk. The number-one trending topic was #ririspurplehair.

"So . . ." Opal stammered, tucking a strand of her brown bob behind one ear, "your mom really let you dye it?"

"Nope," Iris said. She had never talked to anyone about her hair before, and she wasn't really sure what to say. Except the truth.

"You did it as an act of rebellion! Against the boarding school establishment!" Scarlet said, raising her fist in a salute. "Power to the Purple! That's so rock n' roll!"

"No," Iris said, almost apologetically, because that did sound like the kind of thing an artist would do. "I just . . . it just . . ." she faltered. "I woke up one day and it was like this."

Scarlet arched an eyebrow in surprise. Opal raised her two. "Oh, it's just 'naturally' purple, wink-wink!" Cheri said, batting her lashes, which she'd just decorated with hot pink extensions.

"No, really," Iris said, running a hand through her curls and feeling self-conscious. "I know it sounds crazy, but it's true."

That very first morning Iris woke up with purple hair, she was scared. She hid in the bathroom and cried in the shower and tried and tried to shampoo it out. But the suds just rinsed down the drain alone, leaving the purple behind. For one desperate moment Iris even considered cutting it all off, but the vision of a purple crew cut only made her cry more.

Eventually, after she'd stood in the shower so long her fingertips began to pucker, she'd shut off the water and wrapped herself in her bathrobe. With the heel of her hand, she'd wiped the condensation off the mirror in an oval shape, and she'd faced her drenched ringlets. Wet, they appeared even darker, almost black. But not black. Purple. Deep purple.

Iris had worked through the knots with a wide-tooth comb, her eyes tearing up again whenever she yanked on an especially gnarly tangle. Then she let her curls air-dry like she always did. They looked exactly the same. Shiny. Springy. Healthy. Just purple.

Over pancakes, Iris had pretended like everything was breakfast-as-usual. Like having shocking purple hair was NBD. She knew her mom was already all preoccupied with moving and getting her job back at the FLab, and she didn't want her to flip. To flip anything but pancakes. "Please pass the maple syrup," she'd said, and her mother did.

Mom hadn't said anything that first morning, or any morning since. Maybe she just didn't know what to say.

And now, at the sleepover, Iris could see that her three best friends didn't know what to say, either. But at least they were trying to understand.

"You just woke up one day and it was purple," Scarlet finally repeated.

Iris could hear the skepticism in her voice.

"Is there a history of purple hair in your family?" Opal offered helpfully.

"No," Iris said, struggling to remember her "own it" resolution. "Apparently I'm the first. Lucky me?"

She bowed her head toward the middle of the circle so that the girls could see her hair was purple all the way to the roots.

Scarlet propped up on her knees to inspect it closely. "That *is* crazy," she stated bluntly, sitting back again.

Cheri swatted her on the knee. "I think it's blue-tiful," she said as she lined up her nail polishes for the pedicure portion of the evening. "The color goes *purrrfectly* with your eyes."

"Thanks," Iris said, wishing she could be as fashion-forward as Cheri. "I guess I'm sort of stuck with it." She pinched the end of one of her ringlets and pulled it straight. "There are strands of all these different shades mixed together, from pale lavender to deep purple." She let go, and the lock of hair sprung back into a corkscrew. "The colors remind me of . . . of Claude Monet's famous painting of water lilies!"

(She could have also said Vincent van Gogh's paintings of irises, but that would have been too obvious.)

Because Iris was into art, she thought of comparisons to paintings. Because Scarlet was not, she thought, and then actually said, "The colors remind me of this bruise on my elbow." She pushed up her sleeve to show the girls, pressing the spot with her thumb so that its yellowy edges throbbed.

"Gross!" Cheri said as Opal grimaced.

Scarlet didn't mind. She had earned this particular bruise karate-chopping some stupid boy who had stolen a second-grader's yo-yo, so in a way she was proud of it. "You have to admit it's weird, though," she continued, pulling her sleeve back down. "One day you've got hair like Barbie the doll. The next, like Barney the dinosaur!"

"Seriously, what did your mom say?" Cheri asked. "My mom can't even handle a little lip gloss. Did yours completely freak?"

"Surprisingly, no," Iris answered as she considered her choice of nail polishes. "Which *is* weird. I guess she was just so wrapped up with moving back to Sync City and everything that . . . maybe she thought I was 'acting out'? IDK."

"Oh, yeah, I get 'acting out' all the time!" Scarlet said in sympathy.

"That's funny," Opal said. "If I turned purple from head to toe, I don't think my mom would even notice."

The four girls fell silent again, some of them wondering what colors to paint their toes, and some of them wondering when they were going to play *Pants-Pants Revolution* on the XY-Box, and some of them wondering how much longer they'd have to wait before eating a cupcake, and one of them secretly wishing she had something as special as purple hair, too.

"Anyway," Iris said softly, "enough about my hair. Let's get this party started?" She fumbled in her messenger bag, pulled something out, and placed it in the center of the circle. "Look what I brought."

It was a candle, lavender-blue.

"Ooh," Cheri cooed, sitting up on her sleeping bag as Scarlet dashed to the laundry room, flicked off the lights, and came back with a box of matches.

"I found it in one of our moving boxes," Iris explained, her eyes adjusting to the dark. "It must have belonged to one of my mom's coworkers because it was labeled ELIOT ROPI. But the label was already torn, so I peeled the whole thing off."

"Let's light it, all make a wish, then blow it out together!" Cheri said, as Scarlet struck the match. She touched it to the wick, which quickly burned down to the wax. The flame sprung up, glowing not the warm yellow of a typical candle, but more like a lavender-white. A powdery vanilla scent began to fill the basement.

The four girls knelt around the flame thinking up their wishes, their faces cast in candlelight.

"I have an idea," Opal said in a hush, the pale flame illuminating the hollows of her eyes. "Let's all wish to be Best Friends Forever, and then seal it with a drop of hot wax!"

The other three girls were silent for a second, and Opal started to worry that her idea had been too weird. Until Iris said, "That would be so cool."

"You mean, so hot!" Scarlet corrected.

"Like a BFF ritual!" Cheri gasped.

"We have to do it fast," Scarlet said, her freckles tiny shadows on her candlelit face, "because if my mom comes down and sees us playing with matches . . ."

"Okay, okay," Iris said, picking up the candle. "Opal, it was your idea. You first!"

Suddenly Opal was scared, too. But Iris was right. It *was* her idea. She couldn't chicken out of it.

She stuck her trembling pinkie finger into the center of the circle as Scarlet and Cheri leaned in to watch. "Opal, make a wish," Cheri whispered.

"Iris, don't light our hair on fire," Scarlet added. All four girls started giggling, even Iris. "Shut up!" Iris said, the candle shaking in her hands.

Opal hid her face in her shoulder, wished, and waited. Then she felt the soft, warm liquid drip onto her fingertip. It was as if the oil seeped right into her skin, and the heat spread up her arm and all throughout her body. Opal had never been kissed by a boy, but she imagined it might feel something like this. For a brief moment, there in the dark basement, she was completely happy.

"Okay!" Iris whispered. "Don't rub it off yet!" As Scarlet and Cheri giggled and squirmed, Iris poured drops of lavender wax onto their pinkie fingers, too.

"It makes me feel all tingly!" Cheri squealed, while Scarlet just wrinkled her nose.

"Now do me!" Iris said, passing the candle to Opal.

Opal gripped the thick candle in her small hand, trying not to splash it. It was hard with the wax drop already dry on her other pinkie finger. Above the flame, the two girls' eyes met, and Iris smiled as Opal tipped a small bead of wax onto her pinkie finger, too.

"Now press them all together," Scarlet commanded, as Opal placed the candle back in the center of the circle.

The girls joined their sticky wax pinkies above the flame. Upstairs, they could hear the floorboards creaking as someone walked into the kitchen. But in the darkness they didn't see all the glitter floating up from the floor and hovering in mid air around them.

"BFFs!" Scarlet shouted, then blew out the candle. The glitter wafted back down to   the ground

"Hey!" Cheri said. "I barely finished my BFF wish."

"Sorry!" Scarlet yelled, running back to the laundry room to turn the lights on again. She waved her arms back and forth to clear the smoke from the room. "Thought I heard my dad."

"Well, *I* thought that was simply delicious!" Cheri declared, hugging her arms to herself. Most of the candle oil had been absorbed into their skin, but she rubbed the little bits of wax that remained. Then her gaze landed on Scarlet's glitter-soaker on top of the Blueberry Muffin sleeping bag. "Hey," Cheri said with a twinkle in her eye, "new topic! *Hot* topic!" She reached out to the water gun and with a flick of her wrist set it spinning on its side. "To tell you all the *truth*, I *dare* us to play Confess or Risk!"

Confess or Risk

SCARLET ROLLED HER EYES AND OPAL SHIFTED nervously on top of her sleeping bag.

"I don't know, Cher," Opal mumbled, anxious all over again. What if she picked "confess"? She didn't want to admit she was a teensy bit jealous of Iris's wild purple hair. But she didn't want to lie, either. And "risk" could be worse! Who knew what crazy challenge Scarlet might ask her to take?

Iris sat up straight on her field of Pikachus. "Everyone already knows my secret," she said, almost like she had read Opal's mind, but not exactly. "It's growing out of my head!"

Scarlet was attempting a handstand. "As long as we play videogames after," she agreed, staring at the upside-down movie. All talk, no action always made her restless.

"Then you spin first, RiRi!" Cheri said to Iris, leaning back from the glitter-soaker and moving the bowl of popcorn out of the line of fire. "Because you're the guest of honor."

Opal held her breath. Scarlet tumbled back down onto

Blueberry Muffin. Cheri crossed her fingers, hoping the soaker would land on her. And Iris gave the toy a vigorous twirl. Little bits of glitter spewed out of it as it spun. And when it finally came to a stop, the gun was pointing right at . . .

"Yay, Opal!" Iris said, clapping her hands. Then, imitating the fake solemnity of a talk show host, she held out a fresh lollipop like a pretend microphone and asked, "Opaline Trudeau, Confess or Risk?"

Opal again considered her options. She could always lie. But how would she get out of a dare? "Confess," she gulped.

"Then confess this! What boy do you like at school?" Iris asked mischievously.

Whoa. Didn't see that one coming. Probably should have! But Opal was so caught off guard, she just blurted out, "Albert Feinstein in math." Then she clamped one hand over her mouth.

"*Albert Feinstein?!*" Scarlet shouted loud enough for all three of her brothers upstairs to hear. "The mathlete captain? The *nerd*? You are not for real."

"Oh, I don't know, Scar," Cheri said. She believed in love. She believed that there were as many amazing types of love as there were of nail polish colors. And she especially believed in love against the odds, be it Romeo-Juliet, cobra-mongoose, or nerd . . . er, nerd? "Brainiacs have their charm," she declared in defense of Albert. "Le geek, c'est chic!"

"Maybe," Scarlet retorted, "but do they have the muscle power to carry your books home?"

"Never mind that," Cheri said, her toes curling in anticipation. "What are the top three things you like about Albert, Opal? Is it the way he belts his khakis just under his chest? Or buttons his shirt all the way up to his chin? Or is it the vintage pocket protector? Don't leave out a single detail!" She giggled, tucking her ruby auburn hair behind both ears, all the better to hear Opal with.

"Wait, who is this boy?" Iris asked, unwrapping the lollipop and dipping it in the popcorn. "Did I meet him yet? Is he cute?"

Opal wanted to perish on the spot. She wanted to crawl into a shell and never come out. She realized ruefully that she was sitting on one, not that a Ninja Turtle sleeping bag could save her from her embarrassment now. She looked from Cheri to Scarlet to Iris, speechless.

"Knock-knock, girls!" came a call from the top of the staircase.

Saved by Scarlet's mom, Opal thought with relief, her shoulders relaxing slightly.

"Pizza's here!" Dr. Jones announced. "And we've got a very special delivery person for your sleepover!"

Opal's shoulders shot up to her ears again. For one agonizing second, she imagined that the delivery boy might be Albert Feinstein himself, in which case she was sure she would disintegrate into thin air. But as the figure emerged down the steps, pizza boxes in hand, Opal was almost as shocked as if it had been Albert.

"Candace?" the girls said together.

Standing two steps from the bottom of the stairs was their former babysitter. She looked pretty much the same, just more grown up. Four years more grown up, for those keeping count. She still had dishwater blond hair, but she was working it in a funky geometric bob with ruler-straight bangs. Thick black glasses still framed her gray eyes, though the squarish spectacles were the perfect accessory to prove the chicness of geekness, just like Cheri had said. And she still wore her starched white lab coat, only now it fit over a sleek pencil skirt.

"Hi, girls!" Candace said, peeking out from behind the pizza boxes. "Hi . . ." her eyes goggled behind her glasses ". . . Iris."

"Hey, Candace," Scarlet said as her stomach grumbled. "And hello, pizza!"

The girls swarmed to greet her, Cheri, Scarlet, and Iris each grabbing a pizza box and bringing it over to the table. Only Opal stayed put, hoping her Albert confession would be forgotten, and watching Candace watch Iris.

"*Viomazing*." Candace let the strange word escape her lips, then began rummaging in the pockets of her lab coat.

"Candace is a senior now," the disembodied voice of Dr. Jones called down the stairs. "And as part of her studies, she's interning at the FLab. Isn't that wonderful? She always was so clever in biochemistry! She stopped by to drop off some lab results, and she wanted to say hi to her former babysittees."

"Hi!" Scarlet shouted back, tearing through a slice of pepperoni-marshmallow.

"I really like your short bangs," Cheri said.

From the table, Iris avoided eye contact and tossed over her shoulder, "Cool to see you again, Candace!" No doubt the babysitter was staring at her hair. Everyone stared at her hair. But Iris really didn't want to get into it all over again. Besides, all the talking was making her hungry! The sooner they ate the pizza, the sooner they'd get to the cupcakes.

"Opal, aren't you ravenous?" Cheri asked, sitting down next to her and delicately cutting up her piece with a knife and fork. "Go get a slice for yourself—then you can come back and tell me all about your true love for Albert!" Cheri sighed as she sampled her slice. "Opaline Feinstein. It has a nice ring to it! If you want to put a ring on it . . ."

That was enough to snap Opal out of her thoughts. Candace still didn't seem to have realized that she was even there; that she was back in the group, too. No, Candace's eyes were fixed on Iris. Iris and her precious purple mane. Opal felt invisible, and it all felt oddly familiar. Like a playground nursery rhyme, she could almost hear the voice of seven-year-old Iris chanting in her ear, *Candace? Hey, Candace? Look at me, Candace! Look!*

Cheri poked her in the leg. "Opes?"

Candace was still standing on the second-to-last step, as if frozen in place. But by now she had taken out her smartphone and was frantically scrolling down its screen, only stopping every few seconds to look up at Iris's hair again.

"Um, say, 'Cheese!' girls," Candace said, holding up her phone in camera mode.

"Cheese, girls!" Cheri sang out, stretching the mozzarella from the tip of her slice.

"Cheese, girls!" Scarlet mumbled, chewing on her crust.

"Cheese, girls," Iris said quietly from the table, bowing her head instead of turning around to smile.

"Cheese, girls," Opal murmured, a beat behind the other three.

"That one's going on my Smashface page!" Candace proclaimed, with what Opal thought sounded like forced cheerfulness. From where she sat, it looked as if Candace had aimed the phone at the table. At Iris. Opal doubted she'd even made it into the picture.

And she was sure she could see Candace's left eye nervously twitch.

Saturday = Crazy

WHEN ONE HAS EXPERIENCED THE INTENSE BONDING ritual that is the sleepover . . .

When one has played the party games . . .

When one has confessed deep-down secrets and consumed way too much popcorn, pizza, and cupcakes, not necessarily in that order; has stayed up till midnight talking; and then watched a movie that was maybe too scary and that one's mother would have killed one for watching had she known, a threat more scary than the movie itself . . .

When one has done all these things, and then come out on the other side, into the bright light of morning . . .

One may have what is known as a sleephangover, and one may wish for some alone time.

So it was that Opaline's secret crush was confessed, the strange case of Iris's purple hair was discussed, Cheri's belief in love was professed, Scarlet's skill with glitter was revealed, and Candace returned to their lives. It was, in a word, an epic sleepover. (Okay, two words.)

After the epic came the breakfast. And after the breakfast came the quiet. Cheri, Iris, and Opal parted ways at Scarlet's house on Saturday, each retreating to the solitude of her own bedroom.

Cheri's room felt warm and welcoming after her night away. All her stuffed animals still sat on her bed, awaiting her return. She put her Hello Kitty sleeping bag back in the closet, sat down at her desk, and popped open her laptop. She had homework for math class that she really was in no mood for. Fractions. Instead, she put on a clear top coat to protect her nail polish. Last night, while the other girls had been watching that horrid movie about zombie aliens battling ghost sharks in an abandoned forest cabin, she'd kept her eyes down and concentrated on her pink-and-green checkerboard mani. Now, as she daubed another layer on her fingertips, she noticed a trace of purple running down the length of her pinkie. When she smiled at the memory of the quickie candle ceremony, a delicate, lacelike pattern of purple swirled across her forehead, then faded away. But Cheri didn't see that. Only her stuffed animals did. And they were in no position to tell her!

When she was out of ways to procrastinate, Cheri clicked the link to her math assignment and stared dumbstruck at the numbers that popped up on the screen.

Solve the following system of equations:

3x + 2y = 11

5x − 4y = 11

Oh *swell* no! That couldn't be right. She must have gone to the wrong folder. Whatever this was, sixth-grade math this was not!

Though she bet Albert Feinstein could solve it.

Cheri's mind started wandering again. She imagined Albert in his bedroom on Saturday afternoon, his walls covered with posters of past winners of *The X Variable* (**NOT** among her fave shows). *He* probably finished his homework as soon as he got home. *He* probably had the whole weekend free to do whatever it was Albert Feinstein did on weekends. *Probably just more math homework,* Cheri thought. *And not even for extra credit. For fun!*

Honestly, what did Opal see in him?

Cheri imagined Albert and Opal on their first date. She doubted she could convince Opal to give up her Peter Pan collars, but maybe she could soften the look with a sweet pastel cardi. And if Opal refused to remove her two barrettes, Cheri could at least replace them with rhinestone clips. A dab of pearly shadow would really brighten Opal's brown eyes. It was a start.

As for Albert, change the khakis to cargos, lose the belt, switch the button-ups for a T-shirt, and he might just be a heartthrob-in-training. Though there was no escaping the braces: Cheri wasn't a magician, after all. More to the point, she barely knew Albert. How was she going to get him to let her give him a makeover? How was she going to solve *that* problem?

Cheri concentrated. She concentrated on this imaginary dilemma more than she ever concentrated on her homework. And suddenly, like a bolt out of the blue (whatever that means, though it's what people say), she got the answer. Not to the problem of Albert's wardrobe. To the algebra equation.

"X equals three, and y equals one," Cheri said aloud. She looked at herself in her bedroom mirror, hardly able to believe she was the one doing the talking. Or the thinking. "Using both equations and multiplying them by the same constant, eliminate one of the variables. Multiply the first equation by two, and $6x$ plus $4y$ equals twenty-two. Add this to the existing equation, $5x$ minus $4y$ equals eleven, in which $4y$ negates itself, to arrive at

11x equals thirty-three. Dividing thirty-three by eleven, *x* equals three. The original sum can now be solved: *3x* plus *2y* equals eleven; (3 x 3) plus *2y* equals eleven; nine plus *2y* equals eleven. Since nine plus two equals eleven, *y* equals one."

The audience of stuffed animals were the only witnesses to her flash of brilliance. They smiled back at her encouragingly.

Oddly, Cheri found her spontaneous problem-solving both completely astonishing and perfectly clear. As clear as the top coat she'd just dabbed on her mani. She didn't understand how she understood the math, she just did. It was as if a window had opened up in her brain. And all the birds who knew algebra had flown in to roost.

Cheri faced the computer and back-clicked to the assignment folder, finding the correct one for her class. She figured she'd knock it out in just a few minutes now. *Take that, Albert Feinstein*, she thought with a smile. The makeover challenge no longer seemed daunting at all.

There's math. And then there's aftermath.

Scarlet was back in the basement. Now that all her friends had gone home, she had the un-fun chore of cleaning up after their party. In the harsh light of day, she could see she hadn't quite thought through the fallout from rampant glitter-soaking.

The mini microphone at her ear crackled. She tapped the ToothFayree to respond.

"Yes, Dad, I'll vacuum like I promised! Over," she said, then switched the device to VIBRATE.

But the shiny tiny squares had slipped into every nook and cranny in the space. It was probably going to be sparkling for years to come.

"Bummer, basement," Scarlet said, though she didn't really feel too sorry for the room. *Bits of glitter give it a touch of glamour!* she thought. Then palm-smacked her forehead to stop her brain from talking like Cheri. Her fingernails caught her eye mid-slap. A circle of purple still stained the pinkie where the candle wax had seeped in. And while she'd been agape at the bloody showdown between the zombie aliens and the ghost sharks in the forest cabin, Cheri had given her a stealth manicure! The sneaky diva. Cobalt blue with a sliver of turquoise on the tips.

Grudgingly, Scarlet admitted that she liked it.

She'd overheard Ninja Turtle brother once boast that the more trashed the place, the radder the party. Scarlet scanned the wreckage: videogame disks and Iris's sketches scattered across crumpled sleeping bags, popcorn kernels

mixed with glitter, leftover pizza congealing on the table beside half-empty bottles of soda and juice. What a mess! The sleepover had been a big success.

And my mom stresses that I'm antisocial. She smirked. *Ridic!*

Only crumbs remained of the cupcakes. With the exception of a pink-frosted one that was propped on a pillow like a crown for a princess. Scarlet picked it up and took a bite out of the icing. It was a little stiff after sitting out all night, but still sweet.

Sugar-charged, she commenced the clean-a-thon.

I'll start with the sleeping bags, she thought, picking up the Pikachus and dragging them to the back door to shake out in the fresh air. She imagined the little anime creatures protesting in squeaky cartoon voices. The idea made her snicker.

Dance, you crazy yellow monsters, dance! she thought.

But as she shook the sleeping bag, she realized she was shaking—she was *shimmying*—too.

Weird.

Scarlet did not shimmy.

Climb, kickbox, punch: yes.

But shimmy?

Shaken by the shaking, she rolled up the Pikachus and tucked them on a shelf in the laundry room. Then she walked back to the den for the second sleeping bag.

Except she didn't exactly walk so much as . . . well, *glisser* is the official pretentious French word. But if, like Scarlet, you have never taken ballet, let's just call it gliding. She glid (past tense) over to the Blueberry Muffin bag. Lifted it by two corners. Held it over her head like a banner. And positively skipped out the back door.

Tippy-toe skips!

What the—? Scarlet thought, but couldn't stop. Phantom tendrils of lavender-gray smoke curled up from her heels, evanescing into the air before she ever detected them. She skipped two full tippy-toe figure eights in the backyard, waving Blueberry Muffin from one side to the other, before spinning back into the laundry room.

Scarlet dropped the sleeping bag and body-slammed against the washing machine,

73

panting hard. She stared down at Blueberry Muffin's blank, moon-pie face as if it were possessed.

Maybe it's the leftover cupcake, she thought, heart pounding. *Mom's always telling me to cool it on the sugar.*

She reached down and gingerly lifted up the cover by one corner.

"Don't give me that look," she growled at the giant muffin head. "You're a sleeping bag now, but you'll be a punching bag next if you make me start skipping again!"

Thankfully, Blueberry Muffin stayed mute. Scarlet rolled the bag up tight and slid it onto the shelf next to the boogaloo Pikachus.

One more sleeping bag to go.

She stood in the laundry room doorway. The few steps to the middle of the basement, where the Ninja Turtle waited, suddenly seemed scarier to cross than a six-lane highway.
But Scarlet was not the scaredy type.
She clenched her fists. Furrowed her brow. Jutted out her lower lip. Blew her bangs out of her eyes. Then she lifted her foot and . . .

. . . leaped the entire distance in a single gazelley bound, fanning out her arms and flapping her fingers as she did. She landed on the balls of her feet, bent over from the waist to sweep up the Ninja Turtle sleeping bag like a bullfighter's cape, and in another leap she was out the door and full-on dancing. Left, she dodged, then right, sidestepping a pretend bull, spinning the sleeping bag over her head like pizza dough.

Pizza dough, Scarlet thought, still in mid-spin. *I've got to clear off the table and stuff.* But now, instead of resisting, she gave in. She gave in . . . to the dance!

And in a matter of minutes, not only had she shaken out, rolled up, and put away the last sleeping bag, but she'd bagged all the empty bottles, folded the three pizza boxes, fluffed the pillows, vacuumed the glitter, and, for good measure, performed both parts of the Black Swan pas de deux from *Swan Lake*. A ballet she'd never seen!

"Scarlet Louise!"

Dr. Jones stood at the bottom of the stairs, mouth hanging open. The basement was spotless. And apparently her pugnacious daughter was a covert prima ballerina.

"When did you learn to—?" Dr. Jones spluttered. "Have you been taking—?" For a highly intelligent woman, she was having a hard time completing a sentence. "How—?"

"Beats me." Scarlet stood panting in fifth position in the center of the ~~stage~~ room. "But I was perfect . . ." she murmured, exhausted, and took a bow.

Great. My pinkie is purple, Iris observed as she dabbed a dot of caramel-colored paint on the canvas. Instead of wearing off, it was as if the candle wax had suffused her skin, and now very pale vines of violet veined up her arm. So pale she was sure only she could see them. *Or maybe they were always there and I just never noticed them before,* she reasoned.

She might have been more alarmed if she didn't already have purple hair.

Iris had tucked her curls up into a weathered blue bandanna—sometimes she'd try to pretend they were still blond. And she'd changed into faded denim overalls, which had pockets for all her brushes and pencils and lollipops. She wanted to capture her memory of the sleepover while it was still fresh in her mind. Maybe Scarlet could hang up the picture in her basement. Maybe that would become their clubhouse or something.

Iris and her mom had moved into a glass-walled high-rise in Sync City. From her room, she could see all the way to the river. During the day, the light was everything a young painter could dream of. At night, all the other skyscrapers sparkled like diamonds. Iris adored it: It felt like her bed was floating among the stars.

But a modern apartment wasn't the best place for a clubhouse. That's what basements were for.

Iris had painted Cheri, sitting cross-legged in her ice-cream-cone pajamas, polishing her nails. She'd painted Scarlet, on the prowl with the glitter gun. And now she was putting the finishing touches on Opaline, capturing the soft brown of her eyes.

How sweet that Opal is, crushing on some boy, Iris thought as she painted. *So cute the way she confessed it!* Iris wasn't even sure who Albert Feinstein was, but she was going to find out. Maybe she could help nudge them together. Opal was so shy that this Albert boy probably hadn't a clue he was the object of her affection! But the idea of making Opal happy made Iris happy, and she hummed along as she painted.

When the painting was done, Iris put down her brush, shook her hair out of the bandanna, and popped a fresh piece of bubblegum. The sun had begun to set, shooting dusky beams between the glass and steel buildings. Not too far away, she could see the HQT, with its domed lab atop the forty-second floor. The waning light split into rainbow rays as it filtered through the prisms of the FLab's crystal walls.

Psychedelic, Iris thought, blowing a bubble.

Nearer by, in the eaves of a building across the way, a clutch of pigeons roosted. Twirling one amethyst strand around her finger, Iris wondered what it would be like if the birds were rainbow-colored, too. She closed her eyes and imagined it: pigeons with wings striped red, orange, yellow, green. That would cheer up the whole sky! As she pictured it, she felt like warm waves of light were streaming through her. Like she was riding a sunshine roller coaster! The sensation was so strange Iris opened her eyes again. And the violet aura that she didn't know was glowing all around her vanished.

"*Whoa!*" she gasped, giggling a bit. She blinked to make sure she hadn't been dreaming, and realized her finger was still twisted around the strand of hair.

"Nope," she said to herself, releasing the ringlet. "Still purple. Not a dream."

Then she looked out the window again.

Strutting and cooing along the edges of the opposite rooftop, the pigeons were no longer their muted blue-gray, but a riot of primary colors. Had they really been parrots all along? Or was it . . . ?

"Was it me?" Iris whispered.

Her skin tingled with goose bumps at the thought, and the hair at the nape of her neck stood on end. She watched, amazed and a little afraid, as the candy-feathered pigeons fluttered back and forth. Then—even though she was an artist, not a scientist—she decided to test out her theory.

Iris looked above the pigeons, above the rooftops, to the cotton-puff cumulus clouds. The sunset had already tinged them a mauvey-pink. Iris fixed the image in her mind, closed her eyes, tugged on a tendril of her hair, and concentrated. Once again, she felt as if she were on some dizzying amusement park ride in her mind. Once again, the mysterious violet aura radiated from her. When she dared to stare again, she was one part thrilled and two parts freaked that the clouds had indeed turned the same shocking fuchsia she'd imagined them to be.

And the fuchsia was wow.

"Viomazing!" Iris breathed. Then she jumped on her bed and did a little dance of excitement, whipping her hair back and forth like a rock star.

"But wait!" Iris whispered to herself, calming down a bit. "The birds and the clouds could be mirages." Maybe the fading daylight, and all that pizza from last night, were playing tricks on her. Iris slid down to sit on her bed, and decided to try one more time, indoors. She glanced at the items around her: the easel, her messenger bag, a few boxes yet to be unpacked. Not much to work with. But . . .

"I see a white wall," she said softly as she twisted a strand of her hair, "and I want to paint it . . ." She lowered her eyelids for only a second. Her stomach did a little flip-flop. "Peonies."

A field of frilly crimson and yellow flowers now spread up to the ceiling.

"Viomazing, viomazing, viomazing!" she said, jumping to her feet again. She swept her head from the wall of peonies to the fuchsia clouds and back again, her hair flying back and forth until she was truly dizzy.

"Okay, okay," she told herself, "must chill!" She dug her hands deep into the pockets of her overalls to keep herself from twirling around, took a few deep breaths, then blew another bubble.

She was just wondering what she could "paint"

next when she remembered: She had math homework. Fractions. Too bad she couldn't color them solved!

"Ack!"

The cry cut through Opal's thoughts, and she got up and poked her head out her bedroom door to see what was the matter. In the kitchen, her mother was backing away from the grocery bags, her hands clutched up around her neck.

"Mom?" Opal asked, edging out into the hallway. "Everything okay? You didn't see a cockroach, did you?"

"No, it's—" Dr. Trudeau glanced over at Opal, then seemed to change her mind. "Um, yes, a cockroach," she said, lowering her hands and brushing them toward Opal as if she could sweep her daughter back into her bedroom. "That's all it was. Don't worry, I killed it."

"Oh, eww." Opal shuddered. "There was only one, right? Eww!"

"Don't worry," Dr. Trudeau repeated. "I'll clean it up. Sorry for yelling." She swept her hands at Opal again. "Go on back to your homework. I'll call you when dinner's ready."

Opal couldn't help herself. Icked out as she was, she craned her neck, scanning the kitchen for the crushed remains of the bug. But she didn't see anything.

"Go on," her mother urged, stepping in front of the grocery bags like she was guarding them. "Don't you have math homework to do?"

"Almost finished it," Opal said. But she went back into her room anyway, and had nearly closed the door again when she heard her mother muttering to herself.

So she peeked out the crack.

Over the open lid of the trash can, Opal's mom was holding a fish by its tail. At first Opal couldn't figure out why her mother would throw out a fish she'd just bought at the supermarket. But as the fish, hanging from Dr. Trudeau's fingertips, spun in a slow half circle, the light glinted off its eyes.

Its three flat, gluey eyes.

Opal clasped a hand over her mouth to keep from gasping out loud. In the next second, her mom dropped the fish into the garbage, knotted the bag, and headed out of their apartment, probably to the disposal chute in the hallway.

Disturbed, Opal closed her bedroom door and turned to stare out her window. For an instant she could have sworn the clouds were hot pink. She wished she had a lollipop or a piece of gum or something, as if the sweet taste of candy could erase the hideous sight of the triple-eyed fish from her mind. Instead, she tried to focus on her math homework. Fractions.

She struggled through the problems like she would on any other Saturday, all the more distracted by the freaky fish flashbacks. When she crossed the room to get a book from her backpack, she walked. She didn't jitterbug, jeté, or pirouette. She just walked. And when she stared at her wall, it was the same color as always: beige.

Though her pinkie finger did still have a flush of purple from the wax droplet.

After she finished her homework, Opal unbuttoned the top of her shirt collar, took the barrettes out of her hair, and combed out her brunette bob. The static electricity in the air sparked up the strands until they were nearly as wild as Iris's had been last night at the sleepover.

But still ordinary old brown. She frowned at her pale reflection in the mirror.

Opal didn't know what had been happening with Cheri, Scarlet, and Iris that afternoon. But gradually her thoughts began to shift from the icky Frankenfish to Iris's glorious purple hair. Iris twirling around like a miniature glitter tornado overshadowing everything else in its path. Iris ordering her to bring popcorn and bendy straws to everyone else at the party. Iris forcing her to confess her crush on Albert Feinstein! The thought of the teasing that awaited her on Monday made her cringe.

Opal had spent the last four years exiled at the all-girls' academy. But that was then. Now she was in a new school. A school with boys! Hardly anyone remembered her from before. This was her chance to start over. To be somebody besides "the shy one." The brown-eyed girl in the button-up shirt.

But with artsy Iris and her purple hair getting all the attention, would anyone even notice she existed?

Good thing Opal wasn't caught in the middle of another round of that painful party game, because then she just might be forced to confess this: Opal was beginning to wish Iris had never come back to Sync City.

Under the Fluffula Tree

THE DAY WAS MONDAY. THE MOOD WAS MANIC.
Maybe a group of big-haired ladies back in the 1980s sang
it best: "You wish your bed was already made." Before
they walked like Egyptians into the vaults of music videos,
bangles clanging around their wrists.

Scarlet had yet to strut Egyptian-style, though she had
moonwalked much of the way to school, sometimes moving
so fast she thought she could smell smoke wafting up from
the burning rubber soles of her canvas Converse kicks—a
style of sneakers even more retro than that eighties hair
band. As she waited for the other girls by the fluffula tree
behind the gymporium, Scar kept one hand on the low
Plexiglas wall that bordered the yard, just in case she felt the
urge to spin off into another dance solo.

The curved solar panels of the lopsided-egg-shaped
Chronic Prep building looked dull and dark this early in
the morning. As the day went on, the screens would rotate,

shifting
positions to follow
the sun and lifting to reveal the recycled
bottle-green glass of the school's windows. It
was a very energy-efficient, eco-friendly building.
But Scarlet still thought it resembled a gigantic
kiwi fruit, dropped in a nest of feathery trees by,
she liked to imagine, a monster pterodactylus
soaring over the skyscrapers of Sync City.

Iris called the school building "organic."

She arrived next. Scarlet could easily pick her
out of the sea of school kids thanks to her vibrant
hair. Though after only a couple of days, Scarlet had
already grown used it.
She could hardly
remember what
Iris looked like BTP.
"BTP?" Iris asked

w h e n Scarlet said this
to her.

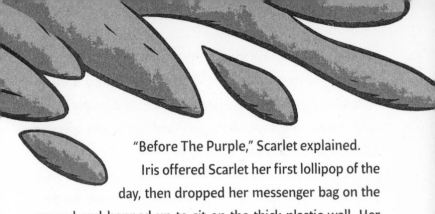

"Before The Purple," Scarlet explained.

Iris offered Scarlet her first lollipop of the day, then dropped her messenger bag on the ground and hopped up to sit on the thick plastic wall. Her long legs swung back and forth in their lace-up boots. "How was the rest of your weekend?" she asked. "Hope it wasn't too much of a chore cleaning up after the party—which, BTdubs, was the best! Your bro bakes crazy good cupcakes." She unwrapped a lollipop for herself and gave it a tentative lick. "Oog, lemon!" she said through puckered lips. "Too tangy for a Monday morning. But can't let good candy go to waste."

"Never," Scarlet agreed. Hers was watermelon, and she sucked on it contemplatively—as much as Scarlet was up to contemplating anything on a Monday, and as much as anyone could contemplate a lollipop. She was really just stalling a little, while she debated whether to tell Iris about her dances with turtles and the *Swan Lake* pas de deux.

87

As Scar Lo mulled it over, the crowds appeared to part, and Cheri skated through, looking fresh as a daisy, even for a Monday. A gold sequined headband sat like a simple crown atop her strawberry-auburn hair, and her waves bounced off her shoulders as she rolled up to the wall. The clandestine rescue pet of the day was a plump bulldog pup, and she'd dressed him to match, with a little gold headband of his own. They looked like a duo out of a Greek roller disco comedy.

(What, you've never heard of a Greek roller disco comedy? The most famous being Sophocles' *Electra Slide*.)

"Cher," Scarlet teased, interrupting this fanciful tangent, "all you're missing is a toga."

"I think it looks fab!" Iris said. "I've got to try wearing a headband like that. Though I don't know if I could handle the roller skates."

"Oh, they're motion-sensitive and GPS-programmable," Cheri explained, pressing an app on her smartphone. "Furi," she said to the screen, "retract wheels."

"Okay, wheels retracting," her phone answered back in a pleasant robotic voice. Scarlet and Iris heard the clicks as Cheri's skates were locked back up inside her platform sandals.

"See? *Très* easy." Cheri straightened her gold sequins. "Also *très* easy: this headband, which I made myself. Iris, I can make you a silver one to set off the purple. And a red one to go with Scarlet's black hair, I think. And for Opal, pearly white. Wouldn't that be pretty? Where is Opal, anyway?"

"Not here yet," Scarlet answered. She hadn't felt any uncontrollable urges to bust into a hustle, even after that fanciful tangent about disco dancing. So she began to relax. When Rhett Smith and his gang edged a little too close to the girls' gathering spot, she straightened up, folded her arms across her chest, and tilted her head to one side, daring him to cross the invisible border into fluffula territory.

"Hey," Scarlet said, turning back to Iris and Cheri. "What happened to your hot dog?"

"Salami? He's back at the Helter Shelter, waiting to be adopted," Cheri said with a sigh. If she could, she would have adopted all the stray animals in Sync City. Her mom had major allergies, so she couldn't even adopt one. Instead, she tried to rotate all the dogs and the occasional pot-bellied pig at the shelter where she volunteered, giving them each a day out to see the world beyond their cages. She hadn't lost a pet yet. But she did have to keep it all on the hush-hush, since you really weren't supposed to "borrow" animals from Helter Shelter. Or bring them to school. That's why it was clandestine. She could have called it the downlow dog of the day, too. But clandestine meant the same thing as secret and sounded more sophisticated. Downlow dog sounded like a yoga pose.

Keeping Jaws the bulldog on a very short leash, and keeping one eye over her shoulder for teachers monitoring the schoolyard, Cheri casually asked the other girls, "Did you finish the math homework?"

Iris groaned. Scarlet was just glad she hadn't asked about the sleepover cleanup.

"I thought it was hard," Iris said, giving the wall light kicks with her heels. Scarlet nodded in agreement.

"Well, three out of two people do find fractions difficult," Cheri said.

"Is that a fract?" Scarlet asked. "You thought it was tough, too?"

"Funny thing about those fractions . . ." Cheri began, ushering Jaws back into her tote bag after he'd peed on the fluffula tree. Then she noticed Opal approaching.

"Too bad we don't have Albert Feinstein to help us with our math homework," Scarlet snickered.

"Shush it, Scar," Cheri said, flapping a hand at her to lower her voice. "Opal was kind of sensitive about that at the sleepover." Cheri still planned to launch Project Nerd Makeover—she just hadn't had a chance to tell the others yet. She hadn't had a chance to tell them about her mysterious amazing math moment, either.

"I thought it was cute, her confession," Iris added hurriedly, before calling out, "Hey, girl!" and waving Opal over.

Opal was wearing her Monday button-up, which looked a lot like her Tuesday, Wednesday, Thursday, and Friday (and Saturday . . . and Sunday) button-ups. Her chocolate brown hair was back in its prim barrettes. They were pulled so tightly from Opal's forehead, Cheri wondered if the strain didn't give her headaches.

"Hey, all," Opal said, but her smile was twisted with suspicion. She couldn't shake the feeling that the other three had been talking about her.

"Hey-ey," the other three chorused, which only made Opal more mistrustful.

After a pause, Iris cleared her throat and said, "Opes, before you got here, we were talking about the math homework. Did you do it?"

Just the mention of the word "math" and Opal blushed fierce as the leaves on the fluffula tree. But she tried to act nonchalant. "Yes," she answered, "on Saturday afternoon. I think I did okay."

"'Cause Cheri was saying that ten out of nine people find fractions impossible," Scarlet added, resisting the urge to dance or make a snarky remark about Opal's crush on Albrainiac.

"Right." Cheri had climbed up on the squat plastic wall next to Iris. Jaws sat in the tote bag between them, his head poking out of the top. "In fact, as I was starting to tell Iris and Scarly . . ."

She waited, making sure no one else was eavesdropping on their convo, then whispered:

"Something weird happened to me on Saturday."

"Me too!" Scarlet and Iris echoed immediately, and the three girls all started gabbling over one another while Opal watched in silence. But before Cheri could explain any further, Scarlet felt a rhythmic wave building inside her. "Oh no!" she blurted out, but it was too late. Her right hand arced up over her head and her left flared downward. Snapping her fingers and tossing her ponytail, she proceeded to dance a flamenco around the fluffula tree. She spun and stomped so quickly none of the other kids even noticed. After she'd

circled the trunk, she came to a stop, hugging the tree to steady herself and digging her heels into the grass.

Cheri, Iris, and Opal stared at her, stunned.

"Ugh!" Scarlet uttered in frustration, turning around slowly to face her friends. "Sorry to interrupt you, Cher, but this . . . this is *my* weirdness from the weekend. I—" Despite the pirouettes and moonwalks, Scarlet scould scarcely scomprehend it herself! She lowered her voice and said somberly, "I seem to be spontaneously dancing."

The three girls burst out laughing.

"You guys!" Scarlet shouted, daring to stomp her foot, even though that might have set off a whole new round of flamencoing. "It's so not funny! It's bizarro! I danced the basement clean in ten minutes flat! And then I performed both the girl *and* boy parts from a ballet I don't even know!"

"In a tutu?" Cheri asked. "I def want to get me a tutu. Who needs a tutu? You do, and me, too . . ."

As Cheri continued her beat poem to tutus, Iris tried to reassure Scarlet. "No, it's great," she said with a kind smile. "It's, um, graceful, Scar."

"What good is graceful?" Scarlet grumped.

Opal couldn't help rolling her eyes: Scarlet thought she could dance. "What about you, Iris?" she heard herself asking, though she wasn't sure she wanted to know the answer. "What's the weirdness that happened to you this weekend?"

"Okay," Iris said from her seat on the wall, leaning forward to tell her story. "Oh, wait!" She leaned back again, dug down into her pockets, then held a hand out to Opal. "Lollipop?"

Opal peered at the pop. Dark Chocolate Raisin. Her favorite. "I'd better not." She could practically taste it. "The doctor says candy might make me hyper." She cast a glance at Scarlet, who had polished off her watermelon lollipop right before her impromptu flamenco performance. Scarlet looked at Opal, too, then gladly grabbed the candy out of Iris's hand.

"Well, you said you didn't want it," she said, tearing off the wrapper with her teeth.

"No worries." Iris pointed to her messenger bag on the grass. "There's more where that came from." As Iris propped herself up on the edge of the wall, Cheri shuffled closer, and Scarlet made the short dash from the tree, gripping the Plexiglas instead. They huddled into a small circle. Then Iris looked straight at Opal with her pale blue eyes. "What's your favorite color?" she asked.

Opal squirmed where she stood. Once again Iris was baiting her with some trick question and she didn't know why! Sticking a lollipop in her face like a microphone! And once again she stammered out an answer she immediately regretted. "Purple!" she said. *Just like your hair.*

"Perfect!" Iris said. "Purple it is. Pinkies crossed!"

But before she could attempt her first public color change, the first bell rang. All the children in the schoolyard started to file toward the oval entrance to Chronic Prep, ready to face a new week of classes. Iris and Cheri each slid down from the wall, Iris slinging her messenger bag over her shoulder and Cheri tucking Jaws into the tote bag The four girls walked in silence under the fluffula tree. But if they had kept talking, they would have agreed: Strange stuff was happening. Weirdness indeed.

And it was only Monday.

MC Cheri

FOR THOSE KEEPING TRACK: THERE'S MATH. AND THEN there's aftermath. And THEN there's Math Episode II: Attack of the Common Denominators.

Yes, this chapter does involve an algorithm.

(And no, *algorithm* is not some mash-up word that describes alligators playing bongos, though that would be awesome.)

But yes! This chapter also involves a flash of brilliance. A hint of romance. A dash of jealousy. And a lavender dog.

Due to the cruelties of alphabetical seating, Opaline Trudeau sat several desks behind her crush, Albert Feinstein. For he was an *F* and she was a *T* and rarely those twain letters did meet in the dictionary. Instead, Opal could only admire Albert—the back of his head, specifically—from afar. She had Iris Tyler as a neighbor in the back of the classroom. While Albert sat right beside Cheri Henderson, up front.

And Cheri got the full frontal nerdity of Albert.

From her vantage point, Cheri surveyed the raw materials of her makeover project. There was hope for Albert Feinstein, she decided. Beneath his thick glasses, he had decent cheekbones. The cleft in his chin could be considered distinguished. And his sandy-colored crew cut had potential to be boy-band-esque in sweep, if only he could stay strong through the growing-out stage.

Yes, Cheri thought with a dreamy smile, resting her own chin on her hand and smiling across the aisle at Albert, *he definitely has future BF potential for Opal.*

Albert was immersed in some mathy mumbo jumbo on his tablet, his nose pressed up against the screen and his mouth-breathing fogging up his glasses. He was completely clueless that one of the prettiest girls in school was staring at him.

Until she barked.

Of course she didn't! It was Jaws, his nose poking out of the mesh tote bag on top of Cheri's textbooks in the rack beneath her seat. But Albert didn't know that. He peeked over the top of his tablet at Cheri, blinking as the sunlight bounced off her gold sequined headband and evaporated the mist on his glasses.

"Why hello!" Cheri said, blinking right back at him. "Have we met? I'm—"

"Rrruff!" As Cheri extended her hand to shake, Jaws let loose another little bark.

"You're r-rough?" Albert stammered, shoving his tablet into his lap so he could return the handshake.

"My hands are rough?" Cheri said, surprised. Moisturizing was an essential step in every manicure. And also: How rude! She made a mental note to include lessons about manners in her makeover.

"N-no," Albert stuttered. "Your name. You said your name was—"

"Cheri, darling," Cher said, the lightbulb going off over her head and making the gold sequins shine even more fiercely. "My name's Cheri. I've just got a bit of a sore throat, that's all."

"Allergies?" Albert asked with a sniffle, offering her a tissue. "Me too." He wasn't used to talking to girls and had no idea what to say next. "I'm Albert, darling. I mean Feinstein!" he said at last.

"I know," Cheri said, doing her best starstruck. "Everybody knows the captain of the mathletes!"

"They do?" Albert spluttered, his glasses fogging up again.

"You even have groupies—wink!" Cheri said, subtly tilting her head toward the back of the classroom, toward Opal. Maybe too subtly, because Albert kept on staring at her.

"Are you okay?" he asked, wondering if Cheri had some sort of nervous tic on top of her sore throat.

She stopped with the head-tilting, figuring she'd better just move on to the next phase in her plan. But before she could get any further, their math teacher, Mr. Grates, shambled into the room carrying a messy stack of textbooks and notepads along with his own computer. His shirttail stuck out from the back of his pants, and his tweedy V-neck had a pseudo suede patch on just one elbow. While Cheri appreciated that no animals were harmed in the making of his sweater, Mr. Grates wasn't exactly cutting edge. The single patch, she was sure, wasn't so much a fashion statement as a hole-fixer.

"Sorry I'm late," Mr. Grates said, dropping the stack of books on his desk and folding his arms in what he probably thought was a hip-hop pose. "Yo yo yo, now let's get ready to fractionate!"

In his quest to make math cool, Mr. Grates always peppered his lectures with little snippets of rapping.

"Holla," Scarlet said drily from a few seats behind Cheri.

"Please take out your assignment from the weekend," Mr. Grates said, leafing through his own folders in search of it, "and switch with the student next to you."

From her seat in the back of the classroom, Opal watched Albert trade tablets with Cheri, wishing *she* could trade places with *her*.

Cheri had just placed Albert's homework on her desk when a single sheet broke free from the notebook Mr. Grates was fanning through. It flew out into the air, then wafted down the aisle to land on the floor between Cheri's and Albert's desks.

$$9 + \frac{5x}{2} = 4$$

$$x + 17 + 3x = 11$$

$$\frac{k}{m} + \frac{1}{c} = x$$

She leaned over to pick it up just as he did, and they bumped heads.

"Owie," Cheri muttered, rubbing the sore spot with one hand. Then she realized she was holding the paper with the other. They both were. Albert tugged it toward his desktop and scanned the page. The flow chart of rectangles reflected in his glasses. "That's some hardcore math," he said to Cheri, because he thought the captain of the mathletes should probably make such a statement under the circumstances. "Even I couldn't do it."

"Affirmative," Mr. Grates said from the front of the class,

where he was still rummaging around for the fractions homework. "That page is from the course I teach at night. Unless you're computating at a community college level, it just might sprain your brain. Yo!"

"My brain *is* hurting. Um, yo," Cheri admitted, tugging the page back toward her side of the aisle. "But I think that's because it knocked into Albert's."

She looked at the page. This time it involved a's and b's, not x's and y's. The chart ran from top to bottom, each step in its own rectangle, sometimes with an arrow doubling back to the top. It reminded her a bit of the monorail map for Sync City. But then the lightbulb flashed again.

"Oh, I get it," Cheri said. "You keep subtracting in two loops until b equals zero. And that's how you figure out a."

Mr. Grates stopped thumbing through his papers. "Respect, respect," he said slowly, "that is correct, correct, Miss Henderson. It's called the Euclidean algorithm, named after the Greek mathematician who came up with it. And it's used to determine the greatest common factor: the largest number that divides both a and b without leaving a remainder."

"I thought yo, I mean so," Cheri said with a smile, handing the page back to the teacher.

"Class, this is an excellent teachable moment!" Mr. Grates exclaimed, all excited, and forgetting all about the fractions homework. He pulled up a chart on his tablet that matched the algorithm on the page, then posted it onto the screen in front of the room. "Miss Henderson, please join me to explain to your fellow students."

Cheri hated to leave Jaws alone at her desk, but she couldn't exactly say no to the teacher. From her smart phone she clicked the wheels back down on her platform skates and rolled to the front of the classroom. As Mr. Grates rapped about algorithms, she pointed out the steps in the flow chart with her pinkie finger.

From his desk, Albert Feinstein gazed at Cheri adoringly, as if she were some Greek goddess of polynomials and nail polish. He stopped only to wipe off his steamed-up glasses on his khakis. But he was breathing so heavy, the glasses just fogged up again.

From her desk, Scarlet stared at her friend, the insta-math queen. *So I guess* that's *the weirdness that happened to Cheri over the weekend*, she thought.

And from *her* desk, Opal gazed at Albert. Even from the back of his head, she could practically see the steam pouring out of his ears. It wasn't enough that Iris forced her to confess her crush on Albert at the sleepover: Now Cheri had to steal him from right under her nose? When all Cheri had to do was bat the lashes of her emerald eyes and toss her auburn hair and she could have any boy she wanted?

It was downright cruel, Opal thought, her stomach in knots. As cruel as the alphabet that conspired to keep her and Albert apart. She sunk down in her seat and tore a page from her notebook into tiny. little. pieces. If only she could find a way to reduce Cheri to zero! To divide and conquer.

"Psst, Opaline!" Iris hissed from behind her. "You said purple, right?"

"Huh?" Opal hissed back, then remembered their convo from the schoolyard. Her so-called favorite color. "Oh, right. Purple."

"Keep your eye on the bulldog," Iris whispered. At the front of the classroom, Mr. Grates was hippening up his algorithm rap with a few robot moves. To keep from challenging him to a break-dance-off, Scarlet had wrapped her ankles around her chair legs.

While Opal watched, Iris set her sights on Jaws, dozing in his tote bag. She closed her eyes for only a second or three, quivered a little . . .

. . . and Jaws's white fur turned a shade that could best be described as lavender.

"Grape googly moogly," Scarlet muttered, spotting the pastel bulldog.

"Iris, did you just color in Cheri's rent-a-puppy?" Opal murmured.

Iris felt dizzy, even a little sick, like some invisible wave had knocked the breath out of her. But she was beginning to get the hang of this color-changing thing. "Yes," she whispered back, "though I was trying for deep purple!"

8

The Freaks Come Out at Night
(And Some of Them Stay Home)

OPAL HAD MADE IT THROUGH THE SCHOOL WEEK. IT hadn't been easy. This time last Friday, she was at Scarlet's sleepover, buttoned up in her pajamas and admitting her now certainly lost-cause crush on Albert Feinstein to the merciless lollipop of Confess or Risk. But this time this Friday, she was safe in her apartment, cozy on the couch as the rain thrummed against the windows.

Her mom had wigged out once more over the groceries when she discovered the broccoli glowed in the dark. If it had three eyes, too, Opal *shudder* didn't want to know. She had enough problems at school and couldn't deal with monster vegetables.

They'd ordered Chinese takeout, to be on the safe side. But that was cool. Opal liked Chinese takeout. She liked to practice her chopsticks technique.

Opal put her chopsticks down in the empty takeout

container and picked up the remote instead. While her mom washed their few dishes in the kitchen, she stayed in the living room and channel-surfed.

Nothing good was on.

Over the past few days, Opal had watched, helpless, as Cheri blew everyone else out of the water with her sudden prowess in math class. Including Albert, who was now following her around in the hallways like one of her stray puppies.

Because Cheri needs another dog, Opal thought in dismay, *like a fish needs a bicycle.*

Scarlet, in the meantime, was still trying to hide her balletomanic outbursts. But rumors were rampant. Opal overheard some seventh-graders who swore they'd seen a punky little ponytailed girl riverdancing in the library. And Rhett Smith dared to post a photo on his Smashface page that showed Scarlet mid-Charleston, dangerously close to the edge of Chronic Prep's indoor infinity pool, about to swing-dance herself into the water. Drama-club kids stage-whispered that she could dance off with a lead in the school play if only she'd audition. It all made Scarlet so mad that she doubled up on her school fights. And double-stepped her way into detention. When she found out about Rhett's Smashface post, she smashed his face with a very graceful left hook to the nose.

Some boys never learn, **Opal** thought, her mind wandering from reckless Rhett to brilliant, and yet equally clueless, Albert.

The TV flickered with images of twisters. A couple in a pickup truck was driving toward the storm. "Wrong way, geniuses," Opal said, pressing the MUTE button and putting the remote down. Silently the tornados spun on screen, while the rain drubbed against the windows.

The peonies in a vase on the coffee table caught her eye, and she ran her fingers over the blossoms. White, with just a hint of red around the edges. Her mom had brought them home days ago, and the blooms were past their peak now, so open they reminded Opal of the frilly tissue paper flowers they used to make in kindergarten.

That was when Iris had normal hair. **Opal** recalled the four of them in their class picture, grinning at the camera. Back then, whenever she was afraid, Opal would hold Iris's hand. Iris always seemed so confident. So positive. So chill. "A natural-born leader," her mom used to say. *Even before her hair turned purple,* **Opal** thought. *And before she could turn things different colors.*

On TV, a tornado ripped a tree from its roots, sucking it up into its vortex.

Slowly—she didn't know why—Opal began to pluck off the pale petals. She dropped them, one after another, in a soft pile on the table. As she did so, a current of white-hot

107

electricity coursed around her, sparking in the darkness of the living room. The charge gently raised her hair off her shoulders, and it floated in midair, as if some invisible twister was lifting it, too. Opal's eyes, normally so warm and brown, clouded over, like milk in a coffee that was spiced with cinnamon powder.

But Opal was as clueless to these changes as she figured Albert Feinstein was to her. She didn't feel any different. After she'd pulled off a few petals, she took pity on the fading flowers. They still looked beautiful even as they wilted, she decided, and she let them be. She swept the loose petals into the empty takeout container and reached for her fortune cookie instead.

Although Opal knew it was just a silly superstition, she snapped it open for the fortune.

You have more power than you can imagine, it read.

Oh, and: *Lucky Numbers: 4, 8, 15, 16, 23, 42.*

"Yeah, right," Opal said aloud. But she didn't throw out the fortune with the plucked flower petals. She rolled it up into a little scroll and hid it in her dresser drawer later that night.

While Opal may have been bumming out about her lack of a freaky talent that Friday night, the other three girls were learning how to deal with theirs.

After a school week of spontaneous solos, Scarlet had to admit defeat. She was now an awesome dancer, whether she liked it or not. She had no idea why. She just was. In the privacy of the family basement, with her older brothers out and her parents absorbed in some storm documentary on TV upstairs, she decided to test her limits.

She stood at one end of the room, balancing on the balls of her bare feet. She gave a last glance to the staircase to make sure her mom wasn't there watching like she had been for the *Swan Lake* matinee. (She wasn't.) And then she concentrated her energy, pliéed, and leaped.

Straight into the basement ceiling.

"Owie," she grumbled, getting up from her face-plant into the carpet.

"Scarlet, what was that noise?" her mother called from upstairs, over the bombastic soundtrack of the TV tsunami.

"Nothing, Mom!" Scarlet shouted back. "Just my head!"

Scarlet waited a few minutes to make sure her mom wasn't coming to investigate further. She listened for footsteps while she dug an old bike helmet out of the toy chest. After she tightened the strap underneath her chin, Scarlet went back to her starting position, crouched down, concentrated, and jumped again.

Smack into the opposite wall.

"Owie!" she moaned, stumbling to regain her balance after her body-slam. "That's gonna leave a mark. Or ten." She looked up just in time to see her dad's favorite painting, of dogs playing poker, crash to the floor. There was a big hole in the Saint Bernard where her elbow had hit it.

"Sorry, dog," she said to the sad-faced hound. For sure her mother was going to bark down again. But all she could hear was the howl of tornados on TV.

That must be some scary storm, she thought as she limped back to the toy chest. She rummaged for the elbow guards she'd worn years ago, when she was training on her skateboard. *Safety first*, she thought, even though by now safety probably ranked about third in the order of priorities. *Might as well buckle on some kneepads while I'm at it.*

As she geared up, she eyed the distance from her starting point to the wall on the other side of the room and considered calling Cheri on videochat. *I bet she could calculate it with just one look.* Even as the idea crossed her mind, Scarlet realized how crazy it would have sounded just a few days ago. Cheri, a math whiz: inconceivable! But even minus Cheri's mathleticism, Scarlet knew the jump was at least the length of three sleeping bags. Which was pretty long.

In bike helmet, elbow guards, kneepads, and bare feet, Scarlet sat down on the bottom step of the basement stairs. She opened a bag of Sour Gummy Babies and bit the head off one. "No pain, no gain," she said aloud, to nobody but the poker-playing dogs. If she practiced, she was pretty sure she could train herself to manage her jumps and bolts and maybe even her pirouettes. It couldn't be any harder than riding a skateboard, could it? After all, that was a toy; this was her own body—even if, these days, it felt out of her control.

Upstairs, the thunder crashed.

Scarlet thought more about it all as she ate a few more babies. *Rumbas and waltzes are probs pointless,* she reasoned. *But maybe this leap-across-rooms-in-a-single-bound thing could be useful . . .*

To be honest, if Cheri had her choice of special talents, she would not have chosen math. She hadn't told this to the other girls because she could sense that Opal . . . well, the whole topic of special talents seemed to stress Opal out. And Cheri couldn't blame her: It was totes whack that all of a sudden Iris was practically a walking rainbow, tiny Scarlet was a tiny dancer, and she could solve trigonometric ratios in her head.

Seriously, though, why couldn't she have caught Scarlet's fever—her dance fever—instead? It's not like she could slow-jam algebra! And Scarlet didn't care one byte about dancing. She probably didn't even remember this anymore, but Cheri would never forget: Once upon a time in second grade, Scarlet had vowed that *absolutely not* would she go to prom. "Oh swell no!" she'd said. Cheri could still hear Scarlet's pipsqueaky voice like it was yesterday—no, really, she could: She'd recorded Scarlet on her smartphone and backed it up on a portable drive. But that wasn't the only reason she'd never forget. The other was because she, Cheri, had been planning her prom dress since way back then. And what did you do at the prom?

Duh. You danced!

Cheri sighed. She was in between clandestine pets for the weekend, so she didn't have any warm puppies to snuggle. She had snuck Jaws back into the shelter, and when everyone else went mental over his pale purple coat, courtesy of Iris, she played dumb. The little lavender bulldog caused such a sensation, though, that people lined up to adopt him. He'd already been taken to a new home. Would his new family still call him Jaws? Cheri wondered.

But puppy withdrawal wasn't all that was troubling her that Friday night. Only since she'd started blowing everyone's minds with her math brilliance did she realize people actually expected her to *be* dumb, not just act it for the sake of a pastel-colored bulldog. And this made her kind of mad, though she wasn't sure why. After all, it's not as if she got her insta-math skills by studying hard or anything ludicrous like that! *Oh swell no,* Cheri thought. In fact, it was all quite backward: Answers would come to her in a flash, and then the steps would rewind in her mind to the beginning of the problem. By the time her brain had followed the steps back to the start, she understood. But it was a bit like learning in reverse. Like knowing how a story ends before you even read the first chapter of a book. And not because you'd already seen the movie.

"Something wrong, kitten?"

Seated at the kitchen table across from her, Cheri's father was elbow-deep in snail mail. But when he heard Cheri sigh, he stopped balancing the checkbook. It fell onto the table, barely covering the electric bill.

"Daddy," Cheri asked, "how come, sometimes, you want to be good at something, but no matter what, you're not? And other things, things you might not even care about, you're good at without even trying?"

Cheri's dad took a sip of his coffee before answering.

"Well," he said, his hands wrapped around his coffee mug, "we don't get to choose our gifts, kitten. If we did, I'd be pitching for the Sync City Protons!" His eyes lit up at this fantasy. "Curve ball!" he called out, throwing a crumpled bill toward the trash bin. He missed.

"Dad, be serious," Cheri said.

"Okay. I guess you could say our gifts choose us," he continued. "What matters is what we do with them. Does that make sense?"

"Maybe," Cheri said. She figured she might as well make the most of her mysterioso math thang: At least it would help her help Opal hook up with Albert. Happiness! Plus it would also help her help her report card hook up with an A+, she hoped. She got up from her seat and gave her father a hug in his chair. Over his shoulders she could see all the bills spread out across the table.

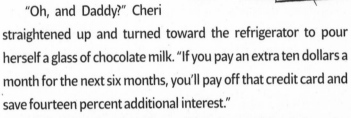

"Oh, and Daddy?" Cheri straightened up and turned toward the refrigerator to pour herself a glass of chocolate milk. "If you pay an extra ten dollars a month for the next six months, you'll pay off that credit card and save fourteen percent additional interest."

Cheri flounced out of the kitchen. "Goodnightie!" she called over her shoulder. "I'm off to my room to paint my nails." She didn't see her dad staring after her, his eyes crossed in astonishment and his coffee going cold in its cup.

Peonies. Iris had "painted" her bedroom wall in peonies again. Something about the rain that Friday night made her crave the cheerful, fluffy flowers. She remembered how they used to make them out of tissue paper in kindergarten class. Now, with nothing but her thoughts, a tug of her hair, and a twitch of her pinkie finger, Iris had covered her walls with the exploding blossoms. In cotton-candy pink, intense magenta, and pure white—with a hint of red around the edges of the petals.

She sat back on her bed, found a blueberry lollipop in a pocket of her overalls, and admired her work. Every night that week, she had practiced with a different landscape: a pebbly beach, a red-sand desert, a snowy pine forest, the surface of a moon. And every morning, before her mom knocked on her door and came in to check on her, she mind-wiped the wall clean again.

She was an artist, Iris told herself, pulling one of her ringlets straight and examining the multi-violet shades of the strands. Artists were supposed to be different. Artists couldn't be afraid of the strange; they had to embrace it!

She looked back at the big peony blossoms covering her bedroom wall. Just for fun, with a few blinks, she drew button-eyed and wide-mouthed smiley faces in their centers. The laughing flowers looked so cheerful, Iris had to smile, too.

But why did my hair turn purple? The question haunted her. It wasn't enough that it just had; there had to be a reason. *And why can I change the colors of all these other things?*

A part of her wished she could ask her mom. At least talk about it. The woman was a scientist, for goodness' sake, working in that big crystal lab high above the fro-yo shop. But something in her gut told her not to. Her mom had already ignored the purple hair. If Iris told her she could turn clouds fuchsia and dogs lilac, the woman might just have a nervous breakdown.

Whatever the reason, Iris had to admit it was kind of cool to have a . . . Iris giggled at the word that came to mind. It sounded so cartoon-geektastic! And yet it fit. It was the *only* word that fit . . .

"But what can I do with it?" Iris said to herself as she stared at the riot of giant grinning peony blossoms bursting from the wall. Okay, it would be a blast to create banners for the gym or backdrops for the school play or whatever. But Iris already liked to do that stuff the old-fashioned way, with paintbrushes and colored markers.

"There must be something more," she said, crunching on her lollipop. "There's got to be more I can do. With. My. *Superpower.*"

She giggled again. Even if it was true, that word was ridiculous.

So the door to this chapter closes with—wait! The door isn't closed yet. It's open a crack. Peer back through, back to that rainy night in Sync City. Each girl was safe as houses (as that expression goes, though it applies to apartments, too, don't worry). Outside, however, down on the city streets, things were getting creepy. Creepy-crawly.

The weeping willow on the other side of the Joan River still cried its amber tears. The lipsticked cattails still smiled their mocking smiles under the acid-yellow lights of the Mall of No Returns. The three-eyed Frankenflounders swam along with the currents, flashing one fish, two fish, red fish, blue fish in the dark waters.

And up on land, a thin man in a trench coat scraped at the door of the twenty-four-hour diner. The rain had soaked his brown overcoat, and it resembled a large, wet, paper bag. A matching brown hat was pulled low on his head.

Once inside, he crouched in a corner booth. He never took off his hat, never even lifted his head when he ordered a slice of shoofly pie. The beehived waitress brought it to him, letting the plate clatter on the table, but still he did not look up. He waited until she was far enough away, back behind the counter teasing her bouffant, before he tasted the sweet molasses cake. As he bent low over it, two spindly green claws shot out from the sleeves of his damp coat. The sharp spines on their edges stuck into the pie and lifted it up to his twitching mandibles. As they sliced through the pie, his one compound eye shot from left to right, and the antenna on the other side of his head slipped out from beneath the hat. With a third tarsal claw—he had four in all—he quickly shoved the quivering feeler back under his hat, then threw a few dollars on the table and scuttled out into the rain again. If the waitress had been paying attention, she might have noticed a pair of pale green wingtips sticking out below the hem of his trench coat.

But the waitress didn't notice because she was too busy clearing the table.

"Humph," she humphed to the fry cook behind the counter. "Talk about your eat and run. Didn't even leave a tip."

Here's a tip, waitress: Thank your lucky stars. Because no, the customer had not left a tip. But at least he had only eaten the pie.

9

Super-Vee-Duper

"NO, FOR REAL."

"Across the whole room?"

"Get out!"

"Ooh, ginormous flower blossoms!"

"But someone's going to patch up the Saint Bernard, right?"

"Your dad's credit card bill. Yawn."

"What about you?"

These are some of the things you say when you are hanging out in the park after school, in what, when you looked back on it later, could be considered the first unofficial meeting of the unnamed group of girls with untested superpowers. Or maybe it's the second unofficial meeting, if you count the sleepover. Let's leave the math to Cheri.

The girls were in Chrysalis Park, sitting atop a small hill—nay, call it a grassy knoll—looking out across the river. After little snippets of whispered conversations all day at school, they were finally free, and ready to face the truth. The truth of what some might call their weirdness, but we might call their awesomeness.

"This is soooo cray-cray," Cheri said as she sat down next to Opal on the park bench. Her clandestine pet of the day was an energetic terrier mix the animal shelter had nicknamed Smelly Barkson. Now that they were out of school for the afternoon, Cheri could let the scruffy pup out of the bag to frolic on the hilltop alongside them. She'd decided Smelly would look stunning in a teal blue. She was just waiting for the right moment to ask Iris.

"True that," said Scarlet. At the peak of the grassy knoll, they were out of sight of the other people in the park, so she was letting herself spiral around the bench like a spinning top.

"Hello, Scar, you're making me dizzy," Cheri said as she followed the blur of her rotating ponytail.

"Hello, Cher, are you sure you weren't already?" Scarlet said. But then she realized that might have sounded mean, so she added, "Just kidding, algebra girl!" and came to a stop.

From where Iris stood, she could see across the river to the garish yellow complex on the other side. The cattails sprouting up on the muddy bank in front of it looked like they were wearing lipstick? That couldn't be right! "Hey, Opal," Iris said, "isn't that where your mom works?"

"BeauTek, yeah," Opal said, glad the conversation had changed from special talents, of which she had zero. "It's kind of an uggo building. It used to be a shopping mall."

"A shopping mall . . ." Iris repeated. She gave her long lilac ringlets a toss as if to shake the strange place out of her mind and turned to face the other three. The light breeze off the river lifted her hair off her shoulders. "But back to more important things," she said, clenching her fists at her sides to contain her excitement. "We . . ." she began in a low voice, taking a step toward the bench.

"Have . . ." Cheri continued, getting to her feet, and getting on board Iris's train of thought.

"Superpowers!" Scarlet shouted, breaking into a rockin' air-guitar solo. The three girls joined hands and jumped around in a circle, screaming and laughing and generally acting goofbally. It was a good thing Iris and Cheri each had

a firm grip on Scarlet, because who knows how high she would have shot into the air otherwise. Smelly Barkson scampered around with them, nipping at the bright purple laces of Iris's lace-up boots. Only after they'd calmed down from their mini freak-out did the three girls realize Opal was still sitting on the bench, silent, watching them.

"Oh, Opal," Iris said, feeling slightly embarrassed by their public display of nuttiness. "It's no big deal, really. I mean, it *is* cray-cray, like Cheri said, but it's not as if purple hair or straight As in math—"

"Or mega-dancing," Scarlet piped in.

"—really makes much difference," Iris continued. "Maybe the straight As! But you're already so good in math it's not like you need a so-called superpower."

Truth be told, Opal was a tad irked by the other girls' hysterical outburst, but she bit her tongue. If she *did* have a superpower, she wouldn't be so silly about it—coloring puppies and rapping with teachers and twirling around trees. She'd take it seriously. "No, it's fine," she said quietly. "It's just, you know."

"I *do* know," Cheri said, sitting down next to Opal again, putting a hand on her shoulder, and looking into her eyes. "But you never DO know, Opal! All this stuff just came out of the blue—"

"Out of the purple," Scarlet interjected.

"Out of the *violet*," Iris said, because she had decided there was no better color to describe her hair.

"Yes, out of the violet," Cheri continued. "That doesn't mean something still might not change for you."

"Whatever," Opal said. The fact that Cheri was being so kind only seemed to make her more angry on the inside. She blinked to keep from crying on the outside. "It's fine, really. It's all good. I think we—" Opal turned away and dabbed her eyes with the cuff of her shirt. She could see the curious yellow BeauTek corporation just across the river, and she wondered what her mom was working on while she sat there in the park. "I think we should test out what you guys can do with your new, you know, 'superpowers.'"

Cheri gave Opal a hug and gave Smelly Barkson a wink. As if in response, the little dog jumped up on Opal's lap and licked her on the chin. "Don't you worry," Cheri said to Opal, visions of Albert Feinstein and her wild romantic schemes swirling in her head. "Special things are in store for you, too. Even if they're not the color purple!"

Scarlet paced in front of the bench impatiently. "Ixnay on this chick flick," she said. "Roll credits, please!" Opal wanted to check out what they could do with their super abilities? After all her crash tests in the basement, Scarlet would be more than happy to oblige.

Opal and Cheri settled back on the bench, Opal with her legs crossed at the ankles and her hands folded in her lap, Cheri twisted sideways, hugging her knees to her chest. Using her science textbook as a cushion, Iris sat down on the grass next to them. From her messenger bag she pulled out her iCan, a lollipop, and her rhinestone stylus, just in case she felt inspired. "Showtime, Scarlet!" she said, tapping a faint drumroll with the stylus.

Scarlet pretended to hold out the corners of a pretend skirt—Scarlet didn't do actual skirts—and curtsied to her audience of three plus dog. They clapped politely, and Cheri giggled. The idea of Scarlet in a skirt was stranger than any of the strange things that had happened recently. But Cheri stopped laughing when Scarlet nodded at her sternly, then folded her arms out in front of her and dropped into a crouch.

She kicked out one leg, then the other. One leg, then the other; onelegthentheotheronelegthentheother! Faster and faster, kicks to the front, then to the side, then to the front, then to the side! She started to turn in place as she kicked, squatting all the while. She flung her arms out and doubled her kicks, two to the front, two to the back, two to one side, two to the other, all while crouched like a Cossack and hopping on the opposite foot. She spun so fast and kicked so hard, her feet started to drill a little hole in the dirt, and pebbles flew up from the ground. At first Smelly Barkson tried to keep up with the little dust devil, running in circles around her and yapping happily. But soon the terrier grew so tired she lay down on the grass next to Iris and put her paws over her eyes.

Just when the girls started to worry that she might kick her way six feet under, Scarlet straightened her legs. Flipped up onto the back of the park bench. Dropped down into a split behind Opal and Cheri. And then snapped back up again and really did rocket into the air. No, for real!

Opal gasped, and Iris scrambled to her feet, worrying that Scarlet might be like a loose balloon carried away on the wind, never to return. But after a scary moment when they weren't sure if they were still watching Scarlet's airborne black ponytail or if that was really just a crow flying by, they could see the rubber soles of Scarlet's sneakers zooming toward them, and all three scattered out of the way.

Scarlet landed in a crouch, right in the small dirt hollow she'd cleared with her kicking feet. Sweeping her head from side to side, she scanned the park for any other observers. But only Iris, Opal, and Cheri had seen her cosmonautics.

"No wayski," Iris said, sitting back down on her science textbook and making a few quick digi-sketches of Scarlet in flight. "That was crayski! Very twirly. With some Slavic on the side. Like the Trepak dance in the *Nutcracker*!"

"Um, if you say so," Scarlet said, straightening her T-shirt, which had billowed out like a parachute on reentry. She was a little out of breath. "I tried keeping track of how many kicks, but I can't keep up with myself."

"Seventy-eight," Cheri said matter-of-factly. "Because I can. And you went fifty-three feet high, F to the YI."

"Cool," Scarlet said, linking her fingers and stretching her arms above her head like a pro athlete. "Although all this supersonic dancing is going to be harsh on my sneakers." She looked down at her feet—the soles of her shoes were already wearing thin. Smelly Barkson scampered over to sniff them. Covered in dust, the dog looked dingier than ever. Cheri could resist no longer.

"Iris, will you change Smelly Barkson to a pretty color, like you did with Jaws?" she asked. "Pretty please? Did I tell you guys? After I snuck Jaws back into the shelter, instant adoption. People went mental over his lavender fur!"

"OMV, really?" Iris said, feeling quite pleased. "So more stray animals might find homes if I colorized them?"

As if she knew the girls were talking about her, Smelly stood up on her hind legs and wagged her tail expectantly.

"Okay, little doggie," Iris said. "I guess I could try again." She took in the terrier, whose wiry fur was a gray-beige mix, like peppered oatmeal. "What shade did you have in mind?"

Cheri gave Smelly a pat on her head. "We were thinking teal—like a bright peacocky green-blue—would complement her eyes. But don't make her a peacock. Keep her a dog. Just peacock-colored."

"Wait, 'we'?" Scarlet interrupted. "Who's 'we'? You haven't told anyone else about our super skills, have you?"

"No, of course not," Cheri said, taking out her tube of lip gloss and dabbling some on. "By 'we' I just meant me and Smelly. When she heard about lavender Jaws, she thought she—"

"Hold. Up!" Scarlet said, hands on her hips. "Smelly Barkson, the dog, told you she wanted to be peacock blue?"

"Uh-huh," Cheri said, tucking the lip gloss back into her bag and then running a finger up the bridge of her nose. "Of course, she didn't *tell* me tell me, because everybody knows dogs can't talk. Now *that* would be beyond the cray. It's more like she thought it to me, and I heard her thought. The same way I can see math, I can hear dogs."

Scarlet slumped down on the ground, speechless. No point stressing about grass stains on her butt pockets, since the rest of her jeans were already so dirty.

"Iris, I thought you could only change colors," Opal questioned, imagining the possibilities, "not actual species?"

"Not that I've tried," Iris agreed. "That would be *too* mutant."

"I figured," Cheri said, running her finger up her nose again. "But considering all the other strange things that have happened lately, there's a one hundred percent chance more strange things could happen. Statistically speaking."

"I see," Scarlet said, getting her snark back. "One more question, Cher. What is the deal with your finger on your nose?"

"I'm pushing up my glasses."

"You're not wearing glasses."

"Imaginary glasses."

"What good are imaginary glasses?" Scarlet spluttered. "And if they're imaginary, why would they slide down your nose?" Cheri was one of her best friends, but the girl could drive a monkey to bananas.

"Now that I have math brains," Cheri answered, "I should look the part. Look smart. I was thinking cat-eye. So I'm practicing. Like you did before with the pretend skirt." The idea of it made Cheri giggle all over again.

"Oh, good grief," Scarlet grumbled. She caught Opal's glance and they both shook their heads at Cheri's kookiness. "Let's just get on with it. Iris, color that puppy!"

Iris wrapped a violet strand around her pinkie finger and fixed her gaze on Smelly Barkson. She closed her eyes for a second or three. As the other girls watched, she seemed to waver within invisible waves of light, and they could almost feel the heat undulating from her. When she opened her eyes again, Smelly was perfectly turquoise.

"Is that close enough?" Iris asked, gripping the arm of the bench to steady herself. She knew from her art classes that turquoise was a little more yellow than teal.

"Totally!" Cheri said, beaming. "Smelly says thanks, Iris! Thank you smelly much!"

"Oh. Good. Grief!" Scarlet repeated.

The blare of a horn from a ferry crossing the river prompted Opal to stand up from the bench. "I probably should get going," she said to the group, hitching her backpack over both shoulders and pulling up her knee socks. "You know, vocabulary quiz tomorrow. And my mom will be home from work soon."

"I'll walk with you," Iris said, gathering up her art supplies and stuffing them back in her messenger bag. "I should get home, too."

Cheri held open her tote and turquoise Smelly hopped right in. "And I should swing by Helter Shelter and sneak back Smelly B," she said cheerfully. "Now that she's such a pretty color, she's positive she's going to get adopted pronto."

"I suppose the dog just 'told' you that," Scarlet said, getting to her feet. She held up her hand to stop Cheri before she could answer.

The four girls trudged down the hill and walked in silence along the orange brick pathway that bordered the river. On the other side, the MALL OF NO RETURNS sign glowed into life for the evening. The warped reflection of the letters rippled on the water's surface.

The park exit was still several lampposts away when a strange shadow slithered across their path, leaving a sticky trail of slime behind. They heard a splash.

"What was that?" Opal asked, a note of panic in her voice. "Did anyone see? Did it go in the river?" She grabbed Iris's hand just like she used to when they were little kids.

"Eww!" Cheri said with a shudder, stepping over the slime marks, which were as wide as the wheel of a monster truck. "Whatever it was, it gave me the creeps."

They continued on toward the exit, looking over their shoulders for any more slimy shadows. As darkness fell, the park seemed more dangerous. With every chirp or chitter or bustle in the hedgerow, the girls jumped, wondering what kind of animal might be making the noise. And not really wanting to know. They still had two lampposts to go when they heard a sharp *smwack-smwack* sound coming from the bushes. They all froze to the spot.

"What should we do, what should we do?" Opal whispered.

"Make a run for it!" Scarlet urged.

"Easy for you to say, Twinkle-toes!" Cheri quietly cried—although, with her gold-dust polish, her toes were pretty twinkly, too.

"Stay calm, girls," Iris said in a low voice. "Act natural. Just keep going. Follow the orange brick path."

"Follow the orange brick path," Opal repeated, squaring her shoulders and clicking her heels together three times.

"Follow the orange brick path!" Cheri breathed, clutching her little blue dog close.

The four girls linked arms, and just as they were about to take their first step, a creature dashed in front of them, halting underneath the lamp's circle of light.

On curdled yellow claws, it turned to face them.

It was as big as a four-door sedan, but much hairier than any car they'd ever seen. Except for its long, rubbery snout, which was fleshy white like a rotting mushroom with a massive handlebar mustache underneath. AND except for its even *longer* ringed tail, which whipped back and forth like a dropped garden hose. Its bulging beach-ball eyes darted from one girl to the other and its crusty lemon claws scratched at the brick path. As its spongy wet nostrils snuffled up to Cheri, it made the *smwack-smwack* noise again.

She gasped, "Oh . . . my . . ."

"Nose!" Scarlet declared. Breaking from the group, she dropped into the same *Nutcracker* squat she'd shown off

before. But instead of cracking nuts, she started kicking schnoz. With flailing feet she pummeled the beast's snout like it was a punching bag. It shrieked at the assault, putting one yellow paw up to protect itself. Scarlet pointed her arms in an arabesque pose and jabbed it in the stomach. As the creature scrabbled toward the water, Scarlet tap-danced down the length of its slithering tail. She jumped off just as it slipped into the river like the mysterious slime-leaver before it.

Scarlet stared at the water defiantly, arms crossed, daring the monster to come back out and desperately hoping it wouldn't. Finally, she turned back to her three friends, stock-still behind her. They stood like that for a second—before they all started screaming at the top of their lungs while they bolted for the exit.

They ran past the last two lampposts, past the park gates, and booked it for the next four blocks straight, until finally they had to stop to catch their breath. Scarlet, too. It occurred to her afterward that she probably could have bounced out of the park in a single bound. But in the fear and the frenzy, she had just kept running alongside her friends.

"That . . ." Iris said between gasps, "was like . . . an opossum . . ."

"On steroids!" Scarlet spat.

"With a mustache!" Opal heaved.

"And a manicure!" Cheri wailed, as Smelly Barkson moaned along with her. "Tell me I didn't almost get eaten by a mutant rat with a yellow manicure!"

"Opossum," Iris repeated, still breathing hard. "Mutant opossum with a manicure."

When their pulse rates finally returned to normal, they realized they were at the crossroads where they would have had to split up anyway. It was too late for them to talk any longer. And nobody knew what to say. Except:

"Thanks for seriously Cossack-kicking, um, mutant opossum snout, Scarlet," Cheri said as Smelly yipped her gratitude.

"Yeah, Scar," Iris said. "Thanks for tap-dancing mutant opossum tail!"

"Oh," Scarlet said with a shrug, trying to sound nonchalant, "NBD." Her chest swelled with pride, but the crackle of her earpiece punctured the bubble pretty fast. "Yes, Mom," she said, making a funny face at the girls. "I'm just a few blocks away!" Then she cupped her ear to cover the small microphone while she said to the girls, "We'd better not tell our parents about this—they'd never let us hang out in the park again."

They all agreed and promised to text each other as soon as they were safely inside their homes. Scarlet strode off one way, Cheri the other.

"Guess we're not the only weirdness going on in Sync City," Iris summed up to Opal, a chill running down her spine. She waved goodbye and hurried toward her apartment building. The evening light tinged her lavender blue.

First the three-eyed fish, **Opal pondered**, *then the glow-in-the-dark broccoli, now a gigantic stache-sporting opossum.* "And I guess weird isn't always good," she said as she stepped away in the opposite direction. The thought scared her. But it also made her a little bit glad.

Amok, Amok, Amok

AND NOW A WORD FROM OUR SPONSOR:

Is all this talk about DayGlo vegetables and mustachioed marsupials bringing you down? Do you long for that innocent bygone time when girls were blonde and dogs kept their thoughts to themselves? Do you firmly believe Russian folk-dancing should not qualify as a mixed-martial art?

If you answered yes to all three of these questions, we're sorry. We can't help you. We have nothing for sale that will stop any of these shenanigans from happening. Alas, we can only distract you for a chapter with snapshots of our heroines' superpowered hijinks as they run amok in Sync City.

So let the wild amoking begin!

Hear Kitty, Kitty

Downtown Sync City.

After school.

Cheri glid (that's how we spell it!) across the sidewalks

on her platform roller skates. She was on her way to Helter Shelter to volunteer for the afternoon. Just as she'd hoped, Smelly was another success story. The dog's now-owner took one look at her beautiful turquoise coat and immediately renamed the little terrier Tiffany Blue. Which Cheri immediately clicked *like* on!

Tiffany Blue was a much more flattering name than Smelly Barkson.

Too bad we can't just turn Albert Feinstein turquoise, she thought. His makeover was going to be more complicated.

Cheri had rolled to a stop at a red light and was imagining who her next clandestine pet would be when a random question popped into her head:

I can has cheezburger?

"Can I have a cheeseburger?" she said out loud, then answered herself. "But that would spoil my dinner. And I'm a vegetarian. And there's no 'z' in cheese."

I can has cheezburger? the question came again, sort of from above. And Cheri realized it wasn't her question at all.

She scanned the fluffula tree branches, searching for the thinker. And then she spotted him: a calico, with a patch of orange over one eye and a patch of black over the other. He was sitting in a nook near the trunk, one paw tucked under his chin pensively.

"LOL, Cat!" she said to the calico, giving him a little wave hello. Then she thought her next sentence, since she didn't want any passersby to see her talking to a tree.

I don't has cheezburger, Cheri answered, *but I'm on my way to Helter Shelter, where they have lots of milk.*

Shelterz no, the calico thought back from his tree branch. *Me needz to b free.*

Cheri shifted her empty tote bag from one shoulder to the other. *I understandz,* she thought back. Cats were so much more independent than dogz. *But it'z getting strange on the streetz. The other nite a giant possum almost haz me!*

This seemed to give the cat paws pause, because he didn't respond right away. Instead, he licked at the bib of white fur on his chest. *I heardz 'bout sum stuff like dat,* he answered at last.

"Then why don't you come with?" Cheri whispered up into the tree. "How 'bout I promise not to takez u in and putz u in a cage? How 'bout I just bringz milk to the back door of the shelter?"

The calico struck his thinker pose again, propping his paw under his chin. *If u promiz,* he said.

"I promiz," Cheri said. "Croz mah hart!" As she gestured an X over her heart, the calico noticed she had tiger-striped nails today. That sealed the deal.

OK, he said, *let me getz my friendz.*

"Ur friendz?" Cheri repeated, and nearly jumped out of her velour romper when the calico stood up on all fours, arched his back, and caterwauled "MEOWR!" into the tree. Cheri just had time to hold open her tote as the cats climbed down. *One, two, three, four . . .*

In the end she counted a dozen. The thoughtful calico waited for all his friends to pile in first, and he couldn't fit, so he perched on Cheri's shoulder, purring in her ear.

Letz roll, he said, and she did.

The oddest part of all wasn't that Cheri was now skating through Sync City with a tote bag full of stray cats and a thirteen on her shoulder. No, it was that all the cats had tails as corkscrewy as curly fries. She was frightened by the sight at first, but the cats were so kind and cute, she didn't feel threatened.

Mmm, curly fries, Cheri thought as she skated, her stomach grumbling. *I bet they would go well with a cheezburger.*

The Good, The Bad, and The Scarlet

The playground.

High noon. (That means lunchtime.)

Scarlet spots a dastardly duo, Duncan Murdoch and his sidekick Bobby McKay, shoving what she reckons to be a seven-year-old off the seesaw and stealing his Game-Boi. In the past couple of weeks, Sheriff Scarlet's been so busy dancing, she's let her anti-bullying patrols slide.

And this is the result. A spike in schoolyard violence, spikier than any volleyball was ever smacked over a net at a picnic. A 10 percent hike, Deputy Cheri calculates, whipping a chart out of her tote bag that illustrates the peaks with a jagged red line.

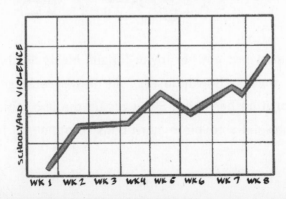

That just won't do.

"Not on my watch," Sheriff Scarlet mutters, hitching up her jeans and heading toward the seesaw. As she approaches, she casts a shadow. A very short shadow. The two thugs don't even notice her till she's right beneath their yeller-bellied noses. From where she stands, she can see their yeller-bellied boogers. It ain't a purty sight.

Scarlet hawks up a loogie, spits it off to the side, and kicks dust over Duncan's high-tops.

"What's the big idea, squirt?" he growls, looming over Scarlet like a bad umbrella. The kind that doesn't know when the sun's come out and it's time to shut up.

Scarlet juts out her lower lip and blows her bangs from her eyes. "Howdy, losers," she drawls, rocking back and forth on her heels. She sizes up the two outlaws: Duncan's got a couple o' horn buds sproutin' out from the top of his head. Bobby's thick tongue stretches back to lick the wax from his ears.

Them's middle-school mutants! she reckons. *Darn tootin' mutants!*

Sheriff Scarlet is disgusted, but undeterred. (Deputy Cheri is just disgusted.)

"I already know you're dumb," she says. "Y'all must be deaf, too, if you haven't heard. This here is my playground. And on my playground, big dumb mutants don't steal from helpless little kids."

"Your playground, huh?" Duncan guffaws, chawing his cud of chewing gum. "Think again, sister. This playground ain't big enough for the both of us."

"There's actually three of you," Deputy Cheri adds, holding up the calculator app on her smartphone screen to prove it.

"And I ain't your sister," Sheriff Scarlet scoffs.

In the background, the seven-year-old lifts his head up and releases a haunting cry, like the howl of a lone coyote calling over the desert. Yup, just like that. Or like a sound effect out of a classic Western. "*Wah-ah-Wah-ah-Aah!*" he wails. It ricochets back off the school building: "*Wah-WAH-wah.*"

"Last chance, varmints," Sheriff Scarlet says. "Or should I say, *varmutants*? Hand over the Game-Boi, walk away, no one gets hurt."

Murdoch and McKay laugh like a couple of hyenas in hoodies. "What are you gonna do, Half-Pint?" Bobby taunts.

A fly buzzes overhead. His tongue snaps out to trap it, like some enormous, mutant bully-frog. "Pinch our ankles?"

"Them's fighting words," Sheriff Scarlet states, plain as vanilla ice cream. "But go ahead. Make my day."

And faster than a chicken can square dance, Scarlet do-si-dos up the side of Duncan Murdoch, rapid-fire tap-dances on his horned coconut noggin till he drops, skips over to Bobby McKay's cracker barrelhead, and does the same.

She stands on top of the two downed thugs like they're a pair of cows she's wrastled at a rodeo. The feller with the horns purty much is!

"Belt," she commands to the gathering crowd, sticking out one hand.

Many belts are offered, but only one is chosen. A nifty canvas strap, just right for knottin'.

Sheriff Scarlet hog-ties the boys together. Pries the Game-Boi

out of Duncan's cold, clammy hands. "Hey, kid," she calls. "Catch." And she tosses it over to the wide-eyed child.

"You take care now, y'hear?" she tells the boy, then leaps six feet into the air to land on the raised end of the seesaw. Balancing there, she gives a tip of the head to the onlookers.

"Yippee ki-yay, momma's boys," she says to the belt-bound bullies before strolling off to fifth-period English.

"Wah-ah-Wah-ah-Aah!" the ghost coyote wails behind her. Yup, just like that.

Color Me Iris

A Saturday morning.

On the Sync City monorail.

Ever since Dr. Tyler learned from Dr. Jones about Scarlet Louise's ballet dancing, she was determined her Iris should take lessons, too. So she signed her up for an intro course at the Cooliard School of the Arts. And Iris took the monorail to the studio.

The first Saturday, all the other dance students *oohe*d and *ahhe*d over Iris's purple hair. But purple hair does not a dancer make. After a couple of disastrous classes, Iris was more convinced than ever: She was an artist. Not a scientist. And NOT a ballerina. She'd leave fifth position and grand pliés to Scarlet, thank you smelly much.

But rather than tell her mom she wanted to bail, Iris struck a bargain with the dance teacher: Instead of dancing,

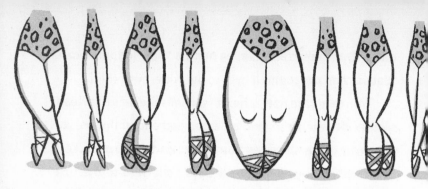

she'd "design" the dancers' costumes (*wink wink*) and "paint" the scenery for their next performance (*winkity wink*). The teacher never did see Iris do it. She'd be instructing a student on her *pas de chat* jumps, and when she looked around again, the rest of the class would be in dramatically patterned leotards, standing before a backdrop of whatever she'd wished for. And Iris would be standing off to the side, a paintbrush tucked behind her ear, twisting one of her very violet ringlets and sucking on a lollipop. It was almost like magic. But the teacher was so happy with the outcome, she decided she'd believe in magic.

Meanwhile Iris didn't care much about all that. It was fun enough to help out the Cooliard kids, but what Iris really liked about her Saturday morning undance class was everything but. Everything but the twirl. Because after Iris had "touched up" the costumes or whatnot (*wink-a-doodle-doo*), she could exit the dance floor and explore Sync City a bit. She loved to go into the museums, practice her sketching, and look at modern art. Some artists painted soup cans, and that was art. Some artists covered skulls in gemstones, and that was art. Some artists even made sculptures out of toilet seats, and *that* was art!

The only thing that wasn't very arty was the creaky old monorail Iris rode to and from Cooliard. It was probably futuristic fifty years ago or whenever it was first built. But now the molded transparent plastic just looked cloudy and dull.

Iris was zooming back home and zoning out that Saturday when a boy got on the monorail and sat down across from her. He was tall and skinny, with a long face and a round mouth. He carried a big messenger bag like hers, slung across his chest. His hair was cool, Iris thought. Shiny black as an oil slick, shaggy on top but shaved on the sides. By the way he smiled at her, she guessed he thought her hair was cool, too.

They were the only two riders in the monorail car.

As the train glid (that's the spelling!) along, the boy glanced up and down the car, then rummaged in his messenger bag.

He pulled out a can of spray paint and gave it a couple of shakes.

Color me intrigued, Iris thought.

Without a word, the boy got up and sprayed a sunny circle on the wall of the car, just to the side of Iris. Then he stashed the yellow can back in his bag, took out a white one, and sprayed a ring of petals around the yellow center.

A daisy! Iris was amazed at how fast the boy could

paint, and how vibrant the painting was. Suddenly, with the sun shining through his graffiti daisy, the scratched plastic wall of the monorail car looked like a glorious stained-glass window.

Iris couldn't resist. She stood up, too, and tugging on her hair, she focused on the wall behind the boy. While he kept spray-painting swirls and sunflowers, she imagined the outline of a funny wolfman monster with furry outstretched paws. And a top hat. She scribbled it with her mind right on the sliding door. The next time passengers boarded the train, it would look like the monster was coming in behind them!

The boy turned around to see Iris's monster just as the doors opened and closed at the next stop. His eyebrows shot up, and he pretended to stagger back from the pretend beast.

Iris giggled. For the rest of the ride, she decorated one side of the train car with cartoon creatures while the boy painted the other. Then they switched places, so that wolfmen walked amongst the daisies.

As the monorail began to slow down, the boy pointed to the upcoming platform. He lifted a pretend top hat of his own to Iris (at least she pictured it as a top hat!), and he dashed out the doors of one end of their car as a police officer boarded at the other.

"What the—?!" the police officer exclaimed, staring at the Technicolor walls of the train car. Daylight streamed through the riot of daisies and werewolves.

"Young lady, did you do this? All by yourself?" the officer asked, eyeing Iris's vivid violet hair with suspicion.

"No, officer!" Iris said, shaking her curls. She held open her messenger bag to show him that it only held lollipops, a sparkly stylus, a digital sketchpad, and a pair of barely used ballet slippers. But not spray paint.

"Because you know it's against the law to deface public property!"

"Yes, officer!" Iris said, nodding vigorously.

He grumbled as he walked up and down the empty car, searching for other suspects. Iris sat down again and waited for her stop. She was already looking forward to next Saturday, and she wondered if she'd ever see the silent graffiti boy again. No matter what, she had a feeling the Sync City monorail wasn't going to be so monotonously monochromatic no mo'!

As the train pulled in to her station, Iris was still envisioning a future chance encounter with the mysterious shock-headed spray painter. She got to her feet and waited for the door to slide open, smiling at the dark silhouette of her top-hatted wolfman, so dapper against all the daisies that surrounded him.

But her smile disappeared as the door slid open. On the other side was a creature way more hideous than her cartoon werewolf. The scowling bald businessman had a furry gray unibrow running above his eyes. It wriggled and twitched, Iris was sure, like a real live caterpillar. As she stared at it, horrified, the man arched the bristly maxibrow in irritation at the purple-haired girl blocking his way.

"Excuse me," Iris whispered at last, slipping past him and off the train. He sssaid sssomething nasssty in return, but all she could hear was the hisssing of a sssnake.

She raced down the platform, clutching her messenger bag and checking over her shoulder that the man wasn't following her. But as the train zoomed out of the station again, she could see the angry charcoal line of his creepy caterpillar brow through the flower-painted windows.

"Ugh!" Iris couldn't help but exclaim, scratching first her hair, then her arms, intensely. It was as if the man's hissed threat had crawled down the back of her shirt. When she finally felt less skeeved-out and itchy, Iris sat down on a seat in the train station and took her iCan from her bag.

An artist has to be brave, she reminded herself as she put stylus to screen.

Iris wanted to sketch Caterpillar Brow Man while the memory—*shudder!*—was still clear in her mind.

Girls Gone Gaga

THE FOUR GIRLS WERE SEATED IN THE FRONT ROW of the balcony at Thinkin' Center. They wore their best clothes—Opal in a cream-colored knee-length dress with pearls bordering the collar and cuffs; Cheri in a sleek cap-sleeved sheath of emerald green satin; Iris in a billowing maxi dress with gauzy butterfly sleeves and three tiers to the skirt. Even Scarlet had made an effort: She still didn't do skirts, but she could deal with her silky black jumpsuit. It reminded her a little of what a ninja warrior might wear. She'd also borrowed a few of her brothers' silver bike chains as necklaces. For sure Cheri would mock her for this, she thought, but instead she complimented Scarlet on her "industrial chic"!

The girls didn't really get why Candace had insisted on taking them to see *Cinderella*. They were just psyched to be out on a school night. And although Scarlet would rather drop and do ten push-ups than admit it, she was secretly kind of excited to see the pretty ballerinas perform.

Ever since Candace saw Iris's purple hair at the sleepover, she'd known she'd have to get the girls out on their own to tell them the truth. Tell them that with great power comes not just fun hair and smooth moves, but great responsibility. So Candace had come up with a ruse. With a wily plan.

Scarlet was dancing on her own, and Iris was taking a Saturday morning class.

What better outing than the ballet?

The lights dimmed, the starburst chandeliers drew up into the ceiling, and the red velvet curtains parted, their golden fringe fluttering like a thousand vanilla wafers. A hush fell over the crowd, and the girls leaned forward in their seats to watch.

On stage, one forlorn ballerina stood in a threadbare tutu by a fireplace while two other ones in hideous gowns fought over a scarf.

"I thought the ballerinas were supposed to be fancy!" Scarlet whispered to Iris beside her as the orchestra played.

Iris whispered back, "You're right! That girl is in rags!"

"I think that's supposed to be Cinderella!" Cheri explained, stretching across Iris to tell Scarlet.

The stout old lady in the row behind them went "Shhhh!" and Scarlet slunk down in her seat while Iris turned and blurted out, "SORRY!"

"Silence, you purple-tressed terror!" the old lady sniped in a high-pitched voice. Shifting on her plentiful bottom, she peered at Iris in disapproval through her ornate opera glasses.

Iris slunk down in her seat, too. She elbowed Scarlet in the ribs.

"Owie," Scarlet whispered. "What?"

"That old lady," Iris said, breathing so close to Scarlet's ear that it tickled. "Did you notice her hair?"

Scarlet twisted around and peeked over the back of her chair. The gilded opera glasses made the woman look like a plump robot. She frowned so deeply when she spotted Scarlet spying on her that her chins doubled.

Scarlet slid down in her seat again.

"IT'S BLUE!" Scarlet whispered much too loudly. So loudly it wasn't a whisper at all.

Iris held a finger up to Scarlet's lips as she said, "But I don't think it's blue like my hair is violet. I think it's supposed to be gray! She's not a mutant, just a crabby old lady."

"The blue-haired battle-ax!" Scarlet said.

The girls tried to stifle their snickers, and the old lady rapped the back of their chairs sharply. She must have been wearing lots of chunky rings, because the girls could hear them scraping against the seats like chalk on a blackboard. Iris and Scarlet both clapped their hands over their ears, but somehow it all only made them giggle more. Iris was trying so hard to hold in her laughter, her eyes started to tear, and Scarlet jiggled in her chair like a Mexican jumping bean.

From the other side of the row, next to Opal, Candace looked at them sternly. "Girls, behave!" she hissed.

The sight of Candace sitting in the theater in her typical white lab coat definitely didn't make things any less funny.

Opal concentrated on the ballet. She felt sorry for poor Cinderella in her tattered tutu, bossed around by those horrible stepsisters. She narrowed her eyes at Scarlet, who was squirming in her aisle seat.

"Candace?" Opal said softly, staring straight ahead again at the stage. "Do you think this is just a fairy tale, or are there fairy godmothers in real life?"

The question caught Candace off guard, and she looked at Opal with a mix of sympathy and surprise. Opal had always been the shyest of the four girls, and honestly, Candace wasn't quite sure what went on inside her head. Not that she knew what went on in any of their crazy tween brains! But Opaline Trudeau was definitely the most . . . *inscrutable* . . . of the bunch. Was she experiencing any strange side effects? Candace didn't notice anything different, and since Opal's mom didn't work at the FLab, Candace had no clue. The last time she'd seen Dr. Trudeau was at that bizarre interview with the BeauTek pocketbook lady.

And she still hadn't answered Opal's question.

"I think . . ." Candace stammered. What could she say? She was a future scientist. Scientists didn't believe in fairy tales! "I'm not aware," she began again, "of any evidence that supports the existence of fairy godmothers." On stage a pumpkin sat, waiting to be changed into a carriage. "But maybe it just hasn't been documented yet."

It sounded lame. Candace knew it. She could never lie to the girls, but from the look on Opal's face she could tell her reply had been disappointing.

"We'll talk more later," Candace leaned in to say, giving Opal's shoulder a squeeze. "For now let's just enjoy the show."

Opal nodded politely, her eyes never leaving the stage.

Even though Iris was quivering with the giggles in the seat next to her, Cheri was trying to watch the ballet, too. But something was bothering her. She sensed a disturbance in the balcony.

Help me, girl in the green dress, a voice pleaded. *You're my only hope!*

Much more delicately than ants-in-her-pants Scarlet, Cheri peeked over her shoulder. The snooty blue-haired lady had her hands folded up under her ample bosom. Cheri peered down past the woman's knees. In the darkness of the theater, she could barely see. The voice came again.

Let me out! it said. *It's hotter in here than a car seat in summer! And grandma's a real crab!*

Cheri realized a teacup poodle was in the lady's handbag, under her seat!

Then came chaos.

It seemed like it happened all at once, but here's how it went down:

Iris, who felt sorry for poor Cinderella just like Opal did, decided to make her ratty rag dress into a stunning, if still shredded, gown of gold. Sprinkled with a print of candy cupcakes like the ones at Scarlet's sleepover. A cupcake dress would definitely capture the eye, and hopefully the heart, of the prince.

But for good measure, with another few blinks, Iris also changed the nasty stepsisters' dresses to the most revolting prints she could think up. One got a skirt covered with grease stains, like she'd showered with a slice of pizza instead of soap. The other one Iris made over with the design of a dented minivan. Because Iris knew the prince would only ever drive one of those sports cars with flames painted on the sides.

Then Iris scattered the scarf that the stepsisters had been fighting over with a pattern of crawling spiders. When they saw the creepy-crawlies, the stepsister ballerinas screamed like opera sopranos, blowing out the lightbulbs all the way up in the starburst chandeliers, and flung the scarf into the orchestra pit. It landed on the conductor's baton. As he waved his arm out to lead the musicians, they saw all the spiders swinging from the stick and they started to scream, too. In harmony. Cymbals clanged and sousaphones squawked; oboes moaned "Oh no!" and French horns swore "Sacré bleu!" One courageous cellist leaped to his feet to sword-fight the spider-baton using his bow.

With confusing costumes and no music, the dancers didn't know what to do with themselves. They came to a halt on the stage, standing around like they were waiting for a bus, not performing a ballet. The audience began to murmur that this was the most avant-garde spectacle they had ever seen. The dancers had switched roles, and now they weren't even dancing!

But someone was about to dance.

To dance her sass off.

Someone in the front row of the balcony who had been fidgeting in her seat since the start of the ballet.

Scarlet leaped to her feet. Jumped on top of the balcony railing like it was a balance beam. And sprung over the orchestra seats to land in the center of the stage. She looked out at the shocked audience. It was so quiet, you could have heard a flower bloom. To silence, she started to perform Cinderella's solo from Act Two, even though the company had barely begun Act One.

"Just dance," Scarlet panted as she pranced. "Gonna be okay, da-da-doo-doo, just dance . . ."

"Shorty, I can see that you got so much energy!" the drummer called from the orchestra pit, getting over his fear of spiders and picking up the beat. The audience settled back in their seats, mesmerized by the ninja ballerina dancing her hip-hop Cinderella.

But were their eyes playing more tricks on them, or was that a tiny white poodle chasing after the stepsister dressed like a minivan?

"Eek!" she shrieked, the license plate on her butt bobbing as she ran.

"Mister Marshmallow!" the blue-haired lady cried from the balcony when she realized her dog was on stage taking a bow-wow. With clicking red claws festooned with glittering cocktail rings, she went to snap up her handbag from under her chair, only to see it open and empty and swinging from Cheri's pinkie finger.

"You really shouldn't take poodles to the ballet in your purse," she said. "The teacup breed much prefers the soothing sounds of smooth jazz. And you really ARE a crab!"

"Well, I never!" the lady huffed, snatching the bag back from Cheri and waddling out of her row to make her way down to the stage. By now, most of the audience was on its feet, clapping along to Scarlet's solo. She came to a stop just as the red-faced, blue-haired old lady mounted the stage to chase Mister Marshmallow as he chased Cinderella's minivan stepsister with the license plate butt.

Surveying the chaos, Scarlet muttered, "Grape googly moogly." Looking for an escape route, she moved toward the wings in controlled catlike leaps.

"Hey! *Pas de chat*!" Iris called from up in the balcony, pointing down at Scarlet's steps. "Whoot! Whoot!" She turned to Cheri and Opal with a wide smile. "I didn't learn how to do those in my undance class!"

Crouched down in her seat, Candace covered her face with the collar of her lab coat and shook her head. This was SO much more out of control than she'd realized.

And it wasn't even intermission.

We Need to Talk

OH, THOSE FOUR LITTLE WORDS. WORDS TO BE AVOIDED at all costs.

1. We.

2. Need.

3. To.

4. Talk.

Do we really? Do we *need* to? Is it absolutely, positively necessary? Because "we" know what those four little words mean. "We" know what *you're* going to say:

We need to talk . . . about your straight-C report card.

We need to talk . . . about your peanut-butter morning breath.

We need to talk . . . about the haircut you gave your little brother.

Or, in the case of our girls: We need to talk about what just happened at the ballet.

Nothing good ever comes after "We need to talk"!

Nevertheless, that's how Candace began the conversation. She had hustled the girls out of the theater at Thinkin' Center and across the avenue to Tom's Diner. Well, she hustled Iris, Cheri, and Opal. Scarlet did the hustle herself.

"What'll it be, girls?" the waitress had asked, pulling a pen from her bouffant to jot down their order. Two white stripes ran up the sides of her towering brown hairdo. She reminded Scarlet of the Bride of Frankenstein in an apron. Luckily, she didn't appear to have any bolts sticking out of her neck.

Opal was about to order when Cheri spoke over her. "Strawberry milkshake, please."

"Butterbeer!" Scarlet shouted, banging her fist on the table. "And don't skimp on the caramel sauce." Then she took a long slug of her water. That Cinderella solo had made her mighty thirsty.

The waitress arched an eyebrow at her, nudging up the white streak above it.

"And I'd like the triple-berry parfait," Iris said, though it was hard to choose from all the sweet options on the menu.

"How 'bout you, hon?" the waitress asked Opal, who shrunk back in the corner of the booth, disturbed by the sight of her bouffant.

"Looks like you could use a stiff butterbeer, too, same as your jittery little friend here."

"Oh, no thank you," Opal said, so softly that the waitress had to bend over the table to hear. Her Oreo-striped beehive towered above Iris like a hairy storm cloud. "Just a hot chocolate for me," Opal squeaked. "With Mister Marshmallows. I mean mini marshmallows!" Opal corrected herself, blushing.

"And one camomile tea." Candace needed to stay calm.

"Got it," the waitress said, snapping her notepad shut and shoving it in her apron pocket. Then she repeated back their order in a weird shorthand that went with the classic-diner vibe: "Pink in a Blender, the Harry Classic—heavy on the sauce—Three in the Snow, and Polar Bears Swim Lake Cocoa. Plus camomile tea for mom."

"Mom?!" Candace spluttered as the waitress walked away. "I hardly look like I'm old enough to be your mom!" Between the funny food names and Candace's anger, the girls burst out laughing all over again. Scarlet covered her nose with her napkin to keep from snorting out water.

"Girls, come on," Candace said. "Sit still. *We need to talk.*"

(Don't say you weren't warned!)

At the sound of those four little words, the four girls did settle down as best as they could, after Iris gave Cheri one last playful kick beneath the table. Candace looked at the four bright faces staring back at her and took a deep breath.

"I know," she said quietly, so that none of the diner's other customers could hear, "about your superpowers."

"What?"

"No way!"

"We don't have any—"

"Uh-uh," Candace said, wagging a finger. "Don't even say it. And don't try to deny it. Don't you think I saw the pandemonium at the ballet?"

"There were pandas at the ballet?" Cheri cried out. "Why didn't anyone tell me?"

"Kung-fu pandas?" Scarlet asked. "Because that would be awesome."

"No, not *pandas*," Candace said. "*Pandemonium.* Chaos. Mayhem. Craziness!"

"Hullabaloo too?" Iris suggested helpfully.

"Hullabaloo too," Candace said, once more observing the girl with the purple hair. "And I think it all started with you."

"Me?" Iris repeated.

"You," Candace affirmed. "Those super-violet strands were a major clue."

"Oh," Iris said, trying to hide behind them.

"So let me get this straight, curly girl," Candace said. "You can turn things whatever color you think of?"

Iris nodded, her purple locks quivering from root to tip. Even though she hadn't hurt anyone with her color-changing, she felt a little bit ashamed. "I only ever did it a few times," she said, her blue eyes blinking back tears. "Mostly in my room. And it helped the dogs from Cheri's shelter!"

"It's okay," Candace said, giving Iris a hug. She'd get the deets about the shelter dogs in her bedroom later. "The first step is admitting it." With one arm around Iris, Candace turned to the table's dancing queen.

"And Scarlet," she said. "Based on your gravity-defying, standing-O, hip-hop ballet solo, I'm concluding you're a power dancer?"

"It's stupid!" Scarlet complained, balling up her paper napkin and tossing it across the diner. "I try not to, but I can't help it!"

"I know you can't." Candace tousled the top of Scarlet's head. "And it's not stupid."

She looked at Cheri, who was toying with her mood ring, twisting it back and forth around her thumb. "Cher," she continued, "you're an overnight math wiz and mind-melding with poodles to boot?"

"Not just poodles," Cheri whispered. "And not just in boots." She took a deep breath and then gushed, "Also terrier mixes. And thirteen stray cats. Usually in my platform roller skates." She lifted one foot up on the booth's padded bench to show Candace.

"Hmmm," was all that Candace said to this news, staring at the rainbow-striped wedges. It was even kookier than she'd expected. She'd better just get it all out in the open.

Opal, sitting at her right side, was fiddling with the condiments. As Candace gazed at her from behind her stern square glasses, Opal fumbled the saltshaker, knocking it on its side. Little grains of salt scattered across the table.

"Don't be nervous, Opal," Candace said, sweeping the loose salt off the table into the palm of her hand and tossing it over her left shoulder for luck. (Even though Candace was a fledgling scientist, she was not above following harmless superstitions.) "We're all friends here. We can trust each other. That's important, guys. Trust."

The other three girls nodded vigorously.

"So spill it!" Candace said with a wink, setting the saltshaker upright again. "What wild power do *you* have? You've done a way better job of keeping it secret than these three chiquitas!"

Opal swallowed. It seemed as if her entire life had turned into one long game of Confess or Risk, and she always had the wrong answer.

"None," she said drily. "I've got nothing. I'm just the same as I've always been."

"Oh, thank goodness!" Candace declared, squeezing Opal's shaking hand. "At least one of you has been spared this insanity." Candace seemed genuinely relieved. But the other three girls looked at Opal with what she was sure was pity.

The bouffant waitress returned with their order: a tray stacked with sugary bliss, with Harry Potter in a Blender and Polar Bears in Pink Snow or whatever the heck she'd called the desserts! She passed them around the table: elegant parfait glasses to Iris and Cheri, a frothy pitcher to Scarlet, and warm mugs to Opal and Candace.

They sat wordlessly for a few seconds, each one tasting her dessert. Cheri sipped her strawberry milkshake, pursing her lips at its sweetness. Iris scooped a blueberry out of her parfait with a long swizzle spork. Scarlet took a big gulp of her butterbeer and exclaimed, "Ahh! Hits the spot!" Then burped.

As Opal bowed her head over her mug of hot chocolate, the white clouds passed over her brown eyes once more. Like mini marshmallows. Or Polar Bears on Lake Cocoa. She winced, blinking to clear her vision, but it didn't help. She could hear the noises of the diner around her: the clink of silverware, the sizzle of burgers and eggs being fried, the chatter of other people's conversations. But the girls at the table said nothing. When Opal could see clearly again, she raised her eyes. The other three girls were engrossed in their desserts, while Candace was distracted by her slippery camomile tea bag, trying to scoop it out of her cup. No one had noticed her momentary whiteout.

Of course they didn't, Opal thought, even though she was relieved.

"Awkward silence alert?" Iris said, offering Opal a blueberry. Opal took it, but squashed it in a napkin once Iris turned away.

Now that they'd finally told a grown-up—well, not a total grown-up, but Candace—about their superpowers, Iris wanted to hear what the babysitter knew. Candace was smart, a teenius: Maybe she could help figure out what was happening to them.

"Candace, is that why you took us to the ballet?" Iris asked. "To test us?"

Candace blew on her camomile tea to cool it down a bit, but that just sent herbal droplets across her glasses. "After I saw Iris at the sleepover," she said, removing them and wiping the lenses with Opal's discarded napkin, "naturally I was curious."

The four girls waited for her continue.

"So I sent up a MAUVe to track your actions."

Scarlet's mouth dropped open. Cheri's eyebrows shot up.

"A what?" Iris asked.

"**M**iniature **A**erial **U**nmanned **Ve**hicle," Candace spelled out. "A, um, drone. It's like a camera in the sky." As she spoke, she placed her glasses on the table and reached inside her bag to take out her smartphone. "I input a few key locations—Chronic Prep, your home addresses—and then had the images filtered back to me."

Candace tapped her phone, then held it up. "See?"

The girls were astonished to see themselves on the screen at that very moment, from just outside and slightly above the diner. Cheri waved tentatively out the window, and Opal watched her waving on the screen of Candace's phone.

"You spied on us!" Scarlet said, stunned.

"Er, yes," Candace had to admit, clicking off the live feed and stashing her phone back in her bag. "But in a good way! Like a 'Big Sister is Watching' way! Just to make sure you were okay!"

"So you saw me change Smelly Barkson in Chrysalis Park," Iris said, putting the pieces together.

"The turquoise dog?" Candace said. "Yes."

"And you saw me flamenco around the fluffula tree?" Scarlet asked.

172

"Your floreos were fabulous," Candace answered, attempting to imitate the swirling hand flourishes of the Spanish dance.

"But how did you know about me and math?" Cheri wondered aloud. "You can't watch math by satellite."

"That's true," Candace acknowledged. "The moms may have also mentioned some things at the FLab . . ."

"My mom is *such* a blabbermouth," Scarlet interrupted, a butterbeer mustache above her mouth. "That's why I never tell her anything! The woman can't keep a secret."

"Well," Candace said, "without tipping them off, I tried to find out from your moms—not your mom, Opal, because she's over at BeauTek, though I guess it doesn't matter, if you haven't experienced any side effects—"

Opal flinched as the babysitter babbled, but Iris cut her off midstream. "Side effects of what?" she asked. Her mind was still reeling from the MAUVe thing.

Candace took a sip of her tea before responding.

"Of Heliotropium."

"Heliowhat?" Scarlet said, confused all over again. The girls shifted uncomfortably in their seats, waiting for Candace to continue.

"He-li-o-tro-pi-um," she repeated slowly, sounding out each syllable. "It's a plant-based derivative altered with subatomic particles."

The girls were even more confused than before.

"It's a destabilized bioorganic compound containing a chain of highly reactive free radicals."

The girls were starting to feel like they were at a foreign film minus the subtitles.

Candace could see the question marks on their faces. She frowned, then tried again.

"It's the goo that got splattered on you at the FLab," she said simply. "Four years ago, when you were just four rambunctious seven-year-olds."

"Oh . . ." Cheri stirred her straw in her strawberry milkshake. It had been four years, but she still wondered what ever became of Darth Odor the skunk, her very first pet.

"I remember that," said Scarlet.

"The talent show!" Opal nodded.

"The drop-kick," Iris said slowly. Then it hit her. "So it's all my fault this stuff is happening to us?" she asked, alarmed.

"No, no, sweetie." Candace shook her head. "It was an accident. If anything it was my fault. I should never have been messing with that serum, especially not with four little girls underfoot. But you know what they say! 'Curiosity killed the—'" Candace caught sight of Cheri and started over. "Er, curiosity got the best of me." An almost dreamy look crossed her face as she thought back to it. "There I was in the FLab, all those chemicals at my fingertips, like a kid in a candy shop! I'd read on some sci-fi conspiracy blogs that a top-secret formula was being developed at the HQT. A formula that could alter fundamental biogenetics. So when I found the Heliotropium in a box labeled CLEANING SUPPLIES next to the lab skeleton . . . well, you know the rest."

"I thought we washed off all the slime in the safety showers," Opal said. She could still hear that electric thunderclap. The memory of the missing Skeletony still sent a shiver down her spine.

"Those showers were like water slides times one hundred," Scarlet agreed.

"I thought so, too," said Candace. "I certainly hoped so. But as soon as I saw Iris's hair, that night at your sleep-do-over, I knew I was wrong. That your bodies had absorbed the serum, and that a sixth, supernatural element had been added to your DNA. What I can't figure out is, after four years, what triggered your reactions now? What activated them?" Candace picked up her glasses and put them back on. The lenses were smeared with blueberry mush from Opal's napkin. Candace pulled them off again, puzzled. Then she dunked them in her water glass, swished them around, and started cleaning them anew.

"The candle wax." Opal thought back to the tingly sensation on her skin. "The purple candle wax."

"What candle?" Candace asked. "The blogs did report that any remaining serum was condensed into waxlike columns. Did you come into contact with it?"

"Candace?" Iris squeaked. "How do you spell . . . ?"

"Heliotropium? H-e-l," Candace began quietly, glancing over her shoulder to make sure the bouffant waitress wasn't jotting *this* down on her notepad, "i-o-t—"

"Eliot Ropi!" Scarlet hissed, thumping the table with her tankard again. "Obviously *not* your mom's coworker, Iris!"

"So it *is* all my fault," Iris whispered, her voice wavery. "I found a candle in one of our moving boxes. I brought it to the sleepover . . ."

Her voice trailed off and the girls sat stunned in their diner booth. Iris pictured them on a screen somewhere, looking stunned from a satellite view. All the hilarity of the ballet had faded away, replaced by the worry that something might be seriously weird with them. The last drops of Opal's hot cocoa had gone cold, a scummy skin on its surface. Scarlet drained the dregs of her butterbeer, which tasted sickeningly sweet. "Blurgh," she grimaced. "Buzzkill."

"The point is . . ." Candace tried to rally the girls. "The point . . . what is the point?"

"That we're genetic freaks?" Cheri's lower lip started to tremble. "I can't be a genetic freak, not yet! I've never even kissed a boy! Or designed an app! Or—"

"Girls, no, chill," Iris said, remembering to be brave and standing up to speak to the rest of the table. Her butterfly sleeves fluttered around her. "We've got to get

176

a grip. Other than a few funny, um, talents, we're fine! No one can even tell! Except for me and my hair, and most people think that's fake."

"Exactly, that's right, Iris," Candace said from behind her dripping eyeglasses. "There's no need to panic. But—"

"But?!" all four girls cried back at her. If there was a "but," then there probably was a need to panic.

"*But*," Candace repeated calmly, patting Iris on the shoulder so that she'd sit down again, "we need to be careful. This has to be our secret."

"Why?" Opal asked.

"Because . . . well, for one thing," Candace began, keeping her voice low and leaning toward the center of their booth. The girls huddled in to hear her. "We don't yet know the extent of your powers. Everything you can do."

"Or can't, in my case," Opal said glumly. The pearls stitched on her sleeve cuffs scratched against the tabletop.

"And secondly," Candace continued, ignoring Opal's comment for the moment but pausing before she spoke again, "we also don't know who else might be interested in . . . examining you."

"EXAMINING US?!" the girls cried out together again, slamming back in shock against the padded benches.

"Shh, shh, shh, shh!" Candace picked up Iris's swizzle spork and waved it like a magic wand at each one of them, trying to quiet them down. She should have made them all order the calming camomile tea!

Noticing the commotion, the bouffant waitress sashayed over and took out her notepad again. "Can I get anything else for you girls?"

"No, thank you," Candace answered for the table. "Just the check, please."

"You got it, Moms," the waitress snapped, totaling up the bill, tearing it from her notepad, and handing it to the babysitter. "Tip not included."

Candace scowled after her as she walked away, then dug in her bag for her wallet.

"It's just," she addressed the four girls again as she counted out the money, "you're unique. One of a kind. The only known, uh, 'specimens' with this sixth element, with Heliotropic DNA. And so"—she picked up the swizzle spork again, giving each girl a warning glance before she finished her sentence—"it's possible that, you know, scientists or the government or whoever would want to, er, *probe* you."

She raised the spork sharply, silencing the girls before they could cry out the P word.

"*Probe* is what they do to aliens," Scarlet whispered.

"So we're genetic freaks *and* we're aliens?!" Cheri whimpered, chewing her thumbnail.

"Semantics," Candace said, her thoughts turning off down a side road. She scratched absentmindedly at her bangs with the spork. "An argument could be made that they're one and the same."

Iris cleared her throat and gave the babysitter a poke in the arm. "Um, Candace? Not helping."

"Right, right," Candace said, focusing again on her four charges. "Girls, listen. It's getting late. It's been a wild night. I don't know what the future will bring."

"That's super comforting, Candace," Scarlet muttered.

"But even though you're almost too old now to need a babysitter, you've got me. And," she said, looking at a tearful Cher, "I've got you, babes!"

Iris nodded to her three best friends. "Candace can help us, guys! She works at the FLab. She can find out more about this Heliowhatchamacallit and stuff."

"Totally," Candace said. "Think of me as your . . . as your fairy godmother." She circled the spork at Opal as if she were casting a spell. "Bibbidi-bobbidi-booyah!"

The image of their former babysitter, the brilliant teenius with blunt bangs and geek glasses, as a doddering fairy godmother made the girls smile in spite of all the serious info they'd just downloaded.

"So code of silence on this convo, okay?" Candace urged them. "But you're going to figure this out. And I'm going to help you. AND . . ."

The girls sat up straight, steeling themselves for whatever new and terrifying truth-bomb Candace was about to drop.

"Bring it on, fairy babysitter," Scarlet said. "And what else?"

Candace smiled at them determinedly. *I may not have my doctorate degree in astrogenetics yet*, she thought to herself. *But the evidence is clear: Something did happen to these girls that night four years ago. I was their babysitter, and it's in the babysitter's bible: I'm responsible. Iris has purple hair. Scarlet is dancing. Cheri is a mathematician who can commune with animals. And who knows what's in store for Opal?*

Candace made a decision right there and then. Whatever happened, whatever was going to happen, she would do everything in her power to protect the girls. She had their backs. And their purple hair, their dancing feet, and whatever other weird mutations they had yet to get!

"And you are *not* freaks," she said proudly. "You four are freakin' fantastic!"

"We're viomazing!" Iris shouted, springing to her feet again, her purple curls bouncing up around her. She fluttered back down just as suddenly, all butterfly sleeves. Then she looked to her right and linked pinkies with Candace, turned to her left and linked pinkies with Scarlet. The other girls did the same, Cheri and Scarlet linking pinkies across the table and Opal joining with their trusty teenius.

Just like before, Iris could feel the energy coursing through them. She could see that Scarlet was defiant, and Opal still disappointed, and Cheri a little bit scared. Her head told her that maybe she should be scared of all this spooky alien DNA stuff, too. Strange things were happening in Sync City, things the girls had only gotten a glimpse of. Drooling mutants roamed the streets, the park, even the schoolyard.

But that night in the diner, Iris's heart raced with excitement. Who knew what the four of them could do? And four good friends can handle whatever bad comes their way.

Of Mothers and Mutants

CANDACE WAS ASSISTING AT THE FLAB, AS SHE DID most days after school. The Mothers Jones, Henderson, and Tyler were currently researching whether the centrifugal force exerted by clothes dryers generated a compressed black hole that was to blame for a pandemic of disappeared socks. To test their theory, they'd digi-tagged multiple pairs before tossing them into the spinning chamber. Up on the wall opposite the rock-crystal windows, a massive three-dimensional grid mapping out Sync City glowed electric green. But as of yet, none of the missing socks had popped up on it.

"It's *got* to be a case of too much fabric softener," Iris's mom concluded grimly.

"No doubt," Scarlet's mom agreed, making copious notations on her WiFi clipboard.

"I'll prep the next batch with no softener," Candace offered, "as a control group." In her crisp white lab coat, with her short straight bangs and her black square glasses, she looked very professional (though still no way near old enough to be anyone's mom). In one hand she held a stray striped sock. In the other, Iris's swizzle spork from the diner. Candace had taken it by accident; she must have stashed it in her bag with her wallet? But anyway, she found that brandishing the twirly utensil helped her feel confident. Her high IQ brain knew it was totes illogical to give inanimate objects that kind of emotional importance. But she didn't care. It was just a stupid parfait spork, after all!

Cheri's mom, Dr. Henderson, returned to the room wrapped in a terrycloth bathrobe, with her hair up in a towel. "The pressure in those decontamination showers takes the wave right out my hair!" she declared, knocking at her water-logged ear with the palm of her hand.

Candace sensed an opening. She had to find out whatever she could about Heliotropium for the girls. Maybe there was an antidote. Maybe she could cure them!

"Yes, those showers are fire-hydrant strength, aren't they?" Candace said, trying to sound casual as she sorted an all-argyle load. "I bet they could blast the pigeon poop off a building from a hundred feet below!"

"Interesting you should mention pigeon excrement," Iris's mom mumbled, peering into the dryer, her head spinning round and round with the socks. "Per my observations, the bird droppings down the side of my apartment building appear to be primary-colored. Rainbow-streaked, one might say. A phenomenon I find quite anomalous."

Oh sugarsticks, **Candace** thought. *Iris's pigeons!* What if Dr. Tyler was on to her daughter's color-changing? Candace had to throw her off the trail. "Maybe the birds have added leprechauns to their diet," she suggested, blinking innocently from behind both her glasses and her plastic wraparound safety goggles.

The other two moms tittered at this joke, but Dr. Tyler was not amused. "Don't be ludicrous, Candace," she said drily. "I suppose next you're going to tell me that the sky is pink."

Not the sky, **Candace** thought wryly, *but some of the clouds.* She pressed on with her covert questioning.

"Do you think the showers are strong enough to rinse off, um, say, Heliotropium?" she asked. "Hypothetically speaking."

"Heliotropium!" Cheri's mom exclaimed. She'd been squeezing water from her hair, but Candace's query stopped her mid-rub, and a droplet splashed onto the lab table. "I think you've been reading too many comics, Candace," she continued, kind of condescendingly. "There's no such thing."

"Because if there were," Iris's mom stated from her spot by the sonic dryer, "even momentary superficial epidermal exposure to such a highly unstable liquefied hybrid compound would result in irreversible subcutaneous genetic alterations."

So even though it supposedly doesn't exist, **Candace**

thought cynically, *its impact is documented?* Of course it existed! Candace had stood in this very FLab four years ago, holding a beaker of it in her own two hands. She'd cleaned it off that cute baby skunk!

Those mothers were lying right to her face.

And, Candace realized, as Dr. Tyler's multi-syllabic blather sunk in, *the effects are "irreversible." Permanent.*

Sugarsticks.

"What Dr. Tyler means," Dr. Henderson was explaining in that possibly condescending way again, "is that, from the second it touches your skin, there ain't a hot tub on earth strong enough to wash Heliotropium off DNA!"

"*If* it existed," Dr. Jones added hurriedly, avoiding Candace's begoggled glare and scanning the digital matrix for sock distress signals instead. "Which it doesn't."

"So then you haven't noticed any"—Candace cleared her throat—"Heliotropic-type symptoms here in Sync City?" Scarlet had told her Dr. Jones had walked in on her spontaneous *Swan Lake* solo. And Dr. Tyler had to see her daughter's purple hair every single day. "Or, like, at home?"

The moms exchanged glances. Then all three broke into the titters.

"Oh, Candace," Scarlet's mom said with a tight smile, "you really are adorable."

"Or 'adorkable,' as the kids say," Cheri's mom chimed in, framing the word and her wet head with annoying air quotes.

"And curiosity *is* the hallmark of a top scientist," Iris's mom stated, back to her typical serious self.

"But you've got to stop reading those conspiracy blogs!" Cheri's mom exclaimed, definitely condescendingly, as she attempted to comb a gnarly knot out of her damp hair. "They'll give you nightmares."

"Now be a dear," Scarlet's mom directed, obviously trying to change the subject, "and dash down to the fro-yo shop for us, would you? When you come back, you can bag and tag the lint for analysis."

"Sure thing," Candace said through gritted teeth, placing a laundry basket on the long lab table and picking up her bag. As she walked to the elevator, she jabbed the spork into her thigh to keep from losing her cool. Emotions were an irrational response for a future scientist, she reminded herself. Otherwise she just might have screamed.

Moments later, riding the rock-crystal elevator down to the fro-yo shop, Candace remembered that she wasn't a full-fledged scientist yet. So she did allow herself a small scream of frustration. How could three such brilliant women be so blind? Their daughters were developing superpowers right before their eyes, and they refused to see it. "Mothers in denial," Candace muttered. It sounded like the name of a play by some intense Russian dude with a beard. Probably was. But it was also the truth. The truth that the moms couldn't handle.

Grown-ups could be so closed-minded.

Then I guess it really is on me, **she resolved.** *College applications. Interning at the FLab. And being the secret guardian for a fierce foursome of supergirls. But I can do it. I got the girls into this Helio of a mess. So it's my job to keep them out of trouble. I'll just have to keep investigating on my own.*

She tapped the spork in the palm of her hand thoughtfully. Later that night she'd definitely have to log on to see what her fave bloggers were buzzing about.

As the elevator descended, Candace stared out the see-through walls at the skyscrapers and spires of Sync City. The afternoon sun cast the cityscape in gold, and the light-emitting diodes started to flicker to life. Every so often, a silver-helmeted aeroscooterist zipped past, navigating between the buildings and the birds. Candace could just imagine Iris looking out at the same view and marveling at the utter sparkliness of it all.

But this afternoon Candace noticed something new. The elevator moved so swiftly, and she was speeding down from so high up, that she only caught a glimpse and wasn't sure what of. Strangely shaped shadows, skulking toward the river in lumbered, clumsy gaits. Dotted here and there throughout the city's streets, but all moving in the same direction. Almost as if they were answering the same call.

Huh, **Candace thought.** *Must be some big concert on the piers tonight.*

That's what she *thought*. What she *felt*, in the pit of her stomach, was *uh-oh*. Even though she knew the gut check was not a scientific way to measure anything at all. She felt *uh-oh* because, despite what the beehived waitress at the diner might have said, Candace was nobody's mother. And she wasn't in denial.

Candace couldn't see exactly who—exactly what—was stumbling toward the river. Into the river. Onto the ferryboats and across the bridges.

But even if she could see, she still wouldn't know what she was looking at.

A "man" in a paper-thin trench coat with spindly green claws, one bulbous eye, and bright green wingtips sticking out above his shoes?

A waddling "hippowomanus" with thick gray skin, webbed feet, and stumpy tusks jutting up from her bottom jaw, chomping at the air as she grunted, "Hungry, hungry . . ."?

The lawyer in a three-piece pinstriped suit and silken ascot, his lips stretching to hide his five rows of shark teeth? A long-necked dental hygienist with three Adam's apples beneath her pelican beak? The pig-nosed, pink-faced chef? The squat little piano teacher with paws like a three-toed sloth? Two middle-grade boys: one sprouting the rounded horns of a cow, the other whipping out a frog's tongue? A two-faced cheerleader! (No, really: Her hair hid the second

face on the back of her head, but her second nose still stuck out. And up.)

And on the other side of the river, greeting them as they stumbled under the acid-yellow archway into the Mall of No Returns, Develon Louder, president of the BeauTek Corporation. With Opal's mom, Dr. Trudeau, standing by her side, trying not to tremble as she logged in each new arrival on her tablet.

What was that your gut said again, Candace?

Uh-oh.

14

Special of the Day

CUE THE DEEP BASS MOVIE TRAILER MAN VOICE:

"The brains. The beauties. The jocks. The rebels. And the recluses."

Really it was just Iris, imitating a deep bass movie trailer man's voice. She aimed an imaginary camera, framing an overhead shot of the cafeteria that spanned every corner and every clique.

"Before this day is over," she intoned, *"they'll break the rules. Bare their souls. Take some chances. And touch each other in a way they never dreamed possible."*

Iris brought her pretend camera down to focus in on her three best friends.

"They only met every day. But it changed their lives FOREVER!"

Close-up of them laughing. The camera's kind of shaky because the director is laughing, too.

"*From the studio that brought you* A Slug's Life *and* Honey, I Unfriended the Kids," Iris said, struggling to keep her voice deep. "*Sync City Pictures presents . . .* The Lunch Club. *Now playing in a cafeteria near you!*"

"Iris," Scarlet said, even though she did think the imitation was funny. "No matter how much you make it sound like a movie, this is still just another lunch period." To prove it, she popped open her brother's Batman lunchbox. "PB and J again," she noted, scanning the other girls' plates to see if there was anything worth trading.

Standing at their usual table, Iris pointed out each corner of the tiled cafeteria with her rhinestone stylus. "But look," she said. "Everyone is grouped off. All the nerdy kids are over there."

Opal and Cheri both looked to where Iris was aiming her stylus and saw Albert Feinstein, his back to them, bent over his laptop. The other students at his table—mostly boys— were doing the same.

"And the trendsters hang under the school banner," Iris continued, gesturing to a gaggle—mostly girls—in mostly expensive jeans, showing off the latest tech toys to each other.

"Hey, I'm still friends with some of them," Cheri said, reaching beneath her seat to give a little scratch under the chin to her clandestine pet of the day, an energetic Chihuahua. "Don't hate on them just because they like to dress up!"

"I'm not a hater," Iris said with a wink. "I'm a creator!" She sat down next to Cheri at the table.

"The sporty types are in the middle, making all the noise," Scarlet noticed. As if on cue, Brad Hochoquatro pumped his arms in a Hulk-like grip and bellowed, "Touchdown!" Then spiked his water bottle on the floor. The lunch monitor blew his whistle and called foul, throwing a penalty napkin on the mess while Brad ignored him and did a knee-knocking end-zone dance.

Scarlet snorted, her feet swinging back and forth beneath the table. "You call that dancing? Please." For a change, she had brushed her hair back into a ballerina's bun. All the kids in their class had been gaping at her all morning, but the girls assured her it looked tight, so she was sticking with it.

Opal glanced around the rest of the room, seeing the cafeteria's social network as clearly as Iris. "And the troublemakers and weirdos kind of hover around the edges," she observed.

"Yup," Iris said. "Everyone has their own little lunch club. *Coming soon to a school cafeteria near you!*"

"Then what are we?" Cheri asked, breaking off a bit of Opal's taco to feed to Dogiego Boneata, the shelter Chihuahua.

"Viomazing?" Iris suggested, before taking a bite of her cheese ravioli, the cafeteria's special of the day.

The four girls laughed at that. Ever since Candace had first muttered the word at the sleepover, one after another they had all started using it. "But seriously," Scarlet pressed, "what does that even *mean*?"

"I think it means . . ." Iris answered, because she'd actually thought about this, thought about it a lot, "that we're *amazing* in a very *violet* way."

"Oh, like that makes sense," Scarlet said, tearing another edge off Opal's taco, to feed herself. "*You're* the only one with purple hair."

"But we all got soaked with the, um, Heliotropium," Opal said in a low voice. "Isn't that what Candace called it? And that's violet."

"Ultra," Iris agreed, also speaking quietly. "And we all absorbed the candle wax. So, like, we're all violet on the inside."

"Violet on the inside," Cheri repeated. She poked at the avocado rolls she'd bought from the salad bar, pushing the wasabi aside. "It's all too weird," she said. "I don't feel any diff—" She stopped midsentence to lean over her seat. "*Again,* Dogiego?" she hissed at the top of the tote bag. "But you just went before PE this morning!"

"Anyway"—Iris skirted her chair a little bit away from Cheri's, just in case Dogiego Boneata decided to go wee-wee—"we have to remember what Candace said. We have to keep our—"

"Superpowers—" Opal murmured wistfully.

"Secret," Iris said. "From now on, I'm keeping my experiments in color to my bedroom wall." *Unless*, she thought, *I ever cross paths with a certain graffiti boy again.*

Cheri gave her an imploring look and pointed toward her feet.

"Okay," Iris yielded. "I'll change the Helter Shelter animals if it's helping them get adopted! But we have to be careful about it."

Cheri nodded eagerly. "Pinkie swear!" she promised.

"And you'd better keep your dog-whispering to, you know, a whisper," Scarlet said, drumming her fingers on the lunch table. "And save the advanced calculus for . . . whatever people use advanced calculus for."

"But what about you, Scarlet?" Opal asked. "Can you control your dancing?"

Maybe she was feeling particularly sensitive because of her hair bun, but to Scarlet that sounded like a taunt. "I'm working on it!" she sniped, tugging at the twist.

Just then the girls became aware of a commotion coming from the other side of the cafeteria, at the border where Nerdsville met Trendster Nation. As they all turned to look, they could see Albert flinching in his chair. Using her plastic spoon as a slingshot, queen-bee mean girl Karyn Karson was lobbing raviolis at his back. They splatted against his white shirt and slid down, leaving tomato sauce skid marks before settling in his seat. Albert was pretending to ignore them. He just kept typing on his laptop keyboard. But there was no way he didn't feel the hot pasta pockets of humiliation as they hit their target: him.

At their table beneath the school banner, Abby O'Adams, Rachel Wright, and all the other trendoids cackled and shrieked like jackals.

"Oh, poor Albert!" Cheri exclaimed. Opal whipped her head around to glare at her, snapping what was left of her taco in half.

"Thanks, Opes," Scarlet said, snatching the last piece right out of her hand and stuffing it in her mouth. She was so mesmerized by the Fling Cheese Incident that she didn't even notice Opal's expression of supreme irkedness.

Iris was more than irked. The bullying of Albert Feinstein made her furious! She knew she was still considered the new girl, and she tried to get along with everyone. But she hadn't forgotten those first few days at school, the snickers and stares and finger-pointing as she walked the hallways with her strange purple hair. She could only imagine how Albert must feel, having to face the same mean girls in math class who had attacked him with their lunch!

It was just wrong.

So wrong.

Too wrong.

"Hey, girls?" Iris said, pulling their attention away from the pastastrophe. "You know that stuff we were just saying about keeping our superpowers on the downlow?"

"Yeah?" Scarlet said, one eye still on the ravioli massacre. Cheri and Opal nodded.

"How about we start that . . . tomorrow?"

The four friends exchanged glances. Iris could tell they all felt the same. Cheri put one hand, pinkie finger up, in the center of the table. "Count me in," she said. The other three followed, linking fingers in a chain. They pounded the table fast, *one, two, three!* then broke apart.

Scarlet stood up and scanned the length of the cafeteria. "Cher," she asked, "about how far—?"

"Time being distance divided by speed," Cheri said, "and the speed of light being 186,000 miles per second . . ." She looked at Scarlet and smiled. "If you go now, you'll be there, like, yesterday."

"And we'll be right behind you," Iris added.

Scarlet nodded. "Cover me," she said. Cheri and Opal stood on either side of her as she dropped into a crouch. And sprung like Spider-Man. If Spider-Man had been a schoolgirl.

As she jetéed across the cafeteria, her ballerina bun finally came loose, and her straight black hair flew behind her like a cape.

She overshot the landing, brushing against the school banner, which fell from the wall to cover the cackling trendoids like a net. Then she bounced back, landing en pointe right in front of Karyn. And just as the girl was about to catapult another ravioli grenade, Scarlet hooked her foot in a coupé, flipping Karyn's entire lunch tray into the air.

Tray and bowl and ravioli spun as if in slow motion high above the trendoids' table while Scarlet backflipped in a blur, beyond the range of the impending fallout. Karyn stumbled to her feet and started to scream, "Nooooo!" But her raviolis came crashing down. Followed by the clunk of her bowl. Followed by the slap of her plastic tray.

The entire cafeteria stared at Karyn in stunned silence. Her trendoid friends clawed their way out from underneath the school banner, then wrapped it around their shoulders like a blanket, trying to shield themselves from the horrible sight: Karyn Karson with a bowl of ravioli on her head, tomato purée streaming down her face like marinara tears.

Psst, Dogiego! **Cheri thought hard.** *See that girl over there, all covered in sauce? Don't her Fugg boots remind you of a fire hydrant? Go, Dogiego, go!*

The hyper Chihuahua didn't need any more encouragement. He leaped out of Cheri's tote bag, not nearly as fast as Scarlet but as fast as a little dog with a little bladder could. Scampered right up to Karyn's ankle. Lifted a hind leg. And did number one on her boots.

"Aaaaaaagh!" Karyn screamed, raising her red sauce hands up to the ceiling.

The cafeteria monitor tooted his whistle again and announced, "Foul! Health code violation! No dogs allowed!" Not that anyone in the cafeteria was listening to him. He ran after the Chihuahua, tearing the banner off the huddled trendoids as he raced past them. They unfurled like balls on a pool table, spinning and slipping in the tomato sauce and dog pee.

The monitor had the banner by the corners, ready to

throw it over the fugitive Dogiego, when the dog seemed to disappear right before his eyes. The teacher skidded to a halt and stared across the floor, under the tables. But all he could see were old linoleum tiles and sneaker scuffs and book bags.

Cheri herself didn't see Dogiego until he jumped back up and burrowed into the safety of the tote bag under her arm. *Oh, there you are!* she thought, relieved. *Good dog!* She felt him settle in the bottom and turn around a few times, getting comfy. When she discreetly peeked inside the bag, she saw a tiny Mexican breed with camouflage fur the pattern of old linoleum tiles and sneaker scuffs.

"Thanks, RiRi," she whispered, looking straight ahead again.

"No problem," Iris said. "We'll change him to something prettier than floor tile later." She stepped to the side, adding, "I'll be right back."

While the rest of the students in the cafeteria were rubbernecking at the ravioli train wreck that was now Karyn Karson, taking out their smartphones and filming videos to post on their Smashface pages, Albert Feinstein took the opportunity to sneak out of the cafeteria. Maybe he could wipe down his shirt in the boys' room or find a clean tee in the gym. He closed his laptop, picked up his backpack, and skulked toward the exit with his head down, hoping no one would notice him. But just as he got to the doors, that artsy new girl with the dazzling purple hair blocked his escape.

Great, he thought, his glasses fogging up. *Another popular girl, just waiting to torment me.*

The girl put one hand on his shoulder, twirled a violet ringlet with the other, blinked her blue eyes for a second or three, and said, "Hi, Albert. Lunch period kind of bites, right? See you later, in math."

And with a bounce of her royal ringlets, she walked back into the cafeteria.

Probably slapped a "Kick Me" sign on my back, **Albert** thought, hurrying out through the double doors and toward the bathrooms. *It's probably stuck to all the tomato sauce.* As he walked, he tried to scratch at his back. He didn't reach the sign he expected was there, but he did brush a couple of embedded ravioli off his butt.

Once Albert got into the boys' room, he dropped his

backpack in front of the door, hoping to stall anyone who might follow him there. Then he tore a paper towel from the dispenser, squirted it with liquid soap, and ran it under the faucet to work up a lather.

But when Albert Feinstein turned around, ready to scrub the back of his shirt by looking at his reflection in the boys' bathroom mirror, he came to a stop. The soapy wad of paper dripped in his fist.

Albert's shirt was spotlessly white. He rubbed his glasses on his thighs and put them back on. But no matter how closely he peered, he could find no trace of the cheese ravioli skirmish. No oily stains. No tomato sauce. And no *"Kick Me"* sign.

Back out in the cafeteria, a frantic Karyn Karson stood in a puddle of Chihuahua pee and pasta sauce, babbling to

the monitor about some giant high-speed superfly that had landed on her table and overturned her lunch. Iris, Scarlet, Opal, and Cheri didn't give her a second glance as they strolled by. From her messenger bag, Iris tore open a pack of spicy cinnamon gum and offered it around.

"Hey, Iris?" Scarlet said, taking a piece.

"Hmm?" Iris answered.

"Why didn't you tell us," Scarlet teased, "that you do laundry?!"

Scarlet leaped just a little to high-five Iris, and Cheri joined in, laughing along. Opal trailed behind, still hungry, and nibbling on Scarlet's abandoned PB and J sandwich.

The grape jelly should have been sweet.

But all she could taste was bitter.

Mwah?

CINNAMON GUM IS SPICY, GRAPE JELLY IS SWEET, AND
Opaline Trudeau is bitter because she's violet on the inside
only. With no superpowers on the outside to show for it.

Iris, Scarlet, and Cheri had gone to Chrysalis Park again.
After their stealth victory over the Fugg-booted bully Karyn
Karson in the cafeteria, they wanted to practice their skills
some more. Cheri thought she might be able to round up a
few stray animals and "be one with the squirrels." Scarlet
had a lot of extra energy to burn. And Iris was up for some
fun with camouflage.

But Opal had begged off sick and walked home alone. She
was sick, sort of. Sick of standing in the shadows of the other
three, with their breathtaking hair and rainbow palette and
infinity bag of lollipops. Their sandwich-stealing and balletic
combat. Their secret psychic shelter pets and math prowess!

Math prowess . . .

Opal thought of Albert, hunched over in the cafeteria,

under ravioli attack. She was surprised to realize that, instead of feeling sorry for him like Cheri had, she was a bit disgusted. Why didn't he stand up to Karyn? Why did he just let her bully him like that?

Next thing you know, Albert, she thought, *Karyn will be ordering you to bring her bendy straws and snatching the tacos right out of your hand.*

Opal input the code to lock her apartment door behind her. Her mom wouldn't be home from work for another couple of hours. She had the place to herself. She dropped her backpack on the floor, peeled off her loafers, then padded into the kitchen and poured herself a cold glass of pomegranate juice.

Cheri's favorite! she thought, downing half of it in one gulp. She put the glass on the counter and pretended to roller skate across the kitchen floor in her socks.

"Look at me!" she said to no one, imitating Cheri's breathy baby voice. "I've got luscious strawberry red hair and the super-shiniest nails! All the animals follow me like I'm Snow White, and the captain of the mathletes wants to be my boyfriend!"

Opal came to an abrupt stop, crashing against the counter. She felt a blinding pain cut across her forehead, and for a moment her vision clouded. "Owie," she said softly, rubbing her temples with her thumbs. It must have been her barrettes, pulled too tight.

That was another thing. The barrettes. Every day, her mom insisted she wear her hair clipped back. But Opal was over the goody-two-shoes look.

She clawed at the barrettes, tearing them out and throwing them across the room. She could feel the sharp sparks of static electricity on her fingertips as she ran her hands through her hair raking out the strands until they were dented waves.

"That's better," she breathed. "But not good enough."

With a twist of her thumb, she undid the top button of her shirt, running her finger around the collar. Then she undid the next button. And the next. And the next. She freed the buttons at her wrists, pulling so forcefully that one popped off, and rolled her sleeves up past her elbows.

"Look at me!" she said again, laughing joylessly at what a joke it all was. "I'm a ballet dancer! And if you don't believe me"—she spun on her tiptoes across the length of the apartment—"I'll beat you up!"

The pain sliced across her forehead once more, and Opal doubled over in the middle of her living room, seeing only a terrifying whiteness.

"Okay, whoa," she said, dropping to her knees on the carpet. She shut her eyes and rocked back and forth, arms covering her head as if she'd been caught in a thunderstorm. When she braved opening her eyes again, the blurry outlines of the coffee table and the couch appeared before her. She was so relieved that she blinked out a few tears.

What was the matter with her? Why was she acting this way? Cheri and Scarlet were her best friends, weren't they? True, Scarlet was always bossing her around and eating her lunch. And yes, Cheri had blatantly gone after the only boy she had ever liked, but . . .

But . . .

Opal crawled over to the couch and climbed up onto it, crouching in one corner and hugging her knees to her chest. Her thoughts moved from Cheri and Scarlet to Iris. How could she imitate Iris, even if she wanted to? The girl could turn things different colors! That was just freaky. But at least Iris was her friend, wasn't she?

"Oh, I don't know," Opal moaned.

She sat like that on the couch in her apartment for a long time, hoping her headache would pass. She sat until the sun went down. She sat in the darkness, staring at the shadows in the room. She felt like a stranger in her own home. Everything seemed different, like she was seeing it for the first time. Like it was somebody else's house and she had stumbled into it by accident.

At last she turned on a light, followed by the TV. The typical chatter of the news anchors helped fill up the emptiness.

Opal stretched out her legs. They were numb from sitting for so long, and pins and needles prickled through them. She placed one foot gingerly on the floor, followed by the other, and stood up slowly, testing her weight. Then she shuffled over to the kitchen sink and dumped the remaining pomegranate juice down the drain. It was too sweet; maybe it had given her the terrible headache. From a bottle in the fridge, she poured herself a glass of pure water instead.

To grab a few ice cubes, she reached into the freezer but quickly recoiled when her fingers touched something gelatinous and sticky. Gaping back at her from between the ice cream cartons and microwave dinners was a freshly frozen Frankenfish. Its scales still flashed blue and red, like a subzero police siren, and it seemed to be ogling her with its three misty fish eyes. She must have poked one of them.

"Ewww!" Opal uttered, slamming the freezer door shut. What was her mom doing, keeping that thing in the fridge?

She stepped back to the kitchen sink and washed her hands with dish detergent, though no matter how hard she scrubbed she could still feel the gummy eyeball on her fingertips. "So gross," she muttered, finally giving up and shaking her hands dry.

She hooked her loafers with two fingers in the heels and slung her backpack over one shoulder. But as she turned to go to her bedroom and begin her homework for the night, something caught her eye.

Her mom's tablet computer. On the kitchen counter all this time.

"That's odd," Opal said aloud. Her mother never went anywhere without that tablet. She must have totally freaked when she realized she didn't have it with her at BeauTek today.

Curious, Opal picked up the tablet and brought it into her bedroom with all her other stuff. She pushed her door closed with her foot.

It didn't take too long for Opal to hack into her mom's tablet. First, she tried a few obvious passwords: Her full name, Opaline Ann. Then just Opaline. Opal Ann. Then just Opal. Her birthday. Her mom's middle name.

Nope. None of those worked.

"What does Mom love more than anything else?" Opal

wondered. Since clearly it wasn't her! She keyed in The FLab, then FLabby, just for fun, then BeauTek. Nope again. Those didn't work, either.

"Hmmm," Opal pondered, taking a sip of her lukewarm water and shuddering at the thought of the flashing fish out in the freezer. Her headache seemed better, at least. She tried to think of anything her mom ever said about work. What was it printed on her employee ID badge, the one she sometimes forgot to take off when she got home?

"Vi-Shush Clearance," Opal recalled. "Vi-Shush . . ."

She keyed in: V-I-S-H-U-S-H.

And the screen glowed to life.

"Score," Opal said, scanning all the icons. Except for one folder called *Press Releases*, they all had weird scientific-sounding names that didn't make much sense to her.

"Eenie, meenie, miney—" Opal circled her finger above the screen, trying to decide if anything was even worth opening. Her mother could come home any minute now. "Mo," she decided, tapping on the icon labeled *Project Mute*.

Maybe it's all the music she doesn't want me to listen to? Opal thought.

Color squares covered the screen, smaller than old-fashioned postage stamps. Opal thought they looked like playing cards in some video game, each one a different character. She pressed the first one, and its picture filled the screen.

What she saw was no character any actress would ever want to play. It looked like a woman, maybe. A woman with gray-blue skin and the thick tusks of a hippopotamus.

"Yikes," Opal said, "talk about your 'before' pictures." She knew BeauTek was a big beauty company, but it was going to take a truckload of cosmetics to make over that woman! She tapped the image again so that it shrunk back down to postage-stamp size.

Next she was confronted by the sight of a grinning, too tan man. He appeared normal enough at first, with his slicked-back hair and his pinstriped suit. But as Opal looked closer, she realized that the man's smile revealed row after row of jagged shark teeth.

"Oh!" she exclaimed, immediately closing that image, too.

She expanded one more image. The creature that filled the screen this time was frighteningly familiar. A giant opossum, larger than a four-door car, with crusty yellow nails and a handlebar mustache under its long, mushroomy snout.

The monster from the park.

Opal scanned down under the image to a small box of text. *Opossumani*, it read, followed by a description, notes about its habitat—

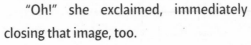

shrubby underbrush, of course—and other details. After that was an alphabet's soup of different chemical formulas and compounds.

"Opal?"

The call came from the hallway, and she could hear the apartment door whir shut. Her mother was home.

"I'm in my room!" Opal called back, shoving the tablet under her pillow and hastily buttoning up her shirt. She'd have to sneak the tablet out again later, maybe after her mom had gone to bed.

Dr. Trudeau poked her head in the bedroom just as Opal was opening up the reading assignment on her own computer.

"Have a good day at school?" she asked.

Opal shrugged.

"Homework, hmm?" Her mom tried to smile, but ever since she'd started working at BeauTek, her face always seemed a bit stiff. "Honey, you don't mind if I order dinner again, do you?" she said. "I'm just too tired to cook tonight."

"Sure," Opal said. "I'm not really hungry, anyway." The image of the three-eyed fish pulsing in the freezer floated in front of her eyes again, and she felt like she could vom.

"Great," her mother said. "I'm just going to take a quick shower first."

Opal waited until the water had been running for a couple of minutes before she took the tablet computer out from under her pillow and opened it up again. As she scrolled through image after image, she wondered: Just what was it her mother did all day across the river at BeauTek? Was it top secret? Is that why the project was called Mute?

If Opal couldn't have superpowers of her own, she could at least find out more about all the other freaks filling her mom's computer folders.

And the streets of Sync City.

Shrieking Violet

CINNAMON GUM IS SPICY, GRAPE JELLY IS SWEET, AND Iris Tyler is violet all over, inside and out. Purple pride, people!

That's pretty much what Iris was feeling in the park that afternoon, hanging with Scarlet and Cheri. After putting vile Karyn Karson in her place ("You got served!" Scarlet joked afterward, imitating Brad Hochoquatro's end-zone dance. "You got served ravioli! On your head!"), Iris was beginning to think that their strange powers could be used for more than just redecorating monorails and perking up dull ballets.

"Maybe," Scarlet said when Iris mentioned this. "But don't forget what Candace said."

"Yeah," Cheri agreed, hugging Dogiego close. He was now fire-engine red, with jaunty black polka dots as accents. "Don't forget there are people who want to PROBE us!"

"I know," Iris said. Still, she felt invincible. If anyone came within fifty feet of "probing" them, she'd cover them in trick mosquito bites. Scarlet could dance them to a pulp. And

Cheri . . . well, Cheri could mess up their tax returns. Then they'd REALLY be in trouble!

They were back on the grassy knoll. Scarlet wanted to dance on a hill, like they did in *The Sound of Music*. Cheri wanted Dogiego to stretch his squat Chihuahua legs before she had to bring him back to Helter Shelter. And Iris, even though she didn't tell the other two this, was curious whether they'd see any more weird creatures. Scared. But curious.

She figured as long as they stuck together and left before dark, they'd be okay.

Iris sat on the bench. She gazed down at the row of fluffula trees that bordered the orange brick path and out to the Joan River beyond them. Then she dug out the rhinestone stylus from the bottom of her messenger bag and tapped open her iCan.

Cheri placed Dogiego next her, snapping his leash around the rusted metal armrest. She gave the dog a pat on the head, then skipped over to join Scarlet, who was throwing down a fierce hip-hop hilltop routine.

"Do you think they'll hold a talent show at school this year?" she asked as she attempted to mimic Scarlet's modern choreography.

"IDK," Iris said. She was concentrating on capturing Scarlet and Cheri in motion, but it was hard because they kept moving.

"If they do," Cheri puffed, "maybe we could perform a dance routine. Scarlet, you could teach us! Opal, too, when she's feeling better."

Iris looked up from her iCan to study them. Cheri was a bit taller than Scarlet—a lot taller in her platform sandals—and was being careful not to elbow Scar Lo in the ear as she tried to pop and lock along. "That could be fun," Iris agreed. "We just need a really cool name for our team."

"Totally," Cheri said. "And matching outfits!" Even as she danced, she was imagining their costumes for this future talent show. Exciting!

"Hey, Scar!" Iris called out. "As long as you don't leap across the gym into the basketball net or something, we might even win!"

"Like I said before," Scarlet shouted back, "*I'm working on it!*" She wasn't really sure how she felt about busting a move in front of the whole school. A wrestling match was really more her groove. Or at least it used to be. This whole superdancing superpower was so confusing! It was messing with the entire way Scarlet saw herself. It was kind of making her crazy.

And the crazier it made her feel, the more manically Scarlet danced.

"Slow down, b-girl!" Cheri gasped. "A mere mortal such as myself"—*huff huff*—"cannot keep up with you!"

"Neither can I!" Iris said. She looked at her sketch so far.

It was a blur of lines and colors: cherry red and licorice black and blue-jean blue.

Scarlet came to a stop and staggered over to Iris, who handed her a fresh piece of gum. Cheri followed, stumbling dizzily toward the bench. She flopped down next to Iris. "That was *très* to the cray," she panted. She took a piece of gum, too. Then she glanced across at Iris's drawing. "Is that supposed to be us?" she asked. Scarlet also leaned over to look at the combustion of colorful lines and narrowed her eyes quizzically.

"Well, it's drawn in a very, um, 'impressionistic' style," Iris explained with a smile.

Cheri smiled, too, but suddenly her face dropped. "OMV!" she cried out. "Where'd Dogiego go?"

Iris and Cheri jumped to their feet and the three girls circled the bench, looking for the red-hot polka-dot Chihuahua.

"Cher, he was just here, I swear!" Iris said. "I was working on my drawing, I was watching you two dance, I thought he was on his leash!"

Cheri grasped the rusty metal armrest. There was a break right where the leash must have slipped through.

"Ooh!" Cheri exclaimed. "Stupid oxidized iron!"

"Wait, so now you're aces at *science*, too?" Scarlet asked.

"It's an equation!" Cheri spluttered. "A chemical equation! And never mind that now! We've got to find Dogiego before it gets dark!" Cheri feared she might freak out. "Iris! OMV, OMV," she stammered, starting to bite off her rose-gold manicure.

"He's bright red," Iris said, trying to calm her. "We'll find him." She faced west, toward the river. The sun had already begun to set. She almost couldn't believe the words that came out of her mouth next.

"We should split up."

Cheri and Scarlet exchanged glances. In the movies, you were *never* supposed to split up in scary dark parks. You were never supposed to split up, period! That was always when bad things happened. What if this time Cheri crossed paths with something a lot less friendly than a curly-tailed calico cat? What if Scarlet couldn't dance away some fresh, freaky danger?

Both girls gulped. But they both nodded.

"I'll take the path along the river," Scarlet offered bravely, hitching her backpack over both shoulders and tugging on the straps to tighten them.

"Okay," Iris agreed, though she didn't like it. "But be careful, because . . ."

"I know," Scarlet said, remembering what they had encountered the last time they were in the park after dark. "I will." Standing there on the hilltop, she touched pinkie

fingers with Iris and Cheri for a split second, so fast the other two hardly even knew she'd done it. And with just one bounce, she was over the grassy knoll and down on the orange brick path.

Cheri would have been majorly impressed if she weren't stressing about her missing Chihuahua.

Iris turned back to Cheri, who was chewing her thumbnail again. "Here's our plan," she said. "Scarlet's got the riverside covered. I'll go into the park toward the uptown exit," she explained. "You go down. Canvas the area, and we'll each circle back toward the middle till our paths cross. Got it?"

"It's got," Cheri said, surveying the park. The landmarks popped up in her head like points on a map. "Either direction is only about a quarter of a mile," she said, "so we should meet at the midway point in under ten minutes." Then she looked the way Scarlet had leaped, toward the sunset. "And with the sun at that angle, I'd estimate we've got about another ten minutes of daylight."

"Then we'd better get going," Iris said, slinging her messenger bag across her body. She put her hands on Cheri's shoulders and gave them a squeeze. "Don't worry," she said. "We're going to find him. He's bright red!"

Cheri nodded, blinking back tears. "He likes tacos,"

she whispered, fumbling with her smartphone to set the GPS with the park bench coordinates.

"We'll have to give him some when we find him," Iris said. "And if anything happens, just shout out . . . *Violets!* At the top of your lungs."

"Violets," Cheri repeated, sniffling. "Go team Violet."

And without another word, the two girls raced off in opposite directions down the hill.

Underneath the fluffula trees and off the park's paved walkways, it was already darker than Cheri expected. Every little crack, snapple, or pop she heard made her afraid, recalling the mega opossum with the mustache. But she kept on searching for little red Dogiego Boneata. She sent her best doggie thoughts ahead of her.

Here, Dogiego! she concentrated. *Yo tengo tacos! And as soon as I take you back to Helter Shelter, I just know you'll get adopted to a wonderful new home!*

She kept thinking these thoughts and listening for a reply as she scanned the shadowy grass for a polka-dot Chihuahua.

Cheri was just about at the midway point in her corner of the park, expecting at any moment to see Iris with her purple curls, and hoping that along with those purple curls she'd see a red dog, when she saw something else. Something definitely not Iris.

A tall man in a dented hat and a thin brown trench coat was stooped underneath the canopy of a tree. It sounded as if he was whispering. Cheri strained to hear but couldn't separate his words from the wind rustling the leaves. She took another step, and her heart leaped into her throat. Little red Dogiego was standing at the man's feet! Cheri wanted to call out, but some instinct stopped her.

Instead, she crept closer, moving as quietly as she could on her platform sandals.

Dogiego! she thought. *Come here! Right now!*

The Chihuahua must have heard her, but instead he skittered back in the grass, never taking his eyes off the man in the thin brown coat. Dogiego curled his lips in a snarl and gave out a low growl.

Cheri was near enough now to hear what the man was saying. But it still didn't make sense. It sounded like *ticka-ticka-ticka-ticka*. She was near enough to see the creases in the man's long coat. The fraying at its hem . . .

The green wingtips sticking out above his shoes?

"Oh!" Cheri gasped just as the man shot out two pointed claws and lifted up the yapping little dog. As he turned around to face her, his hat fell off and two antennae whipped into the air. He fixed Cheri with one bulbous insect eye and his mandibles twitched, *ticka-ticka-ticka-ticka*, hungry for Chihuahua.

"Iris!" Cheri shrieked into the twilight. "Scarlet! Help me, Violets!"

At the sound of her cries, the mantis man scuttled toward the walkway, tucking Dogiego under his armpit like a wriggling polka-dot football. Cheri stumbled after him, her eyes searching the grass for a weapon. Randomly, she spied a lacrosse stick and a single dirty stiletto in the weeds. She didn't have time to think how those two items ever could have ended up in the same place. *Who plays lacrosse in high heels?* she wondered. Then she reminded herself: She didn't have time to think about that! She crammed the shoe in the net so that the spiked heel jutted out of it, and held the lacrosse stick in front of her like a Japanese bamboo shinai.

Where are those kung fu pandas when you need them? she thought in despair. *Probably still back at the ballet!*

"Furi," she commanded her smartphone as she scrambled out of the grass and onto the walkway, "release roller skate wheels."

"Okay," Furi responded in her calm computer voice. "Releasing wheels now."

Cheri almost slipped and fell as the wheels hit the pavement. Almost. But she didn't. As she pushed off with her back leg as hard as she could, the parabolic calculations ran across her mind like digits on a calculator.

"Speed is more important than weight," she muttered, realizing that her stiletto was nowhere near as heavy as an ax. And an ax would have been much better for—eww!—chopping the claws off a mutant mantis man. Which was what she was planning to do. "Speed is more important," she told herself, "because energy is proportional to the square of velocity, but only directly proportional of mass!"

In other words, to rescue Dogiego from the giant mantis man, she was going to have to whack that sucker beaucoup fast with her stiletto stick.

For a lumbering monster in an overcoat, the man moved quickly. Even on roller skates, Cheri couldn't quite catch up to him. "Violets!" she called out again, hoping Iris would hear. Wasn't she somewhere in front of them? The mantis man was getting farther and farther ahead, smaller and smaller in the distance. Dogiego's frightened yelps started to fade.

Then suddenly the mutant came to a complete stop.

Before him appeared a solid brick wall with a bright yellow Under Construction sign in the middle of it. Cheri couldn't recall ever seeing it in the park before. But it now blocked the uptown exit. The mantis man had no way out.

He turned to face Cheri and lifted Dogiego out from

under his coat. With his hideous mandibles scissoring, he held the little dog aloft, about to devour him on the spot.

"*Violets!*" Cheri screamed, skating faster and faster, raising her spiked lacrosse stick over her head. *The antennae!* she tried to think at Dogiego. *Bite the antennae and he'll lose his balance!*

The Chihuahua barked in response, then started to nip at the mantis man's squirming antennae.

Cheri tried to aim her stiletto spike at the mantis man's claws, but Dogiego was wrastling around so much and she was skating so fast. The mutant was just a few feet in front of her now, with a brick wall right behind him. Cheri made a split second calculation and arced the lacrosse stick down low, planning to swing up just in time to bash his claws before she hit the bricks.

But Cheri hadn't counted in the windshield factor.

Which made her rate of acceleration three seconds faster.

Which made the trajectory of her swing—well, just keep reading!

The girl swung up. Hard. And hit the mantis man right between the legs. With the spiked heel on a stick.

"Awrk!" he squawked, dropping Dogiego and clutching in pain at his crotch.

Run, Dogiego! Cheri thought, hoping she could send out one last message before she slammed into the bricks. She covered her head with her arms, thinking, *Goodbye, nose of mine!* There was no way she could decelerate in time. She braced for impact, waiting for the hurt. Any second now, she wouldn't be one with the squirrels, like she had hoped. She would be one with a solid brick wall!

But then she realized. The wind was still blowing through her hair. She was still rolling. She peeked out through her arms, and all she could see was the park's uptown exit.

"Cheri, c'mon!" she heard Iris yell. "Back this way!"

Cheri slid to a stop and twirled around. Directly in front of her was the brick wall. She was on the other side of it. Hearing Dogiego's yelps, she skate-stepped back toward it, until she was face-to-face with the bricks.

She reached out to touch them, and her hand passed right through.

"Whoa," she breathed.

"Cheri, are you okay?" Iris called from the other side.

So Cheri took a deep breath. Pushed off again on her skates. And rolled right through the brick wall.

On the other side, the mantis man lay motionless. Cheri skated past him with a shudder and up to Iris, who stood farther down the path with a panting Dogiego in her arms. She realized she was still gripping the stiletto lacrosse stick, and she passed it to Iris with an embarrassed grin, taking the Chihuahua from her.

"Dogiego Boneata!" she said to the puppy, wagging a finger at him as he happily wagged his tail. "Never, ever run off like that again!" But what she thought was, *I'm so glad you're okay you poor little baby, kiss kiss kiss!*

And Dogiego kissed her back, licking her all over her face with love and doggie spit.

"OMV," she said to Iris, between doggie licks, "did you see that thing?"

"I heard you shout the code word," Iris said, "and I started running. And when I saw that giant bug man heading for the park exit with Dogiego under his arm . . ." Iris didn't finish her sentence, just tugged on a strand of her hair.

"You imagined this whole wall?" Cheri said, amazed. "It looks so real!"

"It was hard," Iris said. "It was like painting on air." She looked tired, and Cheri wondered what kind of effort it must have taken.

With a blink of Iris's blue eyes, the brick wall disappeared, replaced once more by the pathway and park trees that had been there all along. "Let's get out of here," Iris said. "Let's find Scarlet."

The two girls started down the path back toward the middle of the park, Iris now holding the odd lacrosse stick weapon. Cheri skated slowly beside her with the Chihuahua nestled down in the bottom of her tote bag. They were silent, each thinking about the horrible encounter. Until Dogiego began to growl again. And a sound broke into their thoughts.

Ticka-ticka-ticka-ticka . . .

Iris spun around. The mutant mantis man loomed over

her, four tarsal claws scratching out to grab her. "Cheri, get out of here!" she cried as she raised the lacrosse stick. She knew she had to stab him with the stiletto heel, but at the sight of him, so close, she froze. Iris was an artist: She appreciated beauty. And the mantis man was the ugliest thing she had ever seen! Squirmy wormy antennae; one giant compound eye with a hundred little lenses reflecting back at her; the other eye a dull human one, bloodshot and half-closed; and most hideous of all, the jagged-edge mandibles, snicker-slicing toward her.

"Iris!" Cheri screamed. Iris seemed to awake again, and drew back her arm to thrust the lacrosse stick, but . . .

Whomp! A dark shadow passed before her eyes, and the stab of the lacrosse stick met only air. Iris spun a full circle with the force of her jab and looked around desperately for the green-winged enemy.

She saw him crouched on the pavement again. Scarlet was dancing circles around him, pummeling him from gut to butt with sharp fouetté kicks.

"Did somebody call 'Violets'?" she said, giving the creature one last soccer kick.

The three girls stood back and watched the crumpled silhouette of the monster sail across the park and come crashing down in some trees.

"Goal?" Cheri asked.

"Now that," Scarlet said, "was one ugly bugly."

Dogiego barked in agreement.

Iris looked at the other two girls, then up to the sky. "I wonder if Candace was watching THAT on her spy-cam!"

Mwah Ha?

IN THE SPOTLIGHT OF A STREETLAMP, A TRIO OF BEEHIVED
waitresses gather. Imagine them like the Oreo-striped Bride
of the All-Night Diner, times three. Perhaps they're triplets.
Perchance they're clones. This is an imaginary scene. It
doesn't have to make sense.

Three waitresses. Beehives. Streetlamp. Doo-wop.
To the tune of "Downtown." And *a-one* and *a-two* and sing
it, ladies!

When you're alone, and life is making you homely, you can always go

to BeauTek.

When you've got worries, when your earlobes grow furry, there are creams, you know,

at BeauTek.

Just listen to the squeaks of mice trapped in the laboratories,

Test bunnies and test monkeys, the skunk from the start of this story?

BeauTek! Things will be stranger there.

BeauTek! Mutants are changing there.

BeauTek! Freaks will be waiting for you.

Opal didn't put back her mom's tablet computer that night after all. She kept it hidden under her pillow. Her mother was distracted all through dinner, probably worrying about where it was. But she didn't say anything about it, so neither did Opal. As far as her mother knew, she could have lost the tablet anywhere.

And returning it gave Opal the perfect excuse to visit BeauTek. To see for herself exactly what went on there.

It had been capital-A Awkward at school. Supposedly, Iris, Scarlet, and Cheri had lost the Chihuahua in Chrysalis Park yesterday afternoon and there was all this drama finding him, stiletto roller skates and lacrosse sticks or something. Opal didn't really pay attention to what they were saying. She told the girls she still wasn't feeling well. And she wasn't, sort of. Every time she'd dropped off to sleep the night before, a vision of one of the many Project Mute creatures shocked her back awake. If she'd turned on her bedside light, her mom might have noticed. So she just lay there in the dark, picturing all the hideous shark-toothed, sloe-toed, rat-tailed monsters and waiting for the sun to rise.

She was tired.

But the breeze off the Joan River was perking her up a bit. She stood on the deck of the commuter ferryboat, finally getting an up-close look at the neon yellow ex–shopping center where her mother worked. The boat docked, and she disembarked. As she started the short walk up to the entrance, the bobbing cattails seemed to be giving her glossy lipstick smiles? Opal would have blamed it on her sleepless night, but after all the photos she'd seen on her mom's tablet, nothing surprised her.

Past the top of the dock, she hid behind the thick trunk of a weeping willow tree and peered out through its long strands of leaves at the entrance. The Mall of No Returns sign curved above the doorway, its s hanging upside down at the end. It was too early still for the lights to be on, and the tubular fluorescent letters looked dirty, like they hadn't been washed for years.

Opal was considering how to sneak into the lab complex when she spotted a familiar figure waddling toward the entrance.

"Hippowomanus!" she muttered. The mutant was broader than a big gray school bus.

Shoulders hunched under the weight of the tablet in her backpack, Opal dashed out from the cover of the willow tree and walked a few paces behind Hippowomanus. The creature bellowed up to the security cameras, her massive jaws opening wide enough to swallow Opal whole. Opal shook in her shoes, but she stayed put, just out of range of the camera. When the doors slid open for the hippo woman, Opal ducked in behind her.

She'd done it. She'd crashed BeauTek.

Opal hung back, waiting until the Hippowomanus had lumbered out of sight. Then she stepped into the corridors and looked from one storefront to the next. Forever Twenty-Fun. Build-a-Girl Workshop. Cinnaubonpain. But there were no shoppers in the sterile halls of BeauTek. No grandmas resting on their walkers, no moms pushing strollers strung with shopping bags, no teenagers blabbing on their smartphones. The corridors were empty. Opal wondered where everyone was.

She wondered where the Vi-Shush was. Because that was where she was going.

There were so many storefronts, Opal didn't know where to begin. Then she spotted a large sign just ahead of her, situated in front of a fountain shooting up colorful spurts of water.

As she approached the sign, Opal could see it had all the letters of the alphabet on it, with smaller lines running beneath each letter. *Directory*, she read at the top of the board. She scanned to the end of the columns, finding *V*. And there it was, the only store listed for the letter: *Victoria's Shush*.

Victoria's Shush, Opal sounded it out in her head. *Vi-Shush. That must be it. C-3.*

She got on the up escalator. At level B, a harried man in a lab coat passed her, riding down. He was frantically text messaging and never took his eyes off his phone. Opal imagined him forgetting to step off the moving stairs and getting shredded by their metallic teeth.

On the third story, level C, she hopped off the escalator to face the dark pink doors of the Vi-Shush. From what Opal could tell, it was the only store, er, lab, on the floor. With just the mall's food court on the opposite side.

Opal had thought about how she was going to get into the Vi-Shush. Whether she should have taken her mom's employee ID badge out of her bag the night before, or whether she'd have to find a way to pass an eyeball scan or borrow someone else's fingerprints to sneak in, like they did in sci-fi space movies. But in the end, Opal decided simple is as simple does. She'd play the daughter card.

Opal walked straight up to the deep pink doors. And knocked.

From behind them, as she waited, she thought she heard a monkey screech.

She knocked again.

"Access to the Vi-Shush is by special permission only!" came a woman's voice from the other side. "If you have to knock, you're not allowed in."

Opal stood as close as she could to the doors, pressing the side of her face against the glossy pink paint, and said, "Mom? It's me, Opaline."

The doors flew open so fast, Opal nearly fell over.

"Opal!" her mom hissed, yanking her inside and shutting the doors behind her. "What are you doing here? How did you get in? There's a clause in a company contract I drafted that strictly forbids your being at BeauTek!"

"Me personally?" Opal asked. Every time she thought her mom couldn't dis her any more, she found some new and improved and insulting way.

"No, not personally, honey!" her mother answered. "Anybody! If you don't work for BeauTek, you're not allowed to be here!"

Opal shrugged. "But you work here," she said, "and I'm your, um, offspring. Or spawn. Or whatever you call children in bioresearch-speak. So couldn't this be like our own private Take Your Daughter to Work Day?"

Opal's mom sighed. "This isn't that kind of company, honey."

So typical, Opal thought. She'd come all the way across the river on the ferryboat by herself to see her mom at work, and all her mother wanted was for her to leave. "Okay, fine," Opal said sullenly. "But I thought you might need this." She pulled the tablet computer out of her backpack and handed it to her mother.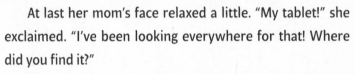

At last her mom's face relaxed a little. "My tablet!" she exclaimed. "I've been looking everywhere for that! Where did you find it?"

"In my top dresser drawer," Opal said. "In between my shirts." It was exactly the kind of ditzoid thing her mother would do. Exactly the kind of lie she'd believe.

"Oops," her mother said, flustered. "I'm such a scatterbrain! I must have stacked the ironing on top of it and then . . . I've just been so busy . . ."

"NBD, Mom. I know." Opal had heard this a hundred times before. Too busy to come to the spelling bee, she'd watch it later on GoobToob. Too busy to host a birthday party, couldn't just the two of them download a movie instead? Too busy to take her for a haircut, scissors were in bathroom.

As her mother clicked open her tablet files and checked through them, making sure no documents had been corrupted or copied, Opal looked around the vast lab. She could see

lavender leopard-spotted rabbits crunching on carrots in their cages. Plummy Rhesus monkeys riding mini stationary bikes. Ferrets whose teeth glowed indigo in the dark. And way back in the corner, beyond the cages and cages of animals and all the barrels and beakers of chemicals, Opal thought she spied the bone-white skull and glittering citrine eye of . . .

Skeletony?

In an instant Opal flashed back to that night four years ago when she got drenched in Helio-goo. When the thunder clapped and the lightning cracked and the lights went out. And when, as she dragged herself off to the decontamination showers, she noticed the skeleton was gone from the FLab.

How did Skeletony end up here?

"Mom," Opal asked, "what is your job exactly?"

Her mother had been so caught up in her computer reunion that she'd almost forgotten about Opal again. She realized with alarm that her eleven-year-old daughter had a 3-D view of the Vi-Shush experiments.

"Never mind that now," she said, ushering Opal back toward the deep pink exit. She grabbed a lab coat off a hook on the door. "Put this on," she said, and Opal obeyed. An ID tag hung from the front pocket. "Dr. S. Cooper," Opal read. The hem of the lab coat hit just above her ankles. "It's a bit big," Opal complained, cuffing the long sleeves.

"Shh, shh, shh, not now, honey, okay?" Opal's mother put a finger to her lips.

"All right, I get it already," Opal groused, rolling her eyes at her mom's lame charades. "Shush means shush!"

Opal's mom smiled weakly, then opened the pink doors a crack and peered out. "It's almost time for the night shift," she said, more to herself than to her daughter. Her eyes searched the empty corridor of level C as she gnawed anxiously on her lower lip. "No one should notice you." She looked Opal in her amber brown eyes. "Just keep your head bowed, go straight down the escalators, and out the front entrance." She flicked her wrist up to check her watch. "I'll meet you at the ferry dock in about a half hour. Can you do that, honey? Just read your homework or something while you wait?"

"Sure, Mom," Opal said, shifting from one foot to the other, trying to get one last look at the rabbits and monkeys and all the way back to the light twinkling in Skeletony's citrine eye. "No problem."

Before she could see any more, her mother turned her around by her shoulders and pushed her out of the Vi-Shush.

"You're welcome!" Opal called out, her voice echoing in the empty corridor.

In response all she heard was the laboratory doors locking behind her.

With her head low and her hands in the pockets of Dr. Cooper's borrowed lab coat, Opal walked to the top of the down escalators. But before she stepped aboard the moving stairs, she paused. Level C was the uppermost floor of the BeauTek complex. The windowed walls opposite the Vi-Shush looked out to the river and the Sync City skyline beyond it. Opal moved away from the escalators and toward the windows instead. Dr. Cooper had left a pair of black sunglasses in the lab coat pocket. Opal put them on. They were too big. But they blocked the sun. And, bonus, they helped with her disguise.

Across the river, the domed top of the FLab stood out from all the other buildings. The HQT was the most famous skyscraper in Sync City. Opal also tried to find her own apartment building, and Iris's. She could see the orange brick path of Chrysalis Park, the crimson leaves of the fluffula trees that bordered it, the small hilltop where she'd hung out with Scarlet and Iris and Cheri.

Even with the threat of mega mustachioed opossums, it was still a nice view.

As Opal's gaze returned to the dock just below the BeauTek building, she decided she wasn't going to go down there to wait for her mother after all. Not right away.

No, she thought, walking away from the windows and toward the food court. *I want a peach soda.*

Either the day-shift scientists were getting a late afternoon snack, or the night-shift scientists were eating an early dinner before they started work, or both of the above. The food court was busy enough, with lines backing up from all the different takeout counters. Thanks to Dr. Cooper's lab coat and sunglasses, no one seemed to notice that Opal was in fact an eleven-year-old girl. *I guess knee socks and barrettes must be trending with the scientific crowd,* she thought. Still, she kept a low profile. Avoiding the lines, she swiped Dr. Cooper's ID card on one of the many automatic snack dispensers. The can of peach soda rotated forward on a mechanical arm, and a small window slid up for Opal to take it. The swipe card made it so easy that she got herself a big piece of chocolate cake as a treat.

She sat down at an empty table.

Having her cake and eating it, too, Opal used the dark sunglasses as an excuse to ogle all the other people in the food court. Lots of scientists, all of them in lab coats, some of them wearing face masks or shower caps or those green doctor pajamas. Each one carrying a laptop or tablet, acting like the busiest person in the world. Definitely too busy to be bothered with her.

But Opal choked a little on a mouthful of cake when she noticed not everyone in the food court was a scientist. Or, more choke-causingly, not 100 percent human. There was the Hippowomanus, loading up on cheesecakes. There was the too-tan shark man, chatting with one of the doctors and flashing his rows of teeth.

They must all be here, Opal realized, her stomach twisting into a knot. *All those creatures from Mom's bizarre desktop flashcards.* The thought terrified her. But it fascinated her as well. Like she was watching video game characters come to life. Something about the sunglasses made Opal feel just hidden enough to stay put. She swallowed the chunk of cake stuck in her throat, washing it down with a swig of peach soda.

Suddenly the food court began to empty. The night shift must have been about to begin. All the scientists and research types streamed out the exit, leaving only the freaks behind. Opal was thinking about leaving herself when one sat down across from her.

She started in her seat, then stayed very, very still.

It took her a moment to recognize who it was. At first she was too fixated on the two smooth horn buds jutting out above his ears, through his shaggy, russet-brown hair. Then it hit her.

Duncan Murdoch? The boy who had once oh-so-charmingly called her a turd? What was *he* doing here? And why did he have horns?!

He stared across the table at her dully, and she could feel the blood rushing to her cheeks. But then she remembered. She was in the lab coat. Shielded by the sunglasses. And like Duncan Murdoch had ever noticed her outside a baked potato costume from kindergarten anyway!

Opal recognized Duncan, but she felt sure that *he* didn't recognize *her*.

What an interesting development . . .

With a guttural *moo*, Duncan reached a hand out toward Opal's cake. Whether it was because of the sunglass protection or the strange location or her lack of sleep, Opal didn't know. But instead of shrinking back, she snapped.

"Hey!" she said, banging the table. "Keep your stinking fingers off my chocolate cake!"

Duncan drew his hand back. Opal couldn't believe it. She could see fear in his eyes. In his big, cow-boy eyes! *Now who's the turd?* she smirked, feeling a rush of power she'd never experienced before. As Duncan pushed away from the table, Opal stood up and shouted after him: "And bring me a bendy straw!"

All the mutants in the Food Court fell silent and turned to look at her.

Opal cleared her throat and sat down again, staring back at all the freaky customers through her black sunglasses. Her heart was thundering in her chest. But, ignoring her fork, she picked up her piece of cake with her bare hands and took a huge bite out of it, certainly getting chocolate icing all over her face and probably on her buttoned-up shirt collar, not to mention the borrowed lab coat. She didn't care. She chewed slowly, savoring the dark, rich flavor. Then she licked the crumbs off her fingers, from pinkie to thumb. It tasted good. And shouting down a mutant Duncan Murdoch tasted even better.

So that's *what it feels like,* she thought, *to be the bosser, not the bossee.*

Opal polished off her cake and cleaned off her hands with a sani-wipe: This being a lab, they were on every table, right next to the ketchup. She got up from her chair, hitched her backpack over one shoulder, and picked up her can of peach soda. She was just about to leave, to make sure she beat her mom to the ferry dock, when another mutant approached her.

This creature had a long neck with folds of skin rippling around it like fleshy necklaces. Its heavy jaws hung down as well, blending in with its neck creases. The bags under its four eyes were so deep, Opal was sure the sunglasses she was wearing would get lost in them. It stooped over her, all its saggy skin flapping above her head, and opened its mouth. When its muscles inched into a grin, the skin folds rolled up with it. The creature had no teeth that Opal could see. She wondered if it wanted to gum her to death.

For the first time that day, she truly feared for her life. What had she been thinking, coming to this crazy place by herself? Her mother was just two pink doors away, and here Opal might be eaten by some sort of walking wrinkle inside the food court of a converted mall!

Still, Opal didn't run. Even when the oversized sunglasses slid down her nose and she was truly eye to eye to eye with the creature, she held her ground.

The mutant stretched out a saggy fist. If it was trying to punch her, it was the slowest punch Opal had ever seen. But then it turned over its clenched fingers and opened them.

Crushed in the palm of its hand were several bendy straws.

Opal sneered as she took one and knocked the rest to the floor. The wrinkled creature crept away, dejected, as Opal pushed the sunglasses back up her nose and popped the straw into her peach soda.

Ha, she thought, her mind reeling as she made her way to the down escalators. *Mutants at my beck and call? Boys from school mooing at my feet? I could definitely get used to this.*

Red Rubber Balls of Doom

"I SO DESPISE DODGEBALL," CHERI SAID, FLINCHING away from an incoming red rubber bomb. "It is *brr-rut-tal* on one's manicure." She held up her metallic kelly green nails to cover her face. "It raises the chance of chips tenfold."

"And I," Iris said, adopting Cheri's dramatic language, "abhor it! Because it's barbaric." Her purple curls were pulled up in a high ponytail, bouncing as she jogged in place. She easily caught a curve ball tossed by Karyn Karson, but instead of lobbing it back, she handed it over to Scarlet. "How is pummeling one another with balls exercise?"

"Dodgeball rules!" Scarlet shouted, jumping just a little too high. She whipped her arm out in a salsa wave and spun the ball right back at Karyn, hitting her on the knee. "Burn!" Scarlet declared. "You got served, Karyn—*again!*"

With the exception of a few of Karyn's trendoid friends, the gym class laughed at Scarlet's joke. Although Karyn didn't know it was superfly Scarlet Louise Jones herself who

had dropkicked the ravioli on her spaghetti-blonde hair, the cafeteria incident was already legendary.

Beneath her black sunglasses, Opal smiled along. Having been bullied by the girl all through primary school, she wasn't exactly a member of the Karyn Karson Fan Klub, either. "Dodgeball has its purpose," she said to the other three girls, catching a ball thrown her way and immediately hurling it back at pudgy Emma Appleby. "It separates the strong from the weak." The ball hit Emma smack on the forehead and she tipped over like a sleeping cow.

The image of a downed cow set Opal chuckling. "Moo!" she laughed beneath her breath, clapping sarcastically as Emma struggled to her feet. Scarlet arched an eyebrow at her teammate and friend.

Standing on the sidelines in her traffic yellow tracksuit, Ms. Skynyrd blew her whistle. "Girls!" she yelled to the PE class, clearly directing her speech at Opal. "No faces! Keep it below the neck!"

Opal held her hands up in a "whaddayagonnado?" gesture. "Sorry!" she called back to the teacher. "Accidenté!"

A new round of balls were thrown. Iris was just about to catch the dodgeball version of a high pop fly when Opal bumped her out of the way and grabbed it for herself. She spun it back instantly, the red rubber ball burning across the pasty white thighs of Annie Barrett. Annie limped off to the benches, rubbing the hot mark on her leg.

"Hey, Opes," Iris said, trying to mask her irritation with a smile, "take it easy, okay? It's just a game."

"Is it?" Opal said, smiling back at Iris from behind her black sunglasses. "Is that all it is?"

As Opal strutted back and forth behind the line, preparing for the next ball assault, Iris said quietly to Cheri and Scarlet, "Does Opal seem different to either of you?"

Cheri glanced over at Opal, who was double-fist-pumping in anticipation. "Well, the sunglasses with the regulation gymporium shorts are a, um, different fashion choice," she said.

"Are you guys talking about me?" Opal challenged, approaching the trio and propping Dr. Cooper's black Stang-Rayz up above her barrettes.

Cheri blushed and hoped it just looked like she was sweating. "Oh, no, Opal, I was just wondering about your sunglasses, that's all. Are they for your headaches?"

"We've hardly seen you the past couple of days," Iris added. "Are you still not feeling okay?"

Opal tipped down her sunglasses again and turned just in time to catch another dodgeball. "Never better!" she answered. She gave the ball a single bounce on the gymporium floor and hurled it back. It hit Julie Nichols square in the stomach and she doubled over, braying in pain. Opal laughed.

"Girls!" Ms. Skynyrd trilled her whistle again, gesturing toward Opal.

Opal flung her arms wide in a "whaddayawantfrom-melady?" pose, then strutted around like that, a rap star in gym class. "You *said* 'below the neck'!" she shouted back to the PE teacher.

Ms. Skynyrd called a time-out as all the balls were gathered up and all the girls already benched were let back into the game. Opal, Cheri, Iris, and Scarlet lined up again, one next to the other, with the rest of their team. Iris balanced on the tips of her toes, ready to catch any red rubber balls.

"Hey," Scarlet whispered next to her. "Do you think the balls would hurt any less if you made them sky-blue instead red?"

Iris gave Scarlet a playful little shove on the shoulder. "Remember what we said! We're only going to use our *ahems* to . . . you know."

"Protect the weak and kick mutant butt?" Cheri muttered.

"What she said." Iris nodded at her.

"Though I have to confess," Cheri admitted from the other side of Iris, "my ability to calculate the projectiles of the dodgeballs *is* helping me not get hit by them!"

Ms. Skynyrd blew her whistle to start the second round of the game. "That's different!" Iris called over her shoulder to Cheri as she sprinted to the centerline to grab a ball. "That's self-defense!"

There was an instant dodgeball massacre in the middle of the gymporium as girls from both teams scrambled to grab balls and bounce them off their opponents at close range. A whole new round of casualties were immediately called out, and the survivors retreated back to their sides.

"Anyway," Opal announced, joining their conversation again, "I'm going to need these sunglasses next week, on the boat."

"What boat? Eek!" Cheri jumped aside, tucking in her butt just in time to miss getting hit. "Are you moving out of your apartment to live at sea?"

"Yeah," Opal said, rolling her eyes behind the dark glasses. "I'm going to be a pirate, Cheri, okay?"

Iris could hear the sarcasm in Opal's voice. She frowned. "No, seriously, Opal," she said before Cheri could ask if that meant Opal would be getting a parrot sidekick. "What's the deal with the boat?" She caught another one of Karyn's feeble throws and paused for a second before she handed the ball over to Scarlet again.

"Thank you smelly much," Scarlet joked, clutching the ball and scanning the other team for her next target. "This is actually fun. And I'm not even using my *ahems*!"

Iris shook her head, but couldn't help but smile as once again Scarlet beaned Karyn with her own dodgeball. To her three friends' surprise, Opal started to sing, "Na na na na, hey hey hey, goodbye!"

As Karyn skulked off to the benches again, Iris did a double take. For a second she thought she saw a thin lizard's tail sticking out from the bottom of the girl's shorts.

While Scarlet continued to hold down the front line, Cheri, Iris, and Opal dropped back a bit, Cheri hiding behind Iris to tie her sneaker.

"The boat?" Iris repeated to Opal.

"The deal is," Opal said, a big grin on her face, "the whole class is going on a class trip. Across the river. On the ferry, Cheri. Or I don't know, maybe on the bus. To my mom's work. The cosmeceutical company. BeauTek."

"We are?" Cheri said, surprised. Honestly, she was more interested in the pirate story and wondered if that was still an option.

"The Mall of No Returns, huh?" Iris said as she scanned the air for round red missiles. "How did that happen?"

"I suggested it to Mr. Knimoy for extra credit," Opal said, obviously proud of herself. "He thought it was a 'highly logical' idea. That it would give the class a chance to see how a real lab worked."

"Okay, cool," Iris said. From the times she'd spent at the FLab, she thought that coloring with chemicals, like the kinds found in oil paints, was more fun than just looking at test tubes and beakers of the stuff, which were always "do-not-touchable." But a tour of the neon yellow mall could be fun. "And hey," Iris added, "the whole class will get to meet your mom!"

The smile left Opal's face and she strutted away to toss another dodgeball. What Iris didn't know was that Opal had yet to tell her mother about the school trip. The woman had been so thrilled by Opal's surprise visit—not—that Opal could only imagine the meltdown to come when Opal showed up with twenty other students. But she'd worry about that later. After her little stare-downs with Duncan Murdoch and the wrinkly mutant, Opal bet she could finally command some respect—from her three super besties and the oblivious Dr. Mom. Her mother might not be happy to see her at her job next week. But Opal had a feeling she'd find some other support at BeauTek. Ugly, horned, fleshy support.

That's what sunglasses were for. To block things that were hard on the eyes.

Gym class was over. Their team had won. Iris easily caught any balls thrown her way. Cheri used math to miss them. Scarlet knocked out Karyn Karson a grand total of four times. And Opal scored really well, too, until Ms. Skynyrd finally called her out for "excessive aggression."

The girls had changed from their gymporium uniforms back into their regular outfits. Iris had taken down her ponytail, and Cheri had dabbed on some plum-tinted lip gloss. As Opal emerged from the girls' room, the other three were surprised to see that she no longer had her hair clipped back in barrettes. Iris spied a streak of solid white running through the brown. It reminded her a little of the long silky hair on WuWu, the shelter Shih Tzu Cheri was toting around today. Iris wondered: Was Opal finally showing some effects of the Heliotropium? If she was and she thought eleven was a little young to go white, maybe Iris could change the streak to another color. *Orange looks nice against brown*, Iris mused, imagining it.

From the bathroom, the four girls walked down the hall to their lockers. On the way, they could see Albert Feinstein approaching in the other direction. Iris couldn't help but notice that the boy was looking better. Still nerdy, but cute nerdy now. Instead of being belted up around his chest, his pants hung below his hips. Instead of pleated-front khakis, he wore straight-leg dark denim. His shirt was still buttoned up to his chin, but his glasses were new. Not so thick and foggy as before.

Maybe our super-save in the cafeteria boosted his confidence a bit! Iris thought happily.

Definitely he's been following my daily style Tweeks! twought Cheri, twilled at the progress of her stealth makeover.

As Albert reached the four girls, Cheri spoke-sang, "Hey, hey, hey, Albert. Loving the new frames. Aviator, am I right?"

Scarlet bit her tongue to stop a snark attack. Albert Feinstein really was not her type, and she totally didn't get what the other three saw in the math geek.

"Hi, Albert," Iris said between licks of her boysenberry lollipop. Despite their life-and-shirt-changing moment in the cafeteria, she didn't think he even knew her name.

Albert smiled awkwardly at Iris, and he mumbled something to Cheri about the math assignment. Then he walked right past them up to Opal at her locker. The other three girls watched, fascinated, and Scarlet scrambled for her smartphone. She sensed a GoobToob moment in the making.

At the sight of Albert, Opal propped the sunglasses on her head like she had in gym class. The streak of ivory hair fell across one of her brown eyes, and from where Iris stood she thought she saw a cloudy mist float across both of them. Clasping her hands in front of her, pointing her toes together, and coyly batting her lashes at Albert, Opal said:

"Whazzup?"

Albert cleared his throat and stammered. "Oh, um, w-what's happening, Opaline?"

"What's happening?" Opal said back, looking him up and down. "Not much."

Iris didn't get it. Wasn't this the same boy Opal had confessed her crush on at the sleepover party? Why was she acting so cool now? Was she just embarrassed in front of her friends?

"Guys," Iris whispered to Scarlet and Cheri. "Let's, you know, give them some privacy."

"Nuh-uh," said Cheri, enraptured. Now that she could see the fruits of her makeover, no way was she missing a minute of love in the afternoon. She stroked WuWu's silky ears and sighed.

"Double nuh-uh," said Scarlet, who was just plain curious. She planned to watch the video later for tips on how to talk to boys, since all she knew how to do so far was bully them.

So Iris turned back to her locker and pretended to be getting her books.

"I just w-wanted to say," Albert was s-still s-stammering, "that I think it's really cool, the class t-trip to BeauTek. Mr. Knimoy told me about it."

"Oh, that," Opal said. Just the mention of it reminded her all over again of how she had to break this news to her mom. She rubbed her eyes. Maybe she was getting another headache. "It's, like . . ." Opal let the sentence trail, and headed off down the hallway, lost in her own thoughts.

"Okay, um, see you in class!" Albert called after her.

Scarlet switched her camera phone off and shoved it back in her pocket as she, Iris, and Cheri followed behind. "That was kind of a letdown," she said. "Zero fireworks."

"Maybe you can fix it in editing," Cheri suggested, though she was disappointed, too. The dark denim was a move in the right direction, but obviously she had a lot more work to do on Albert if he was ever to win the heart of the fair Opaline!

"IDK," Iris said to Scarlet and Cheri as they entered their classroom. Opal was already at her desk. "But I think something might be off with Opal. Maybe the Helio-goo is changing her after all. Did you see the way she was pulverizing people in PE?"

"For shizzle!" Cheri said, giving WuWu the Shih Tzu a pat to keep him safe in her bag. Even Scarlet had to admit that Opal's extreme dodgeballing had crossed the fine line from awesome to scary.

"Right when we're getting all super-violety," Iris said, tugging at her hair anxiously, "she's going super-violenty."

As Iris headed off to her seat in the back by Opal, Scarlet turned to Cheri. "Bummer," she said. "I know I boss Opal around sometimes, but I really like that girl."

Cheri arched a skeptical eyebrow at Scarlet, who protested, "And not just for her lunch!"

While she was waiting for class to begin, Scarlet replayed her video of Albert and Opal. When she'd been watching in the hallway, her attention had been on the semi-bumbling mathlete captain. But this time Scarlet focused on her friend. She, too, noticed the stark white line streaking through Opal's hair. It was hard to tell for sure on the small phone screen, but Scarlet thought she also saw Opal's brown eyes cloud over.

Maybe Iris is right, Scarlet thought, wrinkling her nose. *Maybe the Heliotropium is finally taking effect on Opal, too.* Beneath her desk, Scarlet's feet danced a little jig. It reminded her that, so far, the changes had been mostly good, if confusing, for her, Cheri, and Iris.

But what changes were in store for Opaline?

Worst. Hair Day. Ever.

FROM @CHERICHERI: NOTHINGZ CUTER ON A BRAINEE math captain than cool comfy cotton tees. wit plaid shirt over unbuttned. #middleschoolstylee

From @chericheri: nobodee works hightop bball sneakers like mathletes. unlaced tongues out!!! smart n hot #middleschoolstylee

From @chericheri: r u a math boy with braces? bling yr grill wit gold flash meets classy. longer hair = 2 run fingers thru! #middleschoolstylee

From @albertfnumbers to @chericheri: Hey, are you talking to me?

After Cheri witnessed the non-sparks between Albert and Opal, she upped her Tweeking, posting little fashion tips in

140 characters or less. Targeted directly at middle school math boys. She figured that would narrow the field. Albert was brilliant, but sometimes boys could be so *obtuse* about these things.

Obtuse meaning "a person lacking sensibility and awareness." And not "an angle greater than 90 degrees but less than 180," which was also its definition. Just ask your friendly neighborhood geometrician.

On the subject of geometry, just that morning Cheri had joined Mr. Grates in another one of his funky math raps. Standing in front of the class, she hit her flow defining angles, vertexes, and rectilinear, quadrilateral, and polygonic figures, all while Mr. Grates kept interjecting, "Swaggy Swaggy Swaggy!" She even managed to rhyme "parallelogram" with "wham bam, thank you, ma'am," which was pretty {wham} impressive!

In his new high-top sneakers and distressed jeans, Albert sat in the ~~audience~~ class, watching her, dumbstruck. The cascades of berry red hair. The glints of bubblegum pink nails. The mastery of geometric axioms!

She was magnificent.

Do boys swoon? If they do, Albert did. By the time MC Cheri had ~~shut down the club~~ finished the presentation, he had forgotten all about Opaline blowing him off in the hallway the other day. Brilliant, witty, stylish: Cheri and him had *so* much more in common.

And later, after school, when he saw Cheri, bathed in sunbeams, behind the elliptical Chronic Prep building over by the fluffula tree, he worked up his courage and walked over to her.

He only tripped three times on his untied laces.

"Bonjour, Cheri," he said when he finally reached her, surprised at his own boldness. And his recall of French greetings. He placed one hand up against the fluffula trunk and leaned in to talk to her.

"Bonjour, *Alber*," Cheri said with a smile, dropping the "t" like you did in French. Frolicking around on a leash at her feet was Rococo Chanel, coincidentally a French poodle. Cheri always liked it when her day matched her dog. "Having some trouble with those sneakers?" she asked, excited to see that Albert had followed at least one of her Tweeks.

"You know me," Albert said. "Every day I'm shuffling!"

Cheri giggled. It was so funny when nerds tried to act cool! "Just tuck in the laces," she suggested, squinting past him. Iris was supposed to meet her here so that she could give Rococo his own makeover. And hopefully Iris would also have some fresh bubblegum. Cheri gave hers a few chews, then blew out a small pink bubble.

"Um," Albert was saying, "it was really nice of you to send me all those Tweeks." Rococo Chanel gnawed at one of his loose sneaker laces, and he was trying to shake the little dog off without kicking him.

"Oh, the Tweeks," Cheri said, sucking back the bubble. "They're, you know, for anyone interested in math. And fashion. Who follows me on Tweeker." It started to dawn on her that it was possible Albert could have misunderstood her intentions. She thought back to all the times she'd shared her answers in math class. All the Tweeks. To *protect* Opal, Cheri had never actually mentioned a single thing *about* Opal. With all the attention and links to sample sales that she'd been sending him, Cheri couldn't really blame Albert if he thought that the girl crushing on him was . . .

Oh, sugarsticks, Cheri thought in a panic.

Sticks? Rococo Chanel answered. *Fetch? Where?!* The French poodle scampered around Cheri and Albert excitedly, circling the fluffula trunk. And their legs. With his leash.

"The way you rapped about polygons today," Albert said, tottering a little closer to her as the dog leash tightened around his high-tops, "was mind-blowing. Literally. I think I snapped a synapse." He gave a nasal laugh. Cheri had no idea was he was talking about.

"I might have some double-sided tape in my locker," she offered, "to glue it back together?" Over his shoulder, way back at the school doors, she could see Iris's violet ringlets. And Scarlet's swinging black ponytail as she tangoed alongside her. And Opal's dark sunglasses.

Oh swell no, Cheri thought in a panic.

What happened to the sugarsticks? Rococo demanded, wagging his tail impatiently. *I was told there'd be sugarsticks!* The poodle doubled his laps around the tree trunk, and their legs, until he had run out of leash.

"You're so sweet," Albert said, bending closer. Cheri realized with alarm that they were bound at the ankles. "And so funny. Have you ever considered joining the mathletes? I can get you in."

Cheri opened her mouth to answer, and the last thing she saw was the glint of gold on his braces. The next thing she felt were his lips. On hers. His eyes closed, but hers popped open in shock, her lashes brushing against the lenses of his fly new eyeglasses.

It wasn't that bad, really. He tasted like spearmint toothpaste. Though she immediately regretted wearing her long-lasting lip gloss: That just made the kissing stickier.

With both hands, Cheri gave Albert a gentle nudge. He continued smooching on her. She furrowed her brow and pushed a little harder. He still didn't back off. "Mmpf!" Cheri mmpfed. She had no choice. She coughed her gum into his mouth and stabbed one elbow down on his shoulder, like Scarlet had taught her.

Their lips made a gooey *smwack!* sound as they came apart at last. Albert stumbled back in his loose high-tops over Rococo Chanel's leash and landed in the grass. Cheri staggered and flailed, too, hugging the tree trunk to keep from falling down on top of him.

"Oopsie," she huffed, trying to catch her breath and free Rococo from the tangle as Albert struggled to his feet. "Albert," she said, her cheeks flaming as red as her hair, "I'm flattered, really I am. But the thing is, I have this friend, and she—"

"BFFs!" The scream cut through the schoolyard, bouncing off the Plexiglas wall and the solar panels of Chronic Prep. Albert covered his ears and whirled around toward the source. A brown-haired girl in black sunglasses was on her knees in the middle of the yard, pointing at Cheri. As she shouted, her hair rose up around her, one white streak crackling in the wind.

Albert didn't remember it being windy.

"BFFs!" Opal screamed again, tearing off the sunglasses and clutching at her head as if she was in pain. Terrified by the sight, Scarlet had moonwalked back toward the school doors. But Iris tried to approach her. Why Cheri had been sucking face with Albert Feinstein, she had no clue. But she could only imagine how upset Opal must be!

Then again, she did just kind of blow him off the other afternoon?

"Opal . . ." Iris said, slowly walking toward her. When Opal whipped around to face her, Iris no longer saw the shy girl from the sleepover, one of her best friends. White clouds raced over Opal's brown eyes, veined through with electric orange currents. Her hair floated straight up in the air and snaked around in the wind. As Iris stretched a hand out to comfort her, her fingers felt such a jolt that she was shocked off her feet. Flat on her back, Iris stared up at the sky.

Dark clouds covered the sun, and it began to pour.

Albert didn't remember the forecast calling for rain.

"Hold this," Cheri commanded, over at the fluffula tree. She slapped Rococo's leash into Albert's hand. Then she stumbled across the schoolyard in her platforms in the rain.

"Opal!" Cheri cried. She had recently started wearing a *teensy* bit of mascara along with the lip gloss, and it ran in gritty rivers down her cheeks. "It's not what you think! It was an accident! I was only making out, I mean making *over*, him for—" She reached out to Opal and was thrown back by the electrostatic force field, too. Tendrils of black smoke curled up from her burnt manicure. Her beautiful ruby waves broke out in a hideous case of the frizzies.

Opaline stood up in the center of her electric bubble, tiny threads of violet-white lightning fizzing around her. She pointed from Iris to Cheri and over to Scarlet. "BFFs," she said again, her voice quaking. "You said you were my BFFS. And BFFs don't kiss their friend's crush! Or eat their tacos without at least saying the magic word!"

"Oh, *puh-leez*," Scarlet muttered, back at the school doors and out of earshot.

Iris got to her feet and came as close as she dared to Opal's dome. It was as if Opal was encircled by hundreds of crackling electric currents. Iris could see Opal, standing in the middle, her hair on end. But she couldn't quite make out the borders of the dome itself. As soon as one electric line appeared, another one vanished. Like one of those invisible security fences, you might not even know it was there until you'd run into it.

Unless I color it in, Iris realized, thinking back to scenes she'd seen in movies where spies or thieves sprayed dye into the air to expose the tricky maze of laser beams they'd have to crawl through.

With a tug of her now uber-wiry, 360-degree violet afro, Iris cast a pale orange glow over Opal, and the outline of the dome became clearer. Currents coursed and sparked all around it.

"We *are* your BFFs," Iris said, her voice shaking, too, as she approached the electric shield and held a tentative pinkie up just an inch from the live current. "Opal, I know it's been so stressful, starting over at a new school when your mom is always at work and you're stuck dealing with all these changes." Iris had never said it out loud before. She'd been trying so hard to be strong, to be independent, to be brave, that she hadn't even wanted to admit it to herself. But as she spoke the words, she knew this confession was just as true for her as it was for Opal. And she knew their friendship was worth the risk. "It's been hard for me, too," she whispered, a lump in her throat. "We're kind of the same that way." She looked past the pale orange shield into Opal's clouded eyes. "But let's just talk about it, okay?" Iris said, her tears running with the raindrops down her cheeks. "I'm sure Cheri can explain the kissing. And you and Scarlet can do lunch. Her treat!" She tried to smile. "Opal, maybe you're just finally having a chemical reaction to the Helio—"

"Ya think?!" Opal cut her off, laughing harshly from inside her high-voltage bubble. The hatred in her voice shocked Iris much more than the electric current had. Opal dropped back onto her knees, clutching at her head again. "BFFs," she howled, "stands for Big Fat Fonies!"

By now Scarlet's courage had returned, and she edged up to the dome, too. But she knew this was *so* not the time to correct Opal's spelling.

"Or," Opal shouted, "Bad Freaky Fakes!"

Well, at least that sort of made sense.

Scarlet shook her head, speechless. Even her stick-straight hair had fuzzed up, her ponytail resembling a grizzled shish kebab. In the downpour, the three girls stood around Opal, helpless, as she sturmed and dranged (that's German for had a major hissy fit—this is turning out to be a chapter of many tongues!) inside her thunderdome.

"What should we do?" Cheri asked. With her sparkly headband, mascara dripping down her cheeks, and lip gloss smeared all over her face, she looked like a weeping beauty queen in the long ago days before waterproof makeup was invented. Scarlet yelped "Gah!" at the sight of her. Then she started to think about next year's Halloween costume. She didn't know which was mascarier: Shockwave Opal or Meltdown Cheri.

"I have an idea," Iris said. She sounded sad. But determined.

Standing opposite Opal's electric dome, Iris put her hands to her head, too, and closed her eyes.

Across the dome, the pale see-through orange faded away, replaced by not one, not two, but THREE rainbows. Vibrant bands of red, orange, yellow, green, blue, indigo, and, most vibrant of all, violet sparkled above Opal's head.

And at the base of the dome, miniature unicorns gamboled, trotting in circles around Opal's feet.

Opal stared at the sight, gasping. It was a triple rainbow all the way. So intense. A full-on triple rainbow. "OMV," Opal said.

Suddenly, it was as if the rainbows sapped all the angry energy out of Opal. Her hair floated back down, once again obeying the laws of gravity. The clouds left her eyes. The electric dome vanished into thin air, taking Iris's triple rainbow with it, and the skies cleared.

The four girls stood in silence in the center of the schoolyard. Scarlet should have said she was sorry for being such a bossypants. Cheri should have said she was sorry for the trouble with Albert. Opal should have said she was sorry for almost electrocuting them. But no one said anything.

In the background, a French poodle barked.

At last Opal spoke. "Later, *Worst* Friends Forevs," she said sullenly, picking up the stolen black sunglasses from the wet grass and putting them on again. As she backed out of the schoolyard, she called mockingly, "See you tomorrow! On our field trip! And BTdubs, *nice hair!*"

Iris, Scarlet, and Cheri watched Opal walking backward, backward, backward until she was out of sight. Iris thought she might cry again.

"Oh Iris," Cheri whispered, reaching out to clutch a handful of the purple cotton candy that was her gorgeous violet mane. "Worst. Hair Day. Ever."

"And what about the class trip?" Scarlet asked, twisting her frizzy ponytail. "If Opal's gone all evil, no way am I sitting next to her on the bus."

"Or the ferry." Cheri sighed. Now more than ever, she wished that Opal had gone pirate instead.

"I guess we finally know what Opaline's *ahems* are," Scarlet said. She meant it as a little joke, to break the tension and cheer Iris up. But Iris just shook her head. The mustachioed opossum. The monorail commuter with the caterpillar unibrow. The mantis man in the park. It couldn't all just be a coincidence. Something was way wrong in Sync City. And now this.

"We know what Opal's powers are, yeah," Iris said quietly at last. Arms folded across her chest, she lifted her chin and looked up at the sun. She remembered once more that it was a star, too, and its rays seemed to fill her with strength. She couldn't see the waves of light beaming down on her. But she could feel them. A breeze blew her fried violet hair off her shoulders, and she turned her gaze to Scarlet and Cheri. Her pupils were so small, it was as if her eyes were pure color, the palest shade of purple-blue the girls had ever seen. Cheri and Scarlet were mesmerized: Iris practically glowed.

"If we're seriously becoming superheroes," she said, calm again after the storm, "I think our best friend . . . just turned into the bad guy."

Totally (School) Tripping

SO THIS IS WHEN IT GOES DOWN. THIS IS WHERE IT'S AT.
This is what happens four years after four girls were four-ever altered at a sleepover fail in a FLab on the forty-second floor of a Highly Questionable Tower.

This is the day of the class trip.

They were on the school bus, crossing the bridge over the Joan River. The flashing fish and plaid stingrays and octopi with daisified sucker cups still swam beneath the surface, but the girls were too high above to see them.

While Karyn Karson, Brad Hochoquatro, the notorious Albert Feinstein, and all the other students in their class chattered excitedly and pressed their faces to the bus windows to look at the Sync City skyline behind them, Iris, Cheri, Scarlet, and Opal sat with their sound off. Iris tried to digi-sketch the view from the bridge, but the ride was too bumpy. Besides, she wasn't really feeling very inspired. She unwrapped a fresh blueberry lollipop, but everything tasted like broccoli.

Cheri was so upset about what had happened the day before, she hadn't even bothered to paint her nails for the field trip. The bubblegum pink was chipped at the tips and still blackened in the spots where Opal's electroshock treatment had burned it.

"No clandestine pet today, Cher?" Iris asked. The tote bag sat empty between them.

Cheri just shook her head no.

A shiny black ponytail shot up in front, and Scarlet propped her chin on the seat back. She scowled over at Iris and Cheri, her freckles underlining her eyes. Tilting her ponytail in the direction of her neighbor, she mouthed, "AWK-WARD." But she didn't say anything. She couldn't. In spite of her protests to Mr. Knimoy, she had ended up sitting next to Opal after all. The class had chosen partners days before the four girls had their private electrical storm, and Scarlet couldn't get anyone else to switch places with her that morning.

Toot toot! Ms. Skynyrd, who had come along to supervise with Mr. Knimoy, blew her whistle. Even outside the gymporium, she wore her usual traffic yellow tracksuit. It matched the bus perfectly. On any other day this would have cheered Cheri up immediately. And she did briefly imagine a yellow Labrador retriever colored by Iris with black bumblebee stripes to go with both Ms. Skynyrd and the bus. But even that thought didn't make her smile.

"In your seat, Miss Jones," Ms. Skynyrd was saying.

With a roll of her eyes, Scarlet slunk down and turned to face forward. Opal was back in her usual outfit: button-up shirt, Peter Pan collar, pocket protector. And her hair was back in two gold barrettes. But Scarlet knew better. She knew Opal had changed for the bad. She could see the streak of white snaking through her hair.

Scarlet's feet kicked against the seat in front of them, wishing they were Cabbage-Patching, Roger-Rabbiting, Hokey-Pokeying—any dance but here! Not very practically, but very impulsively, she had worn her brand-new ballerina pointe shoes. They were the most delicate pink, with satin ribbons that laced up her ankles. She thought they were *terribly* pretty. And if Rhett Smith or Karyn Karson or anyone else made fun of her for wearing ballet slippers on their field trip, Scarlet swore she'd go old school and pants them.

She cleared her throat.

"My mom packed an extra chocolate pudding cup for the class trip," she offered. "If you want it?"

Behind her black Stang-Rayz, Opal's expression was unreadable. "They have a food court at BeauTek," she said flatly.

"Alrighty then," Scarlet said under her breath, slinking down even deeper in her seat.

When Opal had finally worked up the nerve to tell her mom about the field trip, naturally her mom went mental. Talk about your sturm and drang! She ranted on and on about how there was no way her company would allow it, how it was unfair of Opal to put her in this position, blah, blah, blah. Opal pleaded and pouted right back. She was just on the verge of making it rain in their apartment when Dr. Trudeau gave in. She must have seen the clouds pass over Opal's eyes, because she agreed to ask her boss, Develon Louder, president of BeauTek, for permission.

Dr. Trudeau had presented the request as calmly as she could, standing before Develon, trembling in her Fugg boots—which were so comfortable when you were on your feet all day in a lab. As Develon lifted her black Burkant bag and peered at her through the transparent plastic strip, Dr. Trudeau braced herself for the barrage of cuss words. At least the Burkant might block Develon's projectile spittle.

But the cuss words never came.

"Capital idea, Trudeau," Develon purred instead, lowering her bag once more and stroking it like a kitten with her lacquered red nails.

"Excuse me, sir?" Opal's mom asked meekly. (Clause twenty-nine of the employee contract required that all staff refer to Develon as "sir.")

"PRIMO IDEA, TRUDEAU!" Develon shouted in her usual tone of voice. "What better way to build loyalty to the BeauTek brand than by getting 'em when they're young and impressionable!"

Dr. Trudeau stared at her boss blankly.

"I BELIEVE THE CHILDREN ARE OUR FUTURE!" Develon said. "Our future customers!"

"My thoughts exactly, sir," Opal's mom stammered, realizing that her daughter's pushiness was actually scoring her some on-the-job brownie points.

"But remember"—Develon Louder gave Dr. Trudeau a bump with her Burkant, bustling her out of her office much as Dr. Trudeau had ushered Opal out of her lab—"the sub-sub-parking lot is strictly off-limits."

"Of course, sir." Opal's mom nodded.

"And the Vi-Shush is strictly verboten."

"What's that, sir? Ver-what?"

"VERBOTEN!" Develon Louder shouted. "THAT'S GERMAN FOR FOR*$#@!BIDDEN!"

"Yes, sir!" Dr. Trudeau shouted back as Develon slammed the silver door in her face.

And with a minimum amount of spit, Opal's class was cleared for the field trip.

Now, through the bus's front window, Opal could see BeauTek, beaming like a fortress of bile. They parked out front. With Ms. Skynyrd leading and Mr. Knimoy herding from behind, the students filed off and marched beneath the archway of the Mall of No Returns.

Dr. Trudeau was waiting inside, and Opal went up to her and gave her a super-obvious hug. "Hi, *Mom*," she said, loud enough for everyone to hear.

"Opal, sweetie," her mother muttered down to her, "do you really need to wear those sunglasses in—"

"Yes," Opal cut her off curtly, then beckoned the other three over. They approached with hesitation.

"Mom," Opal said, "you remember Iris, Scarlet, and Cheri, right? You used to work with their moms at that FLabby place?"

"Ah, yes," Dr. Trudeau said. Just the mention of her old job still annoyed her. She looked down her nose at the trio. Dr. Henderson's daughter was wearing too much lip gloss. Dr. Jones's daughter wouldn't stop fidgeting. And Dr. Tyler's girl had the most outrageously violet hair! "Well, enjoy the

283

tour, girls," she sniffed. "Go on and join the group. Sir Louder is about to speak."

Opal stuck her tongue out at the other three as they shuffled to the back of their class.

Once all the students were gathered on the main floor, a stick-thin woman in a wasp-waist pantsuit stepped in front of the fountain. The class fell silent as she lifted what looked like a square black pocketbook in front of her face. Her eyes darted out at them through a thin transparent strip in the bag, and her silver topknot bobbled above it like a loose doorknob.

"Oh-kay . . ." Scarlet murmured. Ms. Skynyrd overheard her and waggled her gym whistle as a warning.

"Welcome, students, to BeauTek!" the woman announced. Her voice ricocheted around the corridors of the former mall. "I am Develon Louder, president of the company. And here at BeauTek, we're in the business of the science of beauty!"

Standing at her side, Dr. Trudeau smiled nervously.

Develon continued her introduction, talking about the company's innovations in the fields of invisible tattoos and innie-outie belly button reversals and toothpastes that scrubbed the sinks they were spit into.

"So enjoy your tour, children," she finished from behind

her black bag. "Enjoy the astounding sight of science in action! And remember, everyone gets a sample of our latest weed-reducing wrinkle cream at the end. And a two percent discount on your first order. In store or online."

"Two percent?" Cheri's head did the math. "That's only two cents on the dollar!"

Develon turned the tour over to Dr. Trudeau and teetered away from the group on her six-inch stiletto heels. As they clicked along the floor, Cheri thought back to the dirty shoe she'd found in the park. The memory of the twitching mantis man flashed through her mind, and she hugged her empty tote bag close to her side.

Opal's mom began to lead the class around level A, talking first about the innovations taking place at the Build-a-Girl Workshop. Iris kept telling herself she should have been interested, being a girl herself. But no matter how hard she tried, she just wasn't that into it. She dragged along at the end of the line with Cheri.

Behind them, Scarlet kept sprinting up the walls and back-flipping off them.

The rest of the class was just filing into the Forever Twenty-Fun lab when something caught Iris's eye. Separate from the group, a certain student in oversized sunglasses was riding up the escalator.

Iris gave Cheri a poke in the ribs and pointed just as Scarlet joined them.

"Hey," Scarlet said, spotting Opal, too.

"Our tour, detour?" Iris suggested.

"For sure," Cheri agreed.

"Okay, hold on," Iris said, concentrating. And in another instant, the three girls were disguised. As acid-yellow Mall of No Returns shopping bags.

"What kind of disguise is this?!" Scarlet spluttered, ducking toward the escalators just as the doors to Forever Twenty-Fun closed.

"No one even shops here anymore!" Cheri hissed, hunching behind her.

"Sorry!" Iris whispered back. "It was the best I could do on short notice!"

And it was good enough, because no one paid any attention to the stray shopping bags riding the escalators.

Opal was a floor ahead of the threesome. By the time Iris, Scarlet, and Cheri reached level C, she was nowhere to be found.

They stood by the top of the escalator. Three stories down, they could see the colored fountain where the skinny lady had given her speech from behind her giant purse. But level C itself was quite empty. It didn't have lots of storefront labs, like they'd seen on level A. Just a food court to one side, with windows that looked out to the river . . .

"Opal told me there was a food court," Scarlet said.

. . . and, to the other side, a pair of deep pink doors.

"Ooh, pretty color," cooed Cheri. "I wonder what's behind them."

Iris scanned level C, from the pink doors to the food court. But there was no sign of Opal. Or anyone else. "Let's go find out," she said.

Slowly they turned, inch by inch, step by step, nearing the pink doors. It was the middle of the morning, and sunlight streamed through the windows behind them. But something about the air-conditioned emptiness of the space made them shiver. "C must stand for Creepy," Iris said. They could hear the constant *whirm-chunka-whirm-chunka-whirm* of the escalators behind them. It sounded to Scarlet like a robot's theme song. She hoped the escalator wasn't secretly a Transformer with shiny steel teeth.

As they got closer to the double pink doors, the girls noticed a sign. In curly script, the engraved brass plate read *Victoria's Shush*. Cheri tipped her head back and calculated that the doors were three times taller than them.

"Want me to try and slam-dance them open?" Scarlet hissed, itching to move.

"Chill, Cha-cha," Iris muttered back. "There's got to be a better way." Her eyes searched the glossy pink doors. Below one brass handle was a small golden circle.

"Cher," Iris said, "what do you think?"

Cheri looked at the old-fashioned lock, then fished in her tote bag and brought out a thin metal file.

Scarlet stared at it with surprise. "What are you carrying that around for?" she asked, her voice bouncing around the empty corridor. "Planning a jailbreak?"

In response, Cheri held the file up to her hand and smoothed down the ragged edge of one of her chipped fingernails.

"Oh," Scarlet said in a low voice, slightly embarrassed. "I didn't think they made nail files like that anymore."

"It's vintage," Cheri murmured back. Then, with Iris and Scarlet covering her, she crouched down and slid the nail file into the lock. She gingerly twisted it this way and that, mumbling, "If I just apply the correct amount of torque . . ."

Scarlet mouthed to Iris, "Torque?" Iris shrugged her shoulders. And they heard a *click*.

"We're in!" Cheri whispered.

Iris gave one of the doors a light push and it slowly creaked open. The girls glanced over their shoulders once more. Level C remained vacant. Eerily so. They tiptoed across the threshold into the Vi-Shush. (They didn't know it was called that. But you do!)

"Hello?" Iris said softly, her eyes scanning the dark lab. But they still didn't see Opal. And they didn't see any scientists, either. And they were stunned by what they did see.

Three rows of long lab tables, all topped with wire cages, all holding small animals.

"OMV," Cheri said, the color draining from her cheeks. "What is this place?"

Each girl took an aisle and walked down it in silence. The tattooed monkeys on mini stationary bikes. The ferrets with glow-in-the-dark teeth. The leopard-print bunnies, the rats with inflatable lips, the featherless chickens, even a tank of three-eyed flashing fish: They saw it all. And it all was *purple*.

"Iris?" Scarlet asked across the aisle. "You didn't *whoa*—!" Before she could finish her sentence, she came crashing onto the floor. "Owie," she muttered, picking up the banana peel she'd slipped on.

"Ook! Ook!" a capuchin monkey with lavender eyelashes hooted behind her, clapping and chortling so hard that he almost lost his footing on his tiny treadmill.

"Laugh it up, fuzzball," Scarlet grumbled, getting to her feet again. "What I was about to ask was—"

"No," Iris said in a low voice, guessing Scarlet's question. "I didn't do any of this. I've only ever changed the color of Cheri's shelter pets. I'd never keep rabbits and monkeys in a lab!"

Hanging from each cage was a small screen. Cheri touched one, and at first an official-looking seal flashed up. She only had a chance to read the words *Project M—* before the seal disappeared, replaced by an image of the animal in the cage. A bunch of data spewed out in a tinny mechanical voice: about the animals, chemicals, and side effects. "Guys," Cheri said, trying to make sense of it. "I think they might be experimenting with animals' DNA. Like, blending genes?" As she stood and stared at the nightmare petting zoo around her, Cheri felt positively vomitous. There were so many purple animals locked up in cages, she didn't know what to do. Her eyes raced from her aisle to Scarlet's to Iris's, and she thought she might faint.

Then a glint of yellowy-green grabbed her attention.

"Skeletony?" Scarlet blurted out too loudly, right as Cheri recognized the skeleton, too. Keeping a lookout for banana peels, Scarlet grapevined over to him. Lifted both his bony hands in hers. And wheeled the lab skeleton around on his stand as if they were waltzing. "How ya doin', old pal?" she said, smiling up into the single citrine gemstone in his left eye socket. "Long time no see!"

"Scar," Cheri said, joining her in the corner of the room. "This is no time for dancing! Don't you think it's strange that the old skeleton from the FLab is here?"

"Sister," Scarlet answered, putting Skeletony's hands down again and rolling him back to his corner, "I think this whole *place* is strange."

The capuchin monkey hooted again, sticking one paw out of his cage. Scarlet realized he was pointing at a fruit bowl, so she went back up the aisle to give him a second banana. She felt sorry for the little guy. If she were locked up in a cage, she'd probably throw her trash all over the place, too.

Project Mute! The phrase floated through Cheri's mind just as she was turning away from Skeletony. She craned her neck, skimming the aisles. There were so many animals! Which one was speaking to her?

Project Mute! The words came again.

"Hey," Cheri said, "one of the animals keeps saying 'Project Mute,' but I don't know which one, and I don't know what it means."

Over here, Cheri my luv! the voice came back. *Middle row, centr! Don't u remember R nite 2gethr?*

Hold on! Cheri thought. Her heart began to pitter-patter. *I'm coming!* With a quick command to Furi, she switched to roller skate mode and glid (*that's STILL how we're spelling it!*) down the middle aisle. Rolling past the caged animals, she felt like she was in a scary-movie supermarket where the shelves were stacked with bunnies and monkeys and mice. But she clenched her jaw and kept her focus, searching for a familiar furry face.

It was as if a symphony burst into song when she saw him.

He was four years older now, though not much bigger than when he was a baby. Running down his back all the way to the tip of his tail, the two streaks that once were white now gleamed a vibrant, almost neon violet against his soft black fur. But even if he hadn't called to her, even if she hadn't seen him, Cheri would have recognized the sweet smell of that skunk anywhere.

"Darth Odor!" she cried with joy. As fast as her fingers could move, she popped the cage open and the skunk scampered out into her waiting arms. "I never forgot that time when we got coated in slime!" she said, squeezing him tight. "Never ever!"

Darth snuggled into Cheri's shoulder, making little *nyuk nyuk* noises. He was so happy to see her, his first love, again. She rocked him in her arms, petting his fur. "And look at your pretty purple stripes! They're *blue-ti-ful*," Cheri baby-talked, kissing the skunk on his snout. "They look just like Iris's hair! You remember Iris, don't you?"

Darth nodded and squeaked. Cheri held open her tote for him to climb in. As he burrowed down into the bag, he sent her the message once more. *Project Mute.*

"He keeps telling me 'Project Mute,'" Cheri said, skating up the rest of the middle aisle to loop around to Iris. "But I don't know what it means."

"I think I do," Iris said, standing in front of a computer screen set up between the cages. Cheri rolled down the aisle toward her as Scarlet foxtrotted up from the other direction. When all three girls were gathered around the computer, Darth poked his head out of Cheri's tote bag. Iris gave the little skunk a welcoming pat while Scarlet and Cheri stared at the screen.

"Ew."

"Seriously?"

"So gross."

"I know, right?" Iris said, turning away from Darth and back to the computer screen. On it were images of hideous creatures, part human, part beast. A lady the size of hippopotami, with webbed feet and enormous tusks.

A man baring a mouthful of shark teeth. A disgusting fleshy thing with layers of neck fat and pockets of skin under its four eyes.

"This is like the nastiest Smashface group in history!" Scarlet said. She didn't know whether to laugh or scream, the photos were so frightening.

"There was a folder on the desktop labeled PROJECT MUTE," Iris explained. Her throat felt dry. "So I opened it." She clicked through more pictures. The mega opossum from the park. A seven-foot mantis in a thin brown trench coat . . .

"Mantis Man!" Cheri yelped, clutching Darth close to her. "BeauTek knows about all these freaky monsters?"

"I think," Iris said, "BeauTek *made* all these freaky monsters."

Scarlet frowned at the onscreen cavalcade of uglies. "So *Mute* must stand for—"

"*Mutants!*" a voice snarled.

Iris whipped her violet ringlets around. Cheri quarter-turned on her roller skates. Scarlet couldn't resist a cancan kick.

Standing in the doorway, silhouetted by the daylight, stood Opal. Sunglasses on. Shirt buttoned. Arms crossed.

And she wasn't alone.

Mwah Ha Ha!

"OPAL," IRIS SAID, HER COLOR SENSE TINGLING, "WHAT are you doing here?"

"What am *I* doing here?" Opal spat back. "This is my mother's company. My mother's lab. What are *you* doing here? And *what* are you wearing?" She snorted. "You three look like a bunch of bag ladies."

Oh, right. They'd been so distracted by the Victoria's Shush Petting Zoo of Horrors, Iris had forgotten to change their clothes back to normal.

"Well, it's not like I'm going to get all dressed up to have tater tots in a food court with a mutant!" Cheri said defensively. She understood the reason why her outfit resembled acid-yellow shopping bags, but still. She prided herself on being fabulous.

"Believe me, I know," Opal said, as a bevy of mutants grumbled and groaned behind her. "You save all your best style tips for *Albert*."

"Oy vey, not this again," Scarlet muttered, raising one slippered foot, then the other, to her knee in a ballerina passé position.

"Opal"—even though Cheri was facing a mutant mob, she still managed to blush at the mention of golden-grill Albert, captain of the mathalips—"I tried to tell you yesterday, that was an accident, I—"

"SILENCE!" Opal commanded with a sweep of her hand. In the shadows the girls could see little electric sparks shooting from her fingertips. She meant for Cheri to shut up, but the murmuring mutants fell quiet, too. Opal smirked beneath her sunglasses. They were like sheep, these mutants. Hideous, deformed, brain-dead sheep.

"New topic!" Scarlet attempted, ready to get off the boringness that was boys. "Opal, we found Darth Odor! From the FLab, remember?" She shot up en pointe, balancing in her toe shoes, trying to contain her energy in teeny-tiny steps. She was the most graceful shopping bag the mutants had ever seen.

Darth stuck his little skunk head out of Cheri's tote bag, but at the sight of electroshocking Opal and her merry band of mutants, he burrowed right back down again.

"He's shy," Cheri babbled. "He probably doesn't recognize you with the sunglasses and the lightning bolts and all." Opal was already so steamed about Albert, Cheri didn't want her to be offended by a skunk, too.

Opal took a step into the Vi-Shush. She took her sunglasses off, tucking them into the pocket protector. And with her cloudy white eyes, she took one look at Cheri.

"You can't kidnap that skunk," she said coolly.

The mutants drooled, "Nooooo," swaying behind her.

"It's not kidnapping if you're rescuing him from experiments in a freaky mall!" Iris shot back, standing in front of Cheri and Darth to protect them.

The mutants moaned, "Ohhhhhhh" when they heard that.

"It's none of your business, Purply Miss Perfect!" Opal snapped, her voice rising and her hair lifting with it. "You think you can go around painting smiley faces on everything, like that will make it all better. But it won't! You can't save the world with lollipops!"

"Maybe not!" Iris shouted back, to Scarlet and Cheri's surprise. Whatever sympathy Iris had felt for Opal the afternoon before was now replaced by righteous anger. "But I'm going to save all these animals!" As she said it, her curls seemed to double in volume, and intense lavender beams began to radiate from her head and hands.

"You and what army?" Opal sneered, her own hair now completely horizontal and fizzing like live wires. "In case you haven't noticed, I've got mine." She hitched her thumb back at the brutes huddled around her.

"I don't *need* an army," Iris said, rock steady. She swung a gleaming hand out behind her, pinkie up. Cheri and Scarlet linked fingers with her. "I've got the ULTRA VIOLETS!"

"The Ultra Wha—?" Opal started to say, but as the blinding purple beams from Iris's hair-halo filled the Vi-Shush, she fumbled to put her sunglasses back on.

"Mutants!" Opal ordered, the white streak in her hair spitting bolts. "Stop them! Don't let them take the animals!"

"Ultra Violets!" Iris ordered right back. "Set the bunnies free!"

As the mutants skulked into the lab, squinting at Iris's ultraviolet rays, Cheri and Scarlet exchanged glances.

"*I think she means us!*" Cheri stage-whispered.

"Oh, right. Duh!" With a smack to her head, Scarlet spiraled into action. From the front of the first aisle, she bounced into a modern dance barrel jump, twisting her entire body around in midair. Tumbling down the aisle, she precision-kicked the locks of the cages *blam! blam! blam!* opening them with her sharply pointed toes. Her black ponytail, glazed a deep purple in Iris's ultraviolet light, slapped against the tops of the cages as she spun. She moved so fast the mutants thought they were looking at a sideways cyclone.

"Awesome torque, Scarlet!" Cheri cheered her on. Even though Scarlet still had no idea what that meant.

"No!" Opal thundered, her voice booming through the lab. She hurled a small lightning bolt at Scarlet but missed the moving target. It exploded into the wall instead. Pointing to an empty canister, Opal called, "Yo, Fleshtacular!" to the mutant who had first brought her the bendy straws. "Monkeys. Barrel. Catch. Now!"

Fleshtacular bowed obediently, shambling toward the canister.

"And you, Rubberoni!" Opal ordered a mutant with a spear-shaped squidlike head. "Wrap up the rabbits already!"

Rubberoni gaggled his moist squid beak in what must have been a "Yes, My Queen" and began suck-suck-suctioning down the aisles with his gummy tentacle limbs.

At first, Cheri tried to count the mutants. But there were too many, and they were too ugly to look at for long. *An entire Ickipedia of style Tweeks wouldn't help these monsters*, she thought, back-skating into the center aisle just as a fat spider-toad came ribbitting toward her on eight hairy legs. *Pity I forgot to pack my stiletto-lacrosse stick.*

Huh? Darth answered.

Never mind, she said to the skunk, ducking beneath the tables as another of Opal's bolts flashed by. *I need your help!* Out of the corner of her eye, Cheri could see that Scarlet was nearly at the end of her row. Hamsters, guinea pigs, and monkeys skittered to the open pink doors, scrambling over the feet, hooves, and flippers of the lunkish mutants. But there were two more aisles to go.

"Feeling not so fresh?" Cheri asked aloud.

Always! The skunk squeaked, poking his nose out of the front end of the tote bag. And poking his tail out the back.

"Here we go!" Cheri skated down the center aisle, opening cages to the left and right. She wasn't as speedy

as superdancer Scarlet. But every time a grabby mutant got so close that Cheri calculated she was within an inch of her  life, she'd think, *Spritz 'em, Darth-O!* And the skunk would stick up his furry butt and shoot a toxic bouquet of rotting brussels sprouts, bathtub mold, and limburger cheese from his tail.

For the mutants with the aardvark snout and elephant trunk, it was particularly pestiferous.

"*Eau*-de-toilet no!" Cheri gasped. She almost could have giggled, but she didn't dare breathe in any more of the overwhelming stench. "Darth, that is too foul for words!"

Vi-Shush stink bomb, **Darth thought back.**

This lab did that to you? **Cheri realized, horrified all over again.** *They turned you into a deadly perfume?* **She tried to roll even faster down the aisle, telling each newly freed animal to run for it.**

In the last aisle, Iris was opening cages, too. She could hear Opal barking commands at the mutants, and their groans as they got skunk-sprayed. Whenever a new-'n'-loathsome one would stump down her aisle, she'd size it up fast, then paint the first thing that came into her mind.

The shark-toothed lawyer got a convertible filled with cash.

The pig-nosed chef got a smorgasbord of cold cuts.

The pelican-beaked dental hygienist got a teething baby.

But when the mutants reached out to grasp the illusion, Iris would erase it in a burst of light and blast them at close range with ultraviolet rays. The kind that burn the skin. Barbecued monsters came crashing to the floor. As she got to the end of her aisle, a small mountain of beasts had piled up.

She looked at the heap with some satisfaction. And felt a sharp claw on her shoulder.

Ticka ticka ticka . . .

Iris swallowed hard. She could feel spindly tarsal blades puncturing her skin. Clawing at her hair. She could hear the scissoring mandibles twitching right next to her ear. She struggled to twist and face Mantis Man, raising her free hand and aiming her UV beams at his bulbous insect eye. Its hundreds of lenses burned away before her like a melting disco ball, but still the snickering mandibles sliced closer.

"Violets!" Iris cried just as *whomp!* Scarlet brought the funk, stomping la cucaracha on the mutant like the bug he was. Cheri ran up to join them, turning her tote bag around so that Darth could unleash his putrid perfume.

"Didn't I kick your butt once already?" Scarlet shouted. "Back for more?"

When Mantis Man was completely crunched, the three girls huddled in the back of the Vi-Shush, near Skeletony.

"Thanks, guys," Iris said, powering down her UV rays to rub her shoulder.

"Urgh, that is *rank*!" Scarlet blurted, pinching her nose and trying to scrape mantis guts off her wrecked ballet slippers. "And I thought *I* brought the funk!"

Sorry, thought Darth.

"Sorry," said Cheri. "It's Darth. I guess his natural stink wasn't funky enough. He told me they'd been developing him as a chemical weapon."

"OMV," Iris said. She spun around and shot a UV beam at the squidhead mutant, who raised his fried calamari tentacles and dropped ten rabbits. They hopped along to the exit. "Did we free all the animals?"

Cheri looked back up the aisles and over the monster mountain. "I think so." Just as she said it, another mutant smashed like a hairy car through the pink doorway and came pummeling toward them.

Cheri screamed as Scarlet dropped into a squat. "Not you again, too!" she bellowed before she started *Nutcracker*-kicking the opossumani in its mushroomy nose once more.

For good measure, Iris aimed a pinkie finger and lasered an ultraviolet line down the top of its snout, then cooked the curly ends off its handlebar mustache. They fell to the floor like ashes from a matchstick.

"Mreeeeep!" the opossumani squealed. Covering its smoldering nose with its yellow nails, it waddled back out of the Vi-Shush with its hairless tail between its legs. Iris gave that a UV blast, too.

"Burn!" Scarlet called after it, punching the air.

Cheri looked down at her hands. "I really should have given myself a manicure last night," she said, shaking her head at her cracked pink polish. "A yellow like that mutant's would have matched this bag outfit."

Tucking a purple tendril behind one ear, Iris gave her a small smile. "Cher," she said, "we just battled a lab full of freaks. You probably would have chipped them anyway."

Cheri rubbed Darth behind his ears. "True," she said. "Our city may be crawling with mutants. And our bestie has crossed over to the Dark Side. But that's no excuse not to look chic."

U don't know the power of the Dark Side! Darth told her.

"And I don't want to!" Cheri exclaimed.

"You don't want to what?" Scarlet asked. Cheri seemed to be arguing with herself, and Scarlet found it confusing.

"Girls, focus," Iris said. "Looks like we smoked or stanked or danced away the mutants. But where's the big bad O?"

That's when the storm started.

Opal stood at the front of the lab, a black cloud swirling above her.

"Scarlet, Cheri," Iris said in a low voice. "Head for the exits. Make sure all the animals escaped."

"But—!" Scarlet protested.

Iris faced her with shining eyes. "Please," she said. "Just go. I'll be right behind you."

"Be careful, RiRi," Cheri whispered. And with a worried frown, she dashed between the raindrops on her roller skates, holding Darth close. Scarlet leaped onto the base of

Skeletony's stand and pushed off, too, riding the lab skeleton like a scooter.

Iris and Opal were alone in the Vi-Shush.

As each girl took a step toward the other, her powers grew. Opal's milky orbs glinted with bursts of orange, and sparks shot off the metal lab tables as she touched them. Iris's violet rays beamed out around her, burning so brightly they curled the edges of the newspapers lining the empty animal cages. When just three steps separated them, they stopped. It was as if the girls were standing in thin air, everything around them obliterated by Opal's coal-black cloud and Iris's ultraviolet light.

"Guess that didn't work out too well with the mutant army," Iris said.

Opal shrugged, small volts shooting up from her shoulder blades. "Beginner's luck," she said. "For you and your . . . what did you call them? Ultra Violets? Cute name. All that's missing is your rainbows."

"No worries," Iris said. With a twirl of her hair and a wave of her hand, she swept a rainbow through the white-violet light. It sparkled brighter than the sun.

Standing under it, Opal's storm system shrunk and she seemed to waver, the white stripes thinning in her eyes.

"Opaline," Iris said softly, trying to see past the cloudiness to the brown-eyed girl she still believed was inside. "It doesn't have to be like this."

"You're right," Opal said abruptly, her thunder rumbling. "And it won't. There are more mutants where those came from, and they can be trained."

Iris tried again. "You know that's not what I mean. This isn't you. I know you had to wait a little longer till you grew superpowers. But now that you have them, why not join us? Why not use them—"

"For good?" Opal cut her off with a caustic laugh. Her frazzled hair curled up on the sides of her face like a sarcastic smile. "Because it's too late."

"Why?" Iris said, taking a step forward. She reached into the back pocket of her shopping-bag miniskirt and pulled out a lollipop. "Why is it too late?"

As Iris went to offer her the lollipop, Opal doubled over in pain. Her electric thunderdome burst out around her, the force of it killing the rainbow and knocking Iris off her feet.

The peace lollipop shattered into hard candy shards.

"Because!" Opal screamed out, clenching her fists and forcing herself to stand upright again. "Because I don't belong with you!"

A thunderclap echoed after her as she ran out of the room.

It's So Not Over

NO, IT'S NOT OVER. NOT EVEN CLOSE. OKAY, THIS *BOOK*
is almost over. But our girls, the Ultra Violets, have only just
begun.

How did they slip back into their field trip unnoticed?
How did Scarlet explain the lab skeleton she brought onto
the school bus? (You already know Cheri is a pro at hiding
pets, so Darth went undetected.) How many curse words did
Develon spew from behind her big black Burkant bag when
she found the Vi-Shush broken into and rained upon, with
all the circuits blown and all the animals gone?

And what fresh evil is going on in the sub-sub-parking lot?

So many questions!

Kind of makes me want to say those four little words: We
need to talk!

Me being Sophie Bell, authoress and tour guide of this
strange and sparkly adventure, who would sincerely love
to share the answers with you, darling readers. For reals,

I would. But my lovely editor, who has hair as lush and lustrous as Iris's, has vowed to hunt me down with a bazooka and force me at spork-point to wear sandals with socks (Ew. Seriously? So gross.) if I don't deliver this manuscript to her by my midnight deadline.

As they say at Therapists 'R' Us, I'm sorry but our time is up.

Besides, we have to save something for the next book, don't we?

But I can tell you this much: Scarlet bluffed. She claimed she'd bought Skeletony in the mall's souvenir shop. Cheri even piped up about the 2 percent discount to make it more believable, and they bought it. Meaning the teachers bought the lie. The girls didn't buy Skeletony. They rode him out of a nefarious lab and down the escalator like a bony Segway. Which you know if you've been paying attention.

That's one question answered.

And here's one last scene:

The story ends where it began, on the forty-second floor of the Highly Questionable Tower in the quartz crystal Fascination Laboratory better known as the FLab. Considering the chaos that occurred at BeauTek, Iris, Scarlet, and Cheri had decided to pay Candace a visit.

Opal, of course, had gone rogue. If only she had gone pirate!

Conveniently, all the moms were out at an astrogeneticist conference that afternoon. If they hadn't been, the girls would have regrouped at the diner. It served way better strawberry milkshakes than the FLab.

The three girls told Candace about what had happened in the Vi-Shush, and suffice it to say she was not surprised. Not surprised one bit! She'd had her suspicions, her *uh-oh* gut check. Now her fears were confirmed.

"Girls," Candace said from her stool at the lab table, "it's worse than I thought. It sounds like BeauTek is some kind of mutant factory inside an abandoned mall! And only *we* know it. And only *you* can stop it with your secret superpowers!" She tapped the table with the spork as she spoke, then reached behind and scratched her back with it.

What? She had an itch.

Cheri sat across from Candace, buffing her iridescent pearl-white manicure on Darth's soft fur. "I don't care if I do have purple DNA or whatever," she said. "I never want to see another mutant again." Her smartphone lay on the lab table, and she peeked at the screen. She'd texted Opal three times, but still no response.

"And I was thinking of trying out for—nobody laugh!— the school musical," Scarlet said, practicing arabesques by the windows. She might have grown an inch since all this power-dancing started. Or maybe she just stood a little taller now. "Wouldn't being a superhero get in the way of rehearsals?" she asked.

"But we can't let mutants take over Sync City, you guys!" Iris said. She sat on the floor by Scarlet, attempting to craft a soft sculpture out of a bunch of stray socks that she'd found in a box. In honor of her lost friend, she'd pinned her long purple ringlets down with two prim barrettes. But her hair was so wavy they kept popping out. "Scar," she said, argyle in hand, "battling mutants is like fending off bullies, on a mega scale."

"Well, since you put it that way . . ." Scarlet said, dipping down into a demi-plié. She had to admit that the thought of another dance-off with some stupid mutant was making her hips shake. And hips don't lie.

"And Cher," Iris said, "who else is going to protect the animals?"

"We've got to protect the animals!" Cheri cried. She couldn't sleep at night knowing there was even one monkey trapped at BeauTek. "But what about Opal?" she asked.

Iris looked to Candace. Just the mention of Opal's name made her heart hurt. She had really tried to be her BFF, but something had gone wrong, and she didn't understand why.

Candace could see the sadness on all the girls' faces. "It might not be too late," she said. Remembering the Heliotropium accident, she felt responsible for Opal, no matter how badly she was behaving now. "She's still one of you. She was here that night, too, and got splattered with the goo. It just made her go evil, instead of good."

"We can't give up on her," Iris said hoarsely, her eyes welling with tears. Her anger at Opal had passed. Now all she felt was compassion. The pain in Opal's voice as she'd run out of the lab still echoed in Iris's mind. "We've got to bring her back."

"Back from the Dark Side," Cheri sighed, brushing back a tear herself. She fed Darth a grape. His favorite.

It was so quiet in the FLab you could hear an atom split. Even Scarlet stood still for a few seconds, wondering if things would have been different if only she'd treated Opal a little more thoughtfully.

Candace surveyed the glum group. This wouldn't do.

"Girls!" she said with a clap of her hands. "Cheer up! You just defeated a bunch of mutants and freed all those animals! That's awesome!"

Scarlet sprung up on her tippy toes again. "It is pretty awesome," she agreed.

"It's viomazing," Cheri added, flashing the V sign from the lab table.

"Majorly viomazing," Candace encouraged them. "You've got the ultra-smooth moves." She winked at Scarlet. "And you've got the ultra-sharp math," she said to Cheri with a tip of her eyeglasses. "And you"—she pointed the shiny spork at Iris—"have got a rainbow spectrum of sparkle, girl. Mix those powers with best friendship, and it's the perfect formula. You've totes got what it takes to save the day. Sync City needs you three!" Then she rested her chin in her hand and thought hard. Hard as only a teenius can. At last she said, "All you need now is a rockin' superhero name."

"Um, Candace?" Scarlet said, spinning around with a smirk. "We got that."

"C'mon, Candace," Cheri giggled. "Try to keep up!"

"Is that so?" Candace said, but she was smiling. "Okay, then. Let's hear it. Who are you supergirls?"

Iris got to her feet, and Cheri dashed over to join her and Scarlet. Standing before the cut-crystal windows, with sunbeams filtering through the prisms, the three girls linked pinkies. "You tell her," Cheri giggled again.

"No, you!' Scarlet bossed.

"No, on the count of three!" Iris said.

"But I thought I had the math!" Cheri joked, giggling even more.

"One..." they counted, "two..." Scarlet shouted, "three!"

"We're the Ultra Violets!" the girls sang together, Iris shaking her purple curls free, Scarlet pirouetting, Cheri giving Darth a hug and a kiss.

All that was missing was a blast of glitter.

The Ultra Violets. Candace sat at the lab table watching them. The fate of an entire city in the hands of three sixth-grade girls?

Yeah, she felt pretty good about it.

Later, as the three girls rode down in the see-through elevator, looking out at the Sync City skyline in all its gleaming glory, Scarlet said, "So I guess we're officially the Ultra Violets now."

"Guess so," Cheri said, holding up Darth so he could enjoy the view. "Though Iris is still the only one violet on the outside."

Before Iris could respond, Scarlet said, "We know, we know, we're all violet on the inside!"

There was a twinkle in Iris's pale blue eyes. "That's *not* what I was going to say!" She tugged a strand of her purple hair, which was wild and wavy once more. "What I was *going* to say is that Cheri is not the only one who can give makeovers." And she closed her eyes for just a second or three.

As Cheri and Scarlet watched, the crystal elevator filled with pure, sparkling light. It was like they were riding a diamond. Cheri reached her hand out, as if she could touch the sky. Then Iris opened her eyes again, and the glitter star dust disappeared.

Cheri's berry red hair now glimmered with a magenta pink tint. Her emerald green eyes shone as she realized it. Magenta went with everything! And Scarlet's straight licorice-black strands glistened with the deepest purple, a rich eggplanty shade.

"Aubergine, it's called," Iris said as Scarlet looked at her reflection in the elevator's walls. "Do you like it?"

"I love it!" Cheri said, while Scarlet just said, "Cool."

"Now that we're *all* violet on the outside," Cheri said, "what superhero-y thing should we do first? Go to the park? Back to the mall, to investigate?"

"Should we hit the mean streets of Sync City and track down some mutants?" Scarlet said, crouching in a samurai warrior stance.

The elevator neared the ground floor, and Iris put on her

messenger bag. "Sounds good," she said, "but I still haven't done my homework! And I'm all out of lollipops. We've got a lot to do if we're going to get to the bottom of this mutant drama—we'd better keep our strength up! So . . ." The elevator doors opened, and she stepped out into the city. The breeze from the river wove through her ultraviolet hair, and an aura of ultraviolet light glowed around her. "Anyone up for some fro-yo?"

Txs, Merci, and XOX!
{Acknowledgments}

STANDING ATOP THE EMPIRE STATE BUILDING IN GOLD platform ankle boots, trumpeting the call through a neon green conch shell, the original Sophie Bell sings out her sincere thanks to the few, the steadfast and true:

Editor Jocelyn Davies, who seemed to have a sixth sense about me and the UVs, and who tracked me down through a blizzard in Istanbul to manifest it. (No, she did.) For her infinite optimism, encouragement, positivity, and patience. For helping me hit the emotional beats. For courageously stetting all the crazy. Thank you, Jocelyn!

Publisher Ben Schrank, certifiably cool for getting it and putting it out there. So proud to be in your house.

Team Razorbill: Erin Dempsey, Empress of Marketing; publicist Marisa Russell; and big beaucoups to editor Rebecca "E is for Awesome" Kilman, for picking up the rhinestone baton and boldly pirouetting into the purple maelstrom, and designer Kristin Smith, who wrangled and

325

tangoed with a monster or two of her own to create such a viomazingly blue-tiful book, who made sure Graffiti Boy was supercute, and who flipped the lyrics, turning what was just a paper bag into a pretty bird.

Chris Battle, for giving the UVs their fabulous look.

Ethen Beavers, who powered the girls through the pages, from the first splatter of goo to the final mutant smackdown.

Micol Ostow, the Gladwellian maven, brilliant and generous and an all-around classy dame, for connecting the dots.

Super-sparkly, bright-eyed late birdie Aimee Friedman! La fille qui m'écoute et me calme. As some idiot once said, "Truck 'em easy." P.S. Hey girl, your books are like your hair: full of delightful twists.

Jeffrey Salane, secret former indie rock star and stealth brother-in-arms.

Barry Cunningham, Officer of the British Empire, the closest I may ever get to royalty, even with the restraining order.

Massive glitter blasts of man tanks for reals, and deep, mascara-destroying, chocolate-covered Buddha gratitude to Jazan Higgins, cosmic guru, beneficent Scorpio, for seeing and believing. Coffee cannot espresso how much your support has meant. Don't stop!

Lastly, the clan: Cornelius, for his dark charms, forever in my heart; Bridget, for hard work and bleached sheets;

Fiona, Eila, and Niamh, the rainbow butterflies. And through the looking glass to Siobhán McGowan: Shine On You Crazy Diamond.

If **SOPHIE BELL** could have just one super-power, it would be to control the frizzies come rain, snow, tornado, or monsoon. Either that or invisible-flying. Like the Ultra Violets, she once had purple hair, and it came at a terrible cost—about fifteen dollars per extension. She lives with many inappropriate shoes in Brooklyn, New York.

CHRIS BATTLE is an Emmy-nominated animation character design artist, best known for his work on the hit Cartoon Network shows *Dexter's Laboratory*, *The Powerpuff Girls*, and *Samurai Jack*, as well as shows for Disney, Nickelodeon, Warner Bros., and more. Chris, his wife, and their daughter make their home in Los Angeles, and they like pancakes.